DECEPTION 2

TINA BROOKS MCKINNEY

Taboo Publishing

www.taboopublishing.com

Taboo Publishing

Deception 2 Copyright © 2014

Tina Brooks McKinney

ISBN: 0-9821089-8-2
ISBN-13: 978-0-9821089-8-7

DEDICATION

Next to God, the only other person that can share this page is my husband, William K. McKinney. I have never known a love like this. This man makes me feel like I could walk to the moon if I were so inclined. I love you honey!

ACKNOWLEDGMENTS

Sometimes you just have to get gangster and take back what is yours. This is one of those times. When I requested my rights back for my book from my publisher, I was told that I had to waive all my past and future royalties. It wasn't enough that they stole from me the entire time that I was with them. They wanted to keep on doing it while they sold my books under the table. Shame on them. If he wants to take me to court for trying to get paid over my own works, then I welcome the opportunity to see him in court!

Thanks to all my readers for your continued support while I go through this transition. I look forward to future works that won't be tainted by greed and deceit.

CHAPTER ONE
TILO ADAMS

I pointed my gun at my lover's brother, Ramón, and pulled the trigger. I didn't feel a thing when his head blew apart splattering droplets of blood and brain matter on my face and arms. The gunshot seemed to reverberate throughout the house, even though I used a silencer. I didn't blink because it wasn't personal. It was business. It didn't bother me that he was only seventeen and hadn't had a chance to experience busting a good nut with someone other than himself, or fish dive between someone's thighs. All that was irrelevant now. He knew too much about me so he had to die. He didn't even get the chance to question what was happening before I pulled the trigger. Turning the gun on my lover, Gabriela, was harder than I thought it would be, but if I didn't take care of her now, she'd hunt me like a rabid dog after what I did to her brother.

Shock and fear paralyzed Gabriela but none of it mattered. Sadly, her fate was sealed the day she had met me. What she believed to be a chance meeting was actually contrived and part of a plan to get close to her family's fortune. Her eyes tripled in size and her feet appeared to be rooted in place, as she watched Ramón's body drop to the floor. I was good until I gazed into her eyes. These were the same eyes that looked at me as we lay naked in bed, face to face, our lips locked in a passionate kiss. I pulled the trigger again. One bullet. Point-blank range. She was with her brother again. Her body folded gracefully onto the floor. Her blood seared my skin, and pierced through the armor around my heart. I could not bear to look so I averted my eyes and stepped over her. Part of me died when I did it - not because of love - but because this was the most heinous thing I'd ever done, and somehow I knew I'd never be the same.

"Sorry, babe," I whispered. I felt horrible as I prepared to leave the house. Gabriela was the only person I'd allowed close to my heart. Part of me wanted to sneak down to the basement and take care of Moses, but it was a risk I wasn't willing to take. The potential for it to backfire, could ruin everything. I would have to deal with Moses at another time. He was going to come at me with guns blazing so I needed to get him before he got me. My original plan was to split the money with him because I thought I wouldn't be able to get it without him. Now that I had it, I saw no reason to share.

Tucking the gun back into the waistband of my jeans, I quickly gathered the money-stuffed envelopes from Ramón and Gabriela fingers. My hands shook as I pulled them free. The effort made me sick to my stomach. I was almost out the front door when I realized I hadn't wiped the place clean of my fingerprints. I took a deep breath before I thoroughly wiped everything I touched, while avoiding looking at the carnage I created. I wished things could have ended differently as I quietly closed the door behind me.

Gabriela and Ramón had known where I lived and I wasn't sure if they'd shared this with Moses. Every time I met with him, I'd always meet him at his office or in his home. So it was essential to take them out of the equation before I could move on to the next step, which was getting far, far away. Deception had a way of unraveling at the most unlikely times.

♠ ♠ ♠

I didn't see anyone lurking on the street or peering out their window as I backed my car out into the street. Something, however, was wrong. My car was literally limping.

"Fuck." I pounded on the steering wheel in frustration. I pushed the car as far as I could away from the house and got out to take a look.

Either my front tire had been slashed or karma had left its calling card. Either way, the car was not drivable. Even if I tried to push it, I would draw too much attention because it made this loud thumping sound every time the tire buckled. Conspiracy theories bounced around in my head. It appeared as if Moses didn't trust me anymore than I trusted him.

"Fuck me." I moaned.

I looked around again. If anyone was there, they were well hidden. I started sweating. I needed to get as far away from my car as possible.

"Think, bitch." I was mad because I hadn't thought about a contingency plan. I kept staring at the tire like it was going to fix itself. Time was not on my side. I had to get moving before Moses discovered what I had done. My heart was racing. I ran back down the street and tossed the gun I took from Moses' office on the front lawn, under the bushes. I turned and raced back to my car.

I opened the car door and stuffed the blood soaked envelopes in my duffle bag. I left my purse on the front seat and the keys in the ignition. I pulled out my switchblade, cut my palm, and smeared blood throughout the car. I wanted them to think I was dead, so they wouldn't put too much effort into finding me. I lowered the window all the way down and left the door open. Fleeing a crime scene on foot was not in my plans but I didn't have a choice. I pulled out a disposable phone.

"Nine-one-one. Is this an emergency?"

"I heard shots being fired. It sounded like it was right next door. Please hurry - someone may have been hurt." My voice was shaky because my shoulder hurt like hell from carrying the heavy duffel bag, but I hoped it added credibility to my call.

"Your name and address?" The dispatcher sounded as if she was reading from a script.

"Do I have to give my name? I don't want to get involved."

"Address?"

It was a trick question, but it didn't matter. I gave them the address of the house next door to the Mendozas.

"Good luck with that," I said to myself after I slammed the phone to the ground and stomped on it. Even if they managed to piece it together, there was no way it could have been traced back to me.

Whoever invented the disposable phone was a genius. Every crook in the country should've been on their knees thanking them.

"Adios, motherfuckers!" I was about to get ghost.

CHAPTER TWO
GREG CARTER

Two Atlanta police officers stood outside of a Tudor-styled house with their Glocks drawn.

"What are you waiting for? Kick the door in." Rome Watson was eager to go in guns blazing. The new recruit waited anxiously for his partner to lead the way.

I said, "I'm waiting for the shift commander to give the okay."

"Fuck that. The caller said shots were fired. Do you want a death on your hands?"

Rome was antsy, but I liked to err on the side of caution. He had no idea what was on the other side of the door waiting for us.

"Let's wait for backup," I nervously replied.

"While you're playing with your dick, I'm going in." Rome took two steps back and kicked the wooden door squarely in the middle.

"Son of a bitch," I mumbled. His actions left me no choice but to crouch down in a defensive posture and hope for the best. I exhaled the breath I'd been holding. I was convinced that Rome was one crazy motherfucker as I followed him into the darkened foyer.

"Police," Rome yelled.

"You're supposed to yell 'police' before you kick in the fucking door, you dickhead." We were committing all types of violations in protocol as we proceeded through the house; however, we were in now and had no choice but to follow through. "You better be right, nigga, 'cause if you're wrong, I'm singing like Jaheim on your ass."

"Aren't you sick of being the puppy that sits on the porch yapping? Come on out and bark with the big dogs!" Rome replied, laughing.

He was riding on an adrenaline high, but I did not share his rush. I was scared. My mind was telling me to get out. I wanted nothing more than to get in my squad car and wait for backup. I wasn't trying to be a hero. Against my better judgment, I followed Rome as we swept the room for signs of foul play. Anticipation caused my heart to beat faster. We cleared the small foyer and Rome motioned for me to go upstairs while he continued into the living room.

Upstairs? Why the hell did I have to go upstairs? Shit! I didn't want to be in the damn house in the first place, so I damn sure didn't want to check out the upstairs. Part of me resented the fact that he took the lead, but the other half of me was relieved. I was a stickler for rules and we were breaking all of them. We should have been back at the station clocking out, but Rome wanted to play super cop.

We were rookies, straight out of the police academy and ill prepared to be handling anything other than routine traffic stops, but Rome was eager to get his feet wet and my dumb ass was following him. I took the stairs slowly, dreading each step.

"Focus, Greg," Rome hissed and pointed at me as I mounted the stairs. He was right. My mind was all over the place. This lack of focus could put both of us in jeopardy. We were knee-deep in shit and there was no turning back. I crouched down even lower as I edged my way up the stairs, constantly looking back. Rome had entered the living room and was soon out of sight.

Rome's deep voice said, "Get on your knees and make like you're touching the ceiling with your hands."

I had no clue who he was talking to. I was tempted to rush back down the stairs, but that could also prove to be dangerous since I had no clue what I was going to find in the bedrooms above. My senses were heightened as I stepped onto the landing. Moving as quickly as I could under the circumstances, I was relieved to find the upstairs empty.

"Clear," I shouted as I made my way down the stairs. I waited to hear Rome give the all clear shout, but it never came. I moved a tad bit faster just to make sure he didn't need any assistance. I stepped over two blood soaked bodies as my heart rate increase. One of the bodies, a boy was obviously dead. The other, a beautiful woman, I wasn't so sure of.

Rome whispered, "She's got a pulse. Call it in while I check the basement." He quickly moved toward the basement door before I could stop him.

His face was flushed red with sweat rolling down his neck.

"Don't you want to wait for backup?" My voice was a little higher than its normal baritone. I coughed, hoping Rome didn't notice the nervousness that was evident in my voice. My hands trembled. I'd never been around a dead body before.

"Why? If the perp is still in the house, we have to catch him right? Get an ambulance before the bitch dies," he shouted as he opened the door and proceeded down the stairs. He was too amped up to notice my hesitation. It was too much. Blood was everywhere as I stumbled trying to get out of the room. I didn't care if Jesus Christ Himself was in here, I couldn't stay. I rushed out the front door to keep from vomiting on the floor, thereby contaminating the crime scene. For the first time since graduating at the top of my class, I had second thoughts about my career choice.

I made the call, but I didn't bother going back inside. I was done. Instead, I waited outside for the paramedics. I was standing next to the squad car when Rome came back outside.

He gave me a hard look and spat on the ground. "Damn, how are you going to leave a brother hanging?"

I couldn't tell whether Rome was joking or if he was actually angry. Truth be told, I couldn't give a hairy tit if he was. I didn't tell his ass to rush down those stairs, and I damn sure didn't tell him to kick down the fucking door. "We'll be lucky if they don't kick our black asses out of the department or worse yet, turn us into meter maids after this stunt." I was angry at myself for wasting the last six months of my life training for a position I had no stomach for.

"Negro, please. We responded to a call because we were the closest unit to the scene. The way I see it, we should get a promotion."

I could tell he was feeling particularly proud of himself, which only made me madder. "Yeah, whatever." I wanted to get away before our sergeant arrived and read us the riot act. The sergeant hated cockiness, and he would've burst a blood vessel if he got one look at Rome strutting around like the only rooster in the barnyard.

"Do you even know if the chick made it?" Rome asked. He didn't bother to mask his disapproval.

"Uh… I don't know. I couldn't get close to her," I lied.

"Let's get back to the station. I got a shell casing from the living room floor. I want to get the guys in the lab to run ballistics on it to see what we can find out."

"Rome, this is a crime scene. You should have left the casing for the detectives." The paramedics had just arrived and hadn't brought out the bodies.

"Oh, now you want to remember our training?" His look of contempt said it all.

"What the fuck is that supposed to mean?" I bluffed, hoping he would leave me alone.

"It means your punk ass choked the fuck up as soon as we got in the house." Rome was a bigmouth fucker and I couldn't stand him.

"Fuck you. If you wind up in the unemployment line, I won't be standing behind you." I got into the car and slammed the door. As far as I was concerned, he could do whatever the fuck he wanted. I just needed to get away from the house, which was sure to be the source of many bad dreams.

CHAPTER THREE
CARLOS MENDOZA

It had been a long time since I'd visited the United States. Were it not for the telegram I received from someone named Tilo Adams, informing me that my brother and confidant, Monte, was dead, I wouldn't be here now. I didn't like the states. It was all so different from where I came from, Bogotá, Colombia. So quite naturally I was feeling a little uneasy when I got off the plane in Atlanta. I wandered through the maze of Hartsfield-Jackson Airport to the baggage claim with one thought on my mind: revenge.

Someone was attacking the members of my family and I was determined to find out who it was. In the message, Tilo claimed that my brother, Monte, was responsible for the death of my wife. It pained me to find out about her passing in such a callous manner, but my wife and I hadn't been close in years. I knew I had a lot of explaining to do and I wasn't looking forward to it.

During the plane ride, I had plenty of time to reflect on where I had gone wrong. I trusted Monte with my family and my life. Turned out he was a snake. It was because of him I stayed in Columbia to run the family business, rather than returning to Atlanta to be with my family. In fact, Monte volunteered to go in my place so he could put my mind at ease and keep an eye on my family while I worked. Short of being there myself, he was the perfect surrogate. He was the last living member of my immediate family. I told him everything and he used it against me.

Unlike me, Monte embraced the American ways of dress and opulence. Although we were brought up with the same type of values, while I was making money, he'd obviously made a deal with the devil and ultimately put my family in danger. The message also told me where to find Ariana, so I decided to start there.

My heart was heavy. I could not believe my own brother had betrayed me in such a fashion right under my nose. I had no idea he was wheeling and dealing and using me to do it.

I gathered my luggage and went to find the driver I had hired to chauffeur me around the city. Learning to drive was never a priority for me. It didn't make sense to me since everywhere I needed to go, was within walking distance. However, this was going to have to change if I intended to make Atlanta my home.

♠ ♠ ♠

Ariana looked like a beautiful angel. She slept soundly in her hospital bed. I didn't want to wake her. When I first inquired about her and they told me she was in the maternity ward, I thought they had made some terrible mistake. I knew I had been absent for most of my children's lives, but I never once imagined what I was missing. At the end of the day, the only person I could get mad with was myself. I made the choice not to visit and now I would have to deal with the consequences.

I leaned over her bed and kissed Ariana's forehead. Despite the circumstances, it was good to see her. I whispered in her ear, "I love you, my child. I hope you know it. Please forgive me for leaving you. I promise I will never leave you again. I will rebuild our family, starting by avenging your mother's death." I left her room with a mission.

It took less than twenty minutes for my driver to navigate through traffic to Private Investigator Moses Ramsey's office. It was an elegant brick building on Peachtree Street. However, the office door was locked when I tried it, leaving me no choice but to knock on it.

"Who is it?" a man's voice shouted from inside. Perplexed, I waited until the door was snatched open. A tall, slender black man glared at me. "What?"

Stunned by his apparent animosity, I stepped back. His lack of professionalism caught me by surprise and raised my guard. "Are you Mr. Ramsey?"

"Son of a bitch—"

"I beg your pardon." I frowned at him over my horn-rimmed glasses unfamiliar with this type of greeting.

"Uh... I'm sorry. Are you Mr. Mendoza?"

"Why, yes. How did you know?"

He just stared at me as if he were looking at a ghost.

I said, "I received a telegram a few days ago stating my children were in danger. She told me Ariana was in the hospital and that I should get here as soon as I could. I stopped by to see Ariana before I came here."

"Ariana? You spoke to Ariana?" His angry demeanor faltered as he stepped back from the door.

"Well, no. I didn't actually talk to her…" I didn't like the vibe I was getting from Mr. Ramsey. Already suspicious, I watched him carefully.

"What can I do for you, Mr. Mendoza?"

"I want you to find this woman, Tilo Adams. She obviously knows what happened to my family. If I find out that she was involved, I want her to pay," I vehemently declared.

CHAPTER FOUR
MOSES RAMSEY

What I really needed was a moment to get my thoughts together, but that was next to impossible with Mr. Mendoza staring up at me like a pale dwarf.

"Excuse my manners. I very surprised to see you." I had been drinking non-stop since I learned of Tilo's deception. The booze was slowing down my thought process.

"Yet you called me by name? How did you know who I was?"

Mr. Mendoza removed his hat when he came into my office and took a seat. He sat down, adjusting his thick glasses on his face. I could not get over how pale he was compared to his daughters. He did not resemble any of his children for that matter.

"I know your family very well. You fit Ariana's description of you perfectly. "May I see your telegram?" This was not making any sense. Why would Tilo contact Carlos Mendoza? He pulled the yellow paper from his wallet and handed it to me and as best I could tell, it was authentic.

"I know how you must be feeling Mr. Mendoza, but I'm not sure going after Tilo is a good idea. The dates on this memo don't jive."

"I don't understand. What is jive?"

"It doesn't add up—make sense." He nodded his head as if he understood.

"Why would she send this telegram? She obviously knows more about my family than I do. I need to find out what else she knows. If she was in any way involved with what happened to my family, then this woman must be punished. If you're not going to help me, I'll find someone else who will."

We sat in silence for a few seconds as I weighed out the pros and cons of his request. Mr. Mendoza scared me when he mentioned Ariana. I needed to find out how much he knew. On the plus side, Mr. Mendoza's job offer would provide me with a valid excuse for pursuing Tilo. On the negative, he would expect progress reports which I wouldn't be inclined to share until I knew which side he was playing for.

The other most important negative was that if I didn't agree to help him, he may hire someone else to unravel the mystery of Tilo's disappearance which could ultimately lead back to me. Accepting Mr. Mendoza's offer became a no-brainer.

"Mr. Mendoza, the letter you showed me was postmarked before the death of your brother, Monte, which makes me think she might be involved."

"Mr. Ramsey my brother spoke of you before, that is why I came to you. I have to know what he was up to."

"Your brother used my services before. At the time, I thought I was dealing with you."

"Why would my brother need a private investigator? For what purpose?"

"The services I perform for my clients are confidential in nature. I am not sure how much of it I should reveal to you."

"What kind of trickery is this? You say my brother pretended to be me then I have the right to know why!"

I felt like I had a noose around my neck and Mr. Mendoza was holding the rope waiting for me to hang myself. I wasn't ready to admit the circumstances of my employment with Monte Mendoza. So I lied to buy myself some time. "He was looking into some missing bonds and money, which we never recovered. Chances are if you find Tilo she will have it. Since the Feds are involved, you may have to turn it over to them if we find it. Are you okay with that?"

"If you find money, you keep it. I only want to find Tilo. I have to know what has happened."

"Mr. Mendoza, finding Tilo is not going to be easy. Nine times out of ten, she has already fled the States, so I may be required to travel out of the country."

"I'm well aware of that. Just draw up the paperwork so you can get started. I have to find what's left of my family." He pushed his glasses back up on his nose and stood up, indicating that our meeting was over.

"Uh, Mr. Mendoza. A lot of things have happened that you might not be aware of. I think you should speak to Ariana first. She is due home from the hospital today. Where are you staying?"

"I'm staying at my house."

"I don't think the police will allow you to go in there yet. They are still investigating your brother's death. Perhaps you should get a hotel room and I'll have Ariana call you when she gets settled in at home."

"You seem very familiar with my family. Why should I trust you?"

"Mr. Mendoza, you came to me, remember? I want to find Tilo just as much, or more than you do."

"Very well, I will wait for your call." He reached over the desk and scribbled his name and number on a pad. With a nod of his head, he backed out of my office.

CHAPTER FIVE
CARLOS MENDOZA

Two Weeks Later

It was hard on me waiting on the call from Mr. Ramsey letting me know it was okay for me to visit my own child. At times, I was resentful but I had to remember I brought all of this on myself by abandoning them. The worse part about the wait was the not knowing. I could understand Ariana's need to rest, but what about the rest of my family?

When Ariana suggested I stay with her, I almost believed everything would be like it was. My heart was flipping around like a fish out of water as I waited for her to answer her door. I wasn't sure if I was expected to hug her or shake her hand. I hated my uncertainty. It was difficult for me to accept my little girl had grown up.

"Hello, Padre," Ariana said.

There was no warmth in her voice. Given the circumstances, it wasn't a surprise. Tears welled up in my eyes. How was I ever going to make them understand that I never meant to leave them? This was the question which tormented me daily as I waited for news and I still didn't have an answer.

"Ariana. It's been a long time." It was a completely inadequate thing to say, but my tongue wasn't communicating with my brain. My hands trembled and I almost dropped my suitcase. I scanned her face, and I could not help but to admire how beautiful she was. With the exception of her eyes, she was the spitting image of her mother, Alelina.

"Yes, it has been. Are you going to come in?" She opened her door wider and I walked into her home, humbled.

I was ashamed of myself for staying away so long. I stood in her living room clutching my bag and feeling like a complete jerk. My suitcase became a lifeline of sorts. It was the only familiar thing in the room. Although I really wanted to hug my oldest child, I didn't know how she would react. She was a woman with enough reasons to hate me for the rest of my life. When I thought of all the lies, I shuddered.

"You can put your bag down over there." She pointed to a corner that I wanted to stand in myself.

I couldn't think of anything to say, so I continued to stand there with my head down.

"Can I get you something to eat or drink?" To her credit, she was trying to make it easier than it should have been. Unlike me, she appeared to be cool and collected.

"No, I'm fine. I'm glad to be here. You are so beautiful." All my sentiments ran together.

Ariana smiled. "Uh, thank you. You, you look the same, except maybe for a little gray in your hair."

I chuckled. At least she remembered me. She sat down on the sofa, and I finally relinquished the death grip on my suitcase and sat down beside her. She patted my hand. It wasn't the hug I craved, but at least she didn't smack the hell out of me. I openly cried with relief.

"Padre, don't. It is what it is. We cannot go back and change things. Now we just have to figure out where we go from here."

When did she become the grown-up and I the child?

"I feel like such a fool. It's so much that I don't understand," I couldn't shake the feeling that I had let my children down..

"Gabriela and I have a bunch of questions for you as well, but why don't we wait to talk about them when we are all together?"

"What of Ramón, where is he?" I looked around the room, hoping to see him peering at me from around a corner or something.

Her cool veneer slipped. I should've known it was bad when Ariana started to cry. I wiped my own eyes and moved to hug her. Finally an opportunity to be supportive.

"Padre, I couldn't tell you this over the phone because I'm still trying to deal with it myself... Ramón is dead. The same woman who sent you the telegram killed him in cold blood."

I pushed her away as anger surged through my body. "The hell you say! Why wasn't I informed immediately," I shouted as I leaped up and started pacing her living room.

Ariana stood as well. "Technically, Padre, we thought you were dead. Your brother had fooled us all."

26

My anger died as quickly as it came. What was left was only pain. "I…uh…wait…oh Jesus." I knew things were bad, but I had no idea they were this bad. I fell to my knees because I just didn't have the strength to stand anymore. My heart constricted in my chest as a pitiful wail emerged from deep in my lungs. "She killed my son? Oh God, no!" It was a punishment. I knew in my heart that God was finally making me pay for all the deception and the lies.

"I'm sorry, Padre. I couldn't let Moses tell you. I had to do it myself." Ariana pulled me off my knees.

I was trembling and I couldn't stop. Too much was happening at the same time. First my wife, my brother, and now my son. Ramón shouldn't have had to pay for my sins. She allowed me the time I needed to get myself together. The scent of her perfume burning my nose.

"Cold blood, what does it mean?"

"It means there was no reason to kill him. The police said she shot him at close range. Since there was no apparent sign of struggle, I can only assume she surprised both of them."

"But why? I don't understand." I paused. *What did she mean? Both of them?* Ramón was the only son I had left and she was telling me he was gone as well. There was no one left to carry on the family name. I buried my face in my hands.

"Gabriela was lucky, but she's not out of the woods yet."

I was too distraught to immediately put the pieces of the puzzle together. I noticed Gabriela's absence, but I assumed she wasn't ready to see me.

"What? Where is she?" My eyes blinked rapidly trying to catch up with my thoughts. My eyes scanned the room frantically trying to make sense out of what she was saying. This was further confirmation that I had fucked up as a parent and as a husband. It was my job to keep my family safe and I failed miserably. My head felt as if it was going to explode; it was so heavy I could barely keep it from bobbing.

"At the hospital … she's in a coma. We are hopeful she'll pull through," Ariana said.

"We? Who is we?" Either she was not making sense or I'd missed some of the conversation.

"My husband and I."

I did a double take. My eldest daughter married? How could I have been so far out of the loop? "You're married? When did this happen?" I was too confused and hurt to get mad. Tilo's letter told me Ariana was in the hospital, but it obviously left out many other details. I was getting exactly what I deserved for not having an active part in their lives. I wrapped my arms over my chest, guarding my heart.

Ariana wore a look of compassion and understanding on her face. Unfortunately, it did not make me feel any better.

"I can't do this right now. It's too much." I paced back and forth while she silently watched me. "I'm sorry. I can't do this." I walked toward the door.

"Padre, you can't keep leaving when times get tough." There was a distinct warning in her voice that pierced through my pain. She was forcing me to be the man I was meant to be. For almost twenty years I had to deny them in order to keep them safe. Now she was telling me all my efforts were in vain, because it still ended the same.

I screamed at her, "What do you expect me to do?" I didn't mean to yell, I just felt so helpless.

"I expect you to sit down and have a real conversation with me. You can't even imagine what it's been like here for us. You owe us the truth. It's the very least you could do. It won't change the past, but it will definitely determine our future."

I felt defeated. There was nothing in my arsenal of lies that I could say which would absolve me from my sins. "Where do we begin?"

"I need some answers. Is it true you and Madre both speak fluently in several languages? If so, how come we never knew this?"

"If I had my way, you would have never found out. It was a shameful part of the life we lived." Before I moved the family to Atlanta, everything about us was a secret. I thought life would be better for them in the States. However, things didn't go exactly as planned. Given everything that had happened, I was willing to share some information but the rest, I would take to my grave.

"That's not acceptable to me. I refuse to continue living in the dark."

I wasn't used to my anyone giving me back talk, especially my children. In my opinion, it was outright disrespectful. However, I hadn't earned her respect in a very long time. I was man enough to accept it. "I know I owe you some answers, but can we go see Gabriela first? I'd rather explain everything to both of you so I only have to go through it once."

"She's still in a coma. The hospital said they would call if her situation changed." Ariana stopped talking and cocked her head.

I heard my grandchild crying somewhere in the house. Her eyes were trained on the ceiling, and I followed her gaze and smiled.

"I'll be right back." She rushed up the stairs to tend to her child.

Moments later, Ariana came down the stairs carrying a small baby wrapped in a blue blanket. She walked past me into the kitchen, gently cooing to the baby. I could hear her moving about the kitchen. I assumed she was fixing the baby's bottle.

"Sorry about that. Your grandson is very demanding." She was beaming with pride, but she also looked nervous.

I, on the other hand, was trying not to break down in tears. "How old is he?" It seemed like the more appropriate question to ask rather than how come you didn't tell me I had a grandson.

"Four weeks old. He was such a tiny baby, he had to stay in the hospital until he got his weight up. He's gained four pounds since we've been home," she answered proudly.

Four weeks? I shook my head as anger fused through my body. My wife had damn near a year to tell me Ariana was pregnant and she hadn't said a mumbling word. My brother had to have known, as well, and that was the hardest pill to swallow because he knew how much I had cried over my sons. He knew how hard it was for me to let my surviving son leave Colombia.

"Huh? Did you say something?" She didn't even look up. Her child had her full attention.

"I wish your mother would have told me." I couldn't keep the remorse from my voice.

She looked at me, then quickly looked away, but not before I saw the distrust in her eyes. "Padre, I asked her not to tell you. We weren't sure how you would react."

"And you feel this way is better?"

"Keep your voice down. I'm trying to get Li'l Moses to go back to sleep so we can finish our conversation."

I was walking a thin line. I wanted to forge a relationship with my daughter, but I was so angry I didn't know if I could keep it inside. "I guess, if all of this hadn't happened, I probably would've never known about your child. Am I right? Is that what you are telling me?" Knowing my family would go to such lengths to keep a secret hurt me to my heart, but I couldn't throw stones. Her mother and I had done the exact same thing so I had to swallow my ire.

I shrugged my shoulders. "Never mind, don't answer that."

Ariana had just taken the baby upstairs to bed when the front door opened.

"Honey, I'm home," the voice called out.

I was anxious to meet the man my daughter married. I heard a loud crash upstairs and the pounding of feet coming down the stairs.

"Ariana, is everything okay?" I came out of the living room and walked right into Moses Ramsey.

His briefcase was on the counter and he was going through the mail. It took me a minute to put two and two together. Then I remembered what Ariana had called the baby.

Moses looked up from the mail, surprise written all over his face. "Carlos, I… shit."

I felt every one of my fifty-six years. "What… Why?" I was too stunned to get mad yet. I knew things had changed with my family, but never this.

Ariana rushed down the stairs so fast, I feared she would fall. "Padre, uh…" Ariana's eyes flashed from me to Moses as tears shined brightly in her eyes.

"Careful," I shouted. But that wasn't what I wanted to say. Looking back at Moses the weight of betrayal doubled. I scowled at Moses. I was angry, but I was going to kill this *chardo* later.

Moses stood next to my daughter, and even if I wanted to deny what was right in front of me, I couldn't. The question was how was it all going to play out. Above all, I wanted to keep my relationship with her husband private.

"You must be Ariana's husband. My name is Carlos. I'm Ariana's father." I extended my hand to Moses and after several awkward seconds he shook it.

"Padre, I told you I was married. This is Moses… my husband."

I waved Ariana off, "we've met." I replied curtly and sat back down on the sofa. Visions of them having sex made my blood boil. How the fuck could Moses not tell me this? Why him? This motherfucker has some explaining to do.

They held hands and I had to physically force myself to unclench my fists. I didn't know what upset me the most, the fact that she was married with a child or that she married a *chardo*. And, more importantly, this particular chardo. There were so many thoughts running through my head, I couldn't speak for a moment.

Ariana said, "Padre, I know you're upset. Moses wanted me to tell you before you got here. We just ran out of time—"

"Mr. Mendoza, despite the circumstances, it's good to finally meet you."

Surprised, my head jerked up. What kind of mockery was this? I was unable to move. Even though I preferred to keep my business relationship with Moses a secret, I wasn't sure I could stomach having him as a son-in-law. Ariana had to know my views on mixed relationships and I felt like Moses had been deceitful so I didn't trust him.

"Padre, say something please." As she watched me with panic stricken eyes.

I didn't mean to hurt her, but I was hurting too. "How long have you two been married?" The words were forced between lips that didn't want to open, but I was curious.

"We got married shortly after the baby was born and Gabriela got shot," Moses stated with a hint of attitude in his voice.

I raised a brow. "Oh really?"

"It wasn't like that, Padre. I used to work for Moses and we fell in love."

Was this supposed to make me feel better? I didn't even know she had a job outside of the home. I stood up to leave because I needed to be alone to think. "It's late, we should talk about this at another time. Would you show me where I will be staying?" I walked over and grabbed my suitcase, anxious to be by myself. I saw Ariana move out of the corner of my eye, but Moses stopped her from showing me the way to the guest room. Instead, he led the way.

"Does this change what we discussed?" Moses asked when we were out of Ariana's earshot.

"Honestly, I don't know. You've certainly given me something to think about."

Our eyes locked, but neither of us said anything else.

CHAPTER SIX
ARIANA RAMSEY

"Honey, the baby is crying." Moses, nudged me in the back and rolled over.

I was beyond tired and a tad bit irritated with him because he didn't get up and give me a break. "Aw, come on. Can't you get him? I just got in bed."

"Ariana, you know I have to go to work in the morning."

Angrily, I threw back the covers and searched in the dark for my slippers as LM's wails got louder. I felt devalued by his response. "Taking care of our child is also a job, and it doesn't end at five o'clock." I stuffed my feet in my slippers. "I'm coming, boo," I mumbled, fighting through the tears that practically blinded me. I didn't want my resentment to fester, so I knew I would have to tell Moses how I felt.

To be honest, I was surprised by the way Moses was responding to fatherhood. He barely touched our child or me either for that matter. He was so different from my first husband, Mike, God rest his soul. I couldn't help but think Mike would have been more hands on. I hated to compare the two men, but I felt like Moses was taking me for granted.

"Mommy's coming, sweetie." His little arms and legs were flailing around as his whimpers became roars when he heard my voice.

I wanted to keep the baby in our bedroom until he got a little older, but Moses felt it would lead to LM sleeping with us indefinitely. I totally disagreed with Moses, but not enough to fight about it. If there was one thing that I'd learned from my previous marriage, it was to choose my battles.

I retrieved a bottle from the refrigerator and placed it in the microwave for twenty seconds to knock the chill off. Part of me was glad LM was making so much noise because that meant Moses wouldn't be able to get a lick of sleep until I returned with the bottle.

"Ariana, are you getting a bottle?" Moses called down the stairs.

I wanted to say something really stupid to him, but I held my lips together, choking back my response. Instead, I ignored him much like he ignored my son's cries.

♣♣♣

By the time I put LM back in his crib, I had cooled down. I just couldn't stay mad when I saw the way my son's eyes danced when he saw me. Like most men, he was only focused on one thing—my boobs. He fought me tooth and nail when I stopped giving him the boobs and traded it for a bottle. I couldn't take the constant tugging on my nipple so I opted to pump my breast instead. "He got it honest." I chuckled, but my good mood soured, almost immediately.

Mike, my first husband and LM's real dad, was killed a few days before he was born. My Uncle Monte ordered Mike killed when he found out I was pregnant. If Monte had his way, LM would have been dead too. A cold chill traveled down my back. I hurried up and got into the bed. Moses patted me on the leg as I burrowed into the sheet.

"Everything all right?"

He was snoring seconds after he asked without waiting for a response.

I moved away from his touch, but I doubted if he even noticed. I allowed my thoughts to wonder if things would have been different if Mike were alive. I loved him, but I wasn't in love with him. I wanted more fire and passion. I believed it was probably my desire for more which got him killed. I started crying, something I found myself doing at least five times a day, and I was unable to stop. Perhaps I would have felt differently if I had had a chance to morn Mike's death before I married Moses, but it was too late to change any of that now

I felt like the only person in my life who hadn't lied to me was my son. As I drifted off to sleep a tiny voice resonated in my mind. "Trust no one," the voice said. It wasn't the voice that sent off warning bells in my head, it was the words themselves. The voice was androgynous, neither male nor female, but it still sounded vaguely familiar. I struggled to keep my eyes open so I could ponder on the identity of the voice, but I fought a losing battle. I was just too tired to think anymore.

♠ ♠ ♠

After Moses left for work, I brought LM into the room with me and placed him in the middle of my bed to change him. It was still early, but my little man looked wide awake. "Hey, sweetie, things are going to be okay. Momma is just going through a rough time."

He smiled at me. The only thing I didn't regret over the last month was the birth of my son. He was the love of my life, and I vowed to do everything in my power to protect him *better* than my parents protected me. Despite everything I knew now, I clung to the belief that they loved us in their own way.

I could not believe how my son was changing. He'd gone from looking like my first husband, Mike, to me and now, strangely enough, was beginning to resemble Moses. I pulled my baby closer to me. He was the only thing getting me through each day.

Moses' lackadaisical attitude toward us was getting on my last nerve. About the only thing he appeared interested in was finding the money and bonds Tilo had stolen from my family. I couldn't care less about the money. I'd been broke all my life, but Moses was determined to find it. He was convinced she was still alive, but I wasn't so sure. If the authorities were willing to write off her death, why couldn't he? As far as I was concerned, she got what was coming to her.

Finding the money was causing a rift in our relationship. I had almost lost my entire family behind it and finding it wasn't worth the risk. If he showed one-tenth of the energy he spent on her with us, we would be a picture-perfect family. Getting him to shift his focus was the hard part.

"Are you awake?" My father came into my bedroom and I inwardly cringed. Having him in my home was something else I was trying to get used to.

My father knew nothing of boundaries. My bedroom door was closed so he should have knocked before he entered. I could have been doing anything before he barged in.

"I'm awake, but could you please knock on my door before you come in? I don't want you walking in while I'm dressing."

His face turned crimson red. I wasn't trying to embarrass him, but I was no longer a child living in his home. Our roles were reversed.

"I'm sorry. It won't happen again." Obviously embarrassed, Padre hung his head as he backed out of the room.

I felt ashamed for lashing out at him, when it was really Moses I was mad at. "Padre, if I didn't correct you, you might walk in on something you don't want to see."

He gave me a blank look as if he had no clue what I was referring to.

I signed. "I'm married now."

His oversized glasses made his pupils look much larger than they actually were. "I understand. I might have just gotten here, but I didn't ride on the short bus." He pointed to the top of his head and twirled his finger.

I almost choked. *Did my father just make a joke?* He kept a straight face, which only made me want to laugh more. I held it in as long as I could until we both burst out laughing.

He said, "It's good you laugh. It's not so good to have this much tension in your life. Not good for the heart."

No truer words were ever spoken. Things were so hectic at the house. With the baby, new husband, a father I didn't know and my sister in a coma, I was strung tighter than a violin. I'd spent several months with an evil imposter who claimed to be my father and I almost died as a result. Now, my real father was back in the picture, and I was having a difficult time learning to trust again. "Come on in, Padre." I patted the bed to let him know it was okay to sit with me.

"How's my grandbaby?"

"I'm sorry, did he wake you?"

"No, not at all. I have been up for a while. Do you want me to take him so you can get some rest?"

I could tell he really wanted to tend to his grandson, but he still had some explaining to do about the past before I could let him hold the future. "No, that's okay. I'm good. I'm about to get up anyway. I want to go to the hospital to visit Gabriela."

"I spoke to the doctors this morning and she is doing good. They say she is awake."

I jumped up, practically flipping LM off the bed in the process. "Are you serious? That's great news. Why didn't you tell me sooner?" I shouted excitedly.

He stood up. "That's what I came up here to tell you."

"Outstanding! I've been so worried about Gabriela. I was beginning to believe she would never wake up." I thought it many times, but never said it out loud. I turned LM on his stomach trying to coax his off to sleep, so I could get dressed for the hospital.

"Padre, can you give me a moment while I get dressed?"

"Of course." He backed out of the room and closed the door.

I threw back the covers and slipped my gown over my head. I wanted to shower, but I also needed to get to the hospital. I picked up the phone to call my brother, Ramón, and stopped cold. I still couldn't believe he was gone. I choked back a sob. My brother was only seventeen when Tilo killed him.

"Shit." I put my nightgown back on and went to the top of the steps and called to my father.

"Yes?" He stood at the bottom of the steps. He looked so uncomfortable, I felt sorry for him.

"I need to run to the basement to see if I can find something to wear. Could you come upstairs and watch the baby? I know he can't move yet, but I don't want to take any chances."

He quickly climbed the stairs with a big grin on his face. I patted his shoulder as we passed on the stairs.

LM was not on the bed when I returned to my room with several pairs of jeans and tops to match. My father was also missing and I began to panic. My heart started beating really fast. I'd asked him to watch over the baby. I didn't give him permission to move him. I threw the jeans on my bed and rushed down to his room. I stopped short at his door when I saw him cradling my son and whispering into his tiny ear. My heart swelled. I could not stop the tears from flowing down my face. I hadn't given my father any credit. I'd forgotten that he used to hold me in the same manner. I silently turned and went to my room to get dressed.

I needed to get to my sister and let her know I was alive and that our father had finally come home. I wasn't sure how I was going to break the news about Ramón. I would just have to cross that bridge when I got to it.

CHAPTER SEVEN
TILO ADAMS

"Do you like it?" The hairdresser swiveled my chair around so I could see my reflection in the mirror.

My new hair was very full and extended past my shoulders. It actually looked good. I hardly recognized myself. "Honey hush! You outdid yourself." I moved closer to the mirror.

She handed me a small mirror so I could see my entire head. I wanted to make sure no tracks were showing. My new do was worth every bit of the five hundred dollars she charged me. "Shit, my own mother wouldn't recognize me."

"That's what a weave is supposed to do. If it doesn't transform your appearance, it's a waste of money."

I completely agreed. I hacked off my locks and got the weave so I could look like someone else. She said, "I'm glad you like it."

She didn't know how lucky she was that I liked my hair. It actually saved her life. Had she fucked up my hair, I would have one more body to dispose of. Going to the hairdresser was a risk I felt I had to take before going to the airport in the morning. While my face was no longer plastered on every news channel in the state, I didn't want to take a chance on getting caught. If she made any mention of my resembling someone, I would have had no choice but to kill her.

"You earned this tip." I handed her an extra two hundred dollars for her efforts. The hairstyle had me feeling very feminine and sexy. The face in the mirror didn't look like a cold-blooded killer or a wanted fugitive. The disguise was perfect and I couldn't wait to test it out.

♠ ♠ ♠

"Tilo, do you want to tell me what we are doing here?"

"Don't tell me that you don't like a little tits and ass, Greg. I know better."

"I love me some tits and ass, but I don't particularly care to pay for my ass if you know what I mean." Greg pulled out a chair and sat down at the small table I had secured in front of the stage.

"Ain't nothing free in life Greg and that includes ass. Order yourself a drink and chill." I took a generous sip of my long island ice tea. It was my drink of choice when I went out.

"That still doesn't explain what we are doing here. I thought you were supposed to be keeping a low profile until you're able to get out of town."

"I am keeping a low profile. My own mother wouldn't recognize me with this hairstyle. Hell, you walked right pass me too when you first came in."

"True, you do look different but I still don't think you should be all out in public. Half the city is looking for your ass.

"The woman they are looking for doesn't look anything like me, so chill out and let's have a little fun."

I pulled two stacks of one dollar bills from my purse and handed one to Greg.

"What's this for?"

"We're about to make it rain up in this bitch. You didn't know?"

"Tilo, come on now. This shit ain't cool. Plus, I don't feel comfortable tipping some other chick with you sitting next to me and shit."

I leaned in closer to Greg. "This ain't about getting your freak on silly. I need a body and we're about to pick one up."

"A body? What the fuck are you talking about? Finish your drink and let's get out of here. All these bitches are getting me hot."

"We're not leaving until we find someone that looks like the old me. She has to be about my size and skin tone."

"What are we going to do when we find her? Beat her over the head and haul her ass out of here," Greg chuckled.

"We're going to arrange a meeting for later. We'll tell her it's my birthday and we want a threesome. When she shows up, you're going to kill her."

"Oh, hell to the no! You ain't catching me up in this shit. You already got me in deeper than I want to be." Greg started to stand up.

"You will if you ever want to see the inside of this pussy again," I answered confidently. I had Greg's nose wide open and he knew it.

"That's not fair. You know I'm down with you like two flat tires, but I ain't trying to kill a bitch for no reason."

"What do you mean no reason? You said it yourself that I needed to lay low. The best way to shut all this down is if the cops think I'm actually dead instead of them speculating on it." I felt myself getting angry. I wasn't used to explaining shit to anybody. If I could have done it without his help, I would have.

"This is insane Tilo. Who do you think you're going to fool? As soon as they run your prints, they are going to know it isn't you."

"They can't run any prints if the body doesn't have any hands or feet for that matter."

"Oh, fuck no. Now you're really tripping. I ain't doing no shit like that."

"Fine, I'll do it. I just need you to get rid of the body."

"What the fuck am I going to do with the body?" Were it not for the loud music, everybody in the club would have heard how upset Greg was.

"I'm doing the hard part nigga. All you have to do is hide the body in plain sight. Stop acting like you are doing this shit just for me too. You want to be able to leave this bitch without the cops all up our ass don't you?"

"Of course I do, but there has to be a better way to do it."

"Who is being a pussy now?" I knew I had him with that one. Greg hated being called a pussy. I wasn't sure why it bothered him so much, but I used it to my advantage.

"Shit, give me that money. You'd better hope this shit doesn't blow up in our faces."

"It won't. Now let's find this bitch so we can get out of here. These bitches are getting me hot. I'm gonna fuck the shit out of you when we get back to the room."

CHAPTER EIGHT
MOSES RAMSEY

"It's been over a month Moses, let it go. If she's still alive, you're never going to find Tilo."

My tolerance for nagging and bullshit were at an all-time low. Lack of sleep and strangers in my home was taking a toll on me. Hearing her voice in my ear was a constant reminder of how Tilo duped me. "Ariana, do we have to talk about this now? I need to get to the office." I didn't have anything pressing going on at the office, but I needed to get away from my wife before I said or did something I couldn't take back. She had been harping on the same subject ever since she came home from the hospital. I might be married to her, but she wasn't the boss of me.

"Are you going to let it go?" she said, always wanting to get the last word in.

I almost lost it. "Yes," I replied gruffly. When we were sneaking around fucking, I never noticed how much of a pain in the ass she could be. But, then again, she didn't belong to me then. She was someone else's problem. Now, thanks to Tilo, she was mine and she clocked my every move.

"Good. I wouldn't be able to take it if something else were to happen to my family. Too many people have already got hurt. I'm sick of all the drama. I just want our lives to go back to normal."

I stopped and looked around the kitchen. Did she honestly believe that what we had going on could actually be conceived as normal? Everything about us, our lives, marriage, and love, were based on a lie. It was moments just like this that I questioned whether I'd ever loved Ariana.

"Moses?" She had this strange look on her face.

"Huh?" I'd tuned her out.

"I asked what time you'd be home?"

"I don't know, babe, I'll call you." I knew that I was being unfair to her by getting an attitude, but I couldn't help myself. She could be so annoying sometimes, especially when she got something in her craw.

"Don't be mad, Moses. I'm only thinking about you."

Lies, she was thinking about herself. "I'm not mad, sweetie. It's all good. I'll see you this evening." I kissed the top of her head. By telling Ariana what she wanted to hear, I brought myself a little reprieve, but I had no intentions of giving up. Unlike the Feds, I wasn't fooled by the little amounts of blood in Tilo's car. They reported her as dead and I wasn't buying it. They weren't privy to her plans of stealing the money and using me to get it. For that reason, I couldn't let it go. The only way I could persuade the Feds to use their resources to find her black ass would be to admit I was in on the shit. That wasn't going to happen. I grabbed my briefcase and went through the garage to get my car. I was so distracted as I drove to work, I almost hit two cars.

"If you don't focus, you dumb fuck, you're going to wrap this car around a pole," I said aloud. Finding Tilo wasn't going to do any good if I killed myself in the process. I pulled over to the side of the road to get myself together. In a way Ariana was right. This Tilo shit was driving me crazy. I imagined seeing her everywhere I went. I was so obsessed, it had me running up on strangers and making a fool out of myself. I wanted to give it up, but I could not get past the bitch tricking me. I didn't take that shit lightly.

When I pulled back into the morning traffic, I had my concentration back and arrived at work with no other mishaps. I caught the elevator to the third floor and pulled out my keys to open the door. I stopped short when I saw Ariana's father standing there. *Great, just what I needed, more bullshit.*

"Mr. Mendoza, is something wrong?" This was the first time that we'd been alone since he discovered I was married to his daughter.

"I wanted to speak with you and I couldn't do it in front of Ariana."

"Come on in." I was suspicious of the visit. I opened the door, turned on the lights, and adjusted the air conditioning. He took a seat in one of the chairs facing my desk.

"Can I get you some coffee or something else to drink, Mr. Mendoza?"

"We don't have to be so formal seeing as you are now family."

I couldn't tell if he was taunting me for a fight. I hoped he wasn't because I was not in the mood. "I guess we are. What do you wish to talk about? I have some other matters that need my attention this morning."

"I heard you telling Ariana you were giving up on finding Tilo. If that's true, I want to know what type of progress you've made and to seek a recommendation for another investigator to finish the job."

"I am still working on it, but your daughter doesn't need to know about it. She wants to let it go."

"I want that bitch to pay for killing my son."

"So do I. Ramón was my friend. He worked here for a short while before—" I felt myself getting caught up and I pulled back.

"Did you know Gabriela opened her eyes yesterday."

I gaped at Carlos in surprise. "Really? I didn't know. I wonder why Ariana didn't mention it to me. Is she talking?"

"I don't know. Ariana went to see her alone while I watched the baby. She must have forgotten to tell you."

While it seemed plausible, I couldn't help but to think there was more to her omission. "I'm sure." I nodded, even though I didn't necessarily believe it. I was ready for Carlos to leave so I could think about my next move. I was going to have to figure out a way to keep my investigation secret until I knew more about their family dynamics. For all I knew, Carlos might have a hidden agenda the same way his brother had. I was not about to be tricked again. "Are you going to see Gabriela today?"

"No, Ariana said I should wait until she had the opportunity to tell her about all that has happened."

"Don't you think you should be the one who explains your own actions?"

He looked at me quizzically. "How very insightful of you. No wonder my daughter chose you."

Was he being sarcastic? I couldn't tell. He sounded like he was proud to have me in the family. I sat back in my chair, speechless. Based on the conversations I'd had with Ariana, I never thought he would accept me.

"Those two have been through a lot in a relatively short amount of time. Understandably, they have trust issues. You will have to work hard to regain theirs, but I'm sure you know this already."

"I wish I could do it all over again only differently. I have to make it up to them."

"Mr. Mendoza, with all due respect, some things can't be undone. It is what it is. We're just going to have to move on and make the best of it."

He stood up. "You're a very wise man. Now find that bitch. I don't have to tell you that time is of the essence." He turned to leave.

"We should continue to keep this between us for the time being. I have to live with your daughter, and she can make my life a living hell."

"Fine, just find her."

If he only knew how badly I wanted to get Tilo. It had been over a month since she'd disappeared and it was driving me nuts. Finding her wasn't all about the money. She played me for a punk-ass bitch, and I was having a difficult time swallowing it. I didn't care if it took me as long as it took to find Bin Laden, I was going to find her.

♠ ♠ ♠

The phone rang.

"Private Investigator Moses Ramsey," I announced as I picked up the phone. My afternoon was turning out to be a busy one. I was flipping through my mail when I heard the voice that haunted me in my dreams.

"Moses, darling."

I dropped the mail. "Tilo." I wasn't surprised by her call. I expected it.

"Do you miss me?" She was laughing, which only incited my anger.

"What do you want, bitch?" I hissed. I didn't even waste my time trying to track her number because I knew she wouldn't be that stupid.

"Are you feeling a little salty with me? You do know that's not good for your blood pressure, right?"

I was so mad, I couldn't even speak.

"Moses, are you there?"

"I'm here. You obviously got what you wanted, so why are you calling me?" I wanted this bitch so badly I could taste it.

"Humph, for what? You won." I punched the numbers again, trying not to pound so loudly on the keys.

"Would you believe me if I said that I missed you?"

"Oh shit," I muttered as the phone slipped from my ear. My dick got hard. She might be a lying, murderous, thieving, cunt, but she was still sexy as hell.

"I'm not going to lie, I would have liked to get to know you better, but you dipped your dick in another woman first. So don't even think about coming for me, or I'll tell her you tried to kill her." The line went dead. She had some nerve talking about where I had dipped my dick when she was pussy-bumping my wife's sister. Her threat was not lost on me. I had to eliminate Tilo, period. Catching her and turning her over to the authorities wasn't an option. This bitch was dead and she didn't even know it.

CHAPTER NINE
TILO ADAMS

We drove into the darkened subdivision slowly. Most of the houses were dark and unoccupied. Our house was the only one on our street with the lights on.

"Holy shit, Tilo. Whose house is this?" Greg asked as we pulled up in front of the two story structure.

"It doesn't belong to anyone yet, it's under contract."

"How did you find this place?" Greg opened his door and stepped out of the car.

"Did you forget I used to work in real estate. I have my ways."

"Damn, Ma, it's perfect. How are we going to get in? Don't they have security in these places?"

"Not really. Once they get under contract, the sellers kind of slack off. I guess they assume the buyer takes the risks. All we need to do is get the door open and I think I can handle that." I pulled a credit card out of my purse and made quick work out of jimmying the lock.

"You've got some skills girlfriend. I'm impressed."

I heard the awe in Greg's voice, but I didn't have time to bask in his adulations.

"Get the bags out the trunk and bring them in."

He came back with the two large plastic bags. "What's all this shit."

I tried not to get annoyed with his questions. He just needed to shut the fuck up so I could concentrate. We needed to get everything set up and give the house a lived in feeling before our bitch showed up.

"Can you light some candles and put the champagne on ice?"

"Yeah, where you want them?"

"In the living room. Be careful what you touch, we'll have to clean it up later."

"What are you going to be doing?" Greg asked while he eyed the bags sitting on the floor.

"Preparing the bedroom. Hurry up because we need to be ready when she gets here. This bitch is on a clock and ain't gonna want to sit around all night. Don't forget we're trying to make her believe it's my birthday."

"I don't think she cares if it's your birthday or not. You're paying her five thousand dollars just to show up. She's going to want that other half."

"She's going to get it too," I said laughing as I picked up the bag and went into the bedroom. The woman we picked could have been my sister from another mother. She even wore her hair the same way that I did before I cut off all my hair. Not that her hair mattered. When I was finished with her, she wouldn't have a head.

I quickly went about dressing the room for our tryst. From the closet, I retrieved the rolls of plastic and the saw that I had dropped off earlier in the day.

"Greg, I need your help."

"What's up?" He asked from the doorway of the bedroom.

"Help me get this plywood on the bed." If he thought it was odd, he didn't say anything as he hauled the plywood out of the closet and positioned it in the center of the bed. I covered the plywood in plastic and ran a few strips under the bed.

"There, we're all set. Once she gets here, things are going to go fast." I pushed Greg out the door and closed it behind me.

"How are we going to get her in the bedroom?"

I pulled a syringe from my purse and waved it in front of Greg. "She will be persuaded. All you have to do is keep her occupied while I give it to her."

"How am I supposed to do that?"

"Damn it, Greg, do I have to think of everything?"

He didn't have time to answer as the doorbell sent us both into a frenzy. I slapped a smile on my face and waved him toward the door.

Greg wiped his hands on his jeans before he opened the door. I could tell that he was nervous and I echoed his feelings. I wasn't sure I was going to be able to go through with my plan. Ever since I tried to kill Gabriela, I'd been suffering from nightmares. However, this was a matter of survival and I always played to win.

♠ ♠ ♠

Greg showed Tiffany into the living room and I jumped into action. I rushed over to greet her with the money in hand.

"Thanks so much for coming. I have your money right here." I opened my arms to give her a hug and plunged the syringe into her neck. She collapsed in my arms. "Help me, damn it, she's heavy," I shouted.

"Shit Tilo. I thought we were going to have some fun first." Greg snatched Tiffany's limp body from my arms and carried her into the bedroom.

"Nigga, we don't have time for pleasure. I can take care of you after you dispose of the body."

"What are you about to do to her? Is she dead?"

"She will be soon. You might want to step out the room. This is going to get ugly."

"Shit, are you sure?" Greg sounded as if he was having second thoughts about being there.

"Just go clean up in the living room and put out those candles. I'll call you when I'm ready."

Without another word, Greg closed the door. I could feel his relief even though he wasn't in the room. "What a pussy," I mumbled.

I went back to the closet and put on some plastic rain gear that I had in the bag. I covered every part of my body, including my face. Grabbing the saw, I approached the bed. My heart was beating faster than I ever remembered it beating before. For a moment, I didn't think I was going to be able to do it. Tiffany moaned and it was just the incentive I needed. There was no way I could allow her to walk out of the house now.

Channeling my inner *Dexter*, I plugged in the chainsaw and switched it on. I averted my head slightly while I sawed off her head. It was a lot harder than I anticipated. The impact of saw on bone sent jarring pain through my arms, but I had no choice but to continue. Tiffany's body jerked around for several seconds before it ceased to move. The smell of blood and shit filled the room. I staggered away from the bed trying not to throw up. It would have been so much easier for me if she had not shit on herself.

I took several calming breaths before I was able to approach the bed again. The plastic was filling up with blood so I wheeled the wet Vac out of the closet and used it to suck up the blood before it could drip to the floor.

I pulled her hands over her next and sliced off both hands at the same time. Now that I was used to the vibrations coming from the saw, they came off pretty quickly. I did the feet in the same manner. Finally, I tossed the head, feet and hands in an empty garbage bag and tied it closed.

Greg was standing outside the door when I opened it. "Is it over?"

"Yeah. We just need to get her out of here."

"Remind me not to fuck with you."

Surprisingly, I didn't feel a thing when I went back to the living room and turned up the bottle of champagne to my lips. I wasn't fooling myself into believing I was a ruthless killer. I knew this time was different because I didn't know my victim. Oddly enough, I felt rejuvenated. I prayed this feeling would last long enough for me to fall asleep tonight.

CHAPTER TEN
GABRIELA MENDOZA

It began with a loud noise, more of a nuisance than anything. But this changed as the sound grew intense. It was so loud it hurt my eardrums and shook me from my deep sleep.

"Make it stop," I moaned, but my spoken plea didn't sound anything like it did inside my head. My lips felt like mush. I had no control over how they formed my words. I twisted my head to the right and felt a blinding pain that infused my brain with white lights. My body tensed from what seemed to be a massive revolt inside my body; every muscle woke up, engaged in some sort of motion. I opened my mouth to scream, but it sounded more like a whelp.

I could feel my arms flailing, legs twerking, torso convulsing, and there wasn't anything I could do to stop them. I only wanted to go back to sleep, but each agonizing movement sent currents of pain to my brain. The noise in my head escalated. If I could've moved my arms, I would have gripped my head to keep it still. Turning it to the right only brought more pain, but I couldn't keep my head still either.

Stop. I heard the word in my mind, despite the clutter in my head, but I wasn't sure if the word came out of my mouth.

Where am I? I tried to open my eyes, but it felt like my lids were taped shut. The more I struggled to open my eyes, the louder the noise in my head became. God, I give up. If you stop this pounding in my head, I'll stop fighting. I waited for the pain to subside, but I could only assume God was otherwise busy or couldn't understand me. My body continued to shake and shimmy on what I assumed was a bed. My arm connected with a solid object causing pain to shoot up my limb. Whatever I hit was major because the pain in my arm was different from the pain in other parts of my body. It radiated up my left arm and centered in my chest.

"We're losing her," someone shouted.

Who the hell was that and who are they losing? The pain in my head subsided somewhat, but my chest was cutting the fool.

"Code blue. Code blue," another voice shouted.

These motherfuckers were getting on my nerves. I felt additional pressure on my chest, and I wanted to tell them to leave me alone. I couldn't breathe. Someone was pressing down on my chest and my nose was covered. I struggled to open my eyes, but they remained glued shut.

Someone shouted, "Clear."

Clear what? I wish these stupid asses would speak English. Couldn't they see I was in need of some assistance? I felt my body lift up off the bed and fall back with a thump. *What the fuck is going on?* Before I could get an answer, my body lifted again and crashed back onto the bed. My entire head was hurting now, not just the right side. I was convinced someone was trying to kill me. But just as suddenly as everything started to lose clarity, everything came into focus. The pain slipped away and my body relaxed.

"I got a pulse." A nurse bent over me and shined a light in my eyes.

"Welcome back," another spoke.

I looked around the room as best I could without moving my head. I was afraid to because I didn't want to re-trigger the pain I was certain was connected to my head.

"You gave us quite a scare," the first nurse spoke.

I tried to speak, but my lips wouldn't cooperate. Frustrated, I started to cry. I didn't understand what had happened to me, but it must have been bad—very bad.

"Don't try to speak. Give the medicine a chance to work. You're okay now."

Was this supposed to make me feel better? If it was, it wasn't working. I wanted to know where I was and, more significant, how I had gotten there. I let my eyes roam the hospital room, searching for anything familiar, but I didn't recognize anything in the room. I lifted my hand and grabbed the nurse's hand before she could leave me. I implored her with my eyes to tell me what was going on.

She reached for a cup with ice chips and coated my lips. "You're at Grady Memorial Hospital. You've been here for about seven weeks and up until yesterday you've been in a coma. You started

62

convulsing yesterday, and we've had to use the crash cart on you three times."

"I almost died?" My words seemed muffled, but she obviously understood.

"Yes, but this is the first time that you've opened your eyes since you've been here; so, hopefully, the worst is over with." She smiled.

"Head hurts." My throat was parched and it hurt to talk.

She gave me a few more ice chips. "We've given you some medicine for it. Try to relax. I'm going to call your doctor and let them know the good news."

Panic overwhelmed me. I didn't want to be left alone. What if I crashed again? "I'm scared." I felt tears roll out of my eyes and puddle in my ears.

"I know, sweetie. I won't be gone long. I'm just going to go up the hall and call your doctor. Your family has been notified. I'll be back before you know it." She patted my hand and she was gone.

I couldn't have held her there if I tried. I closed my eyes and turned my head to the right. My eyes shot open as my brain was infused with pain again. I shifted my body to the left, which also woke up some nerve endings, but I didn't want to make the mistake of turning back to the right. Once I got comfortable, I silently prayed God would wake me up again.

CHAPTER ELEVEN
MOSES RAMSEY

I spoke into the phone. "Dad, I need to speak with you. Is Mom around?" I paced my office nervously. I needed to get something off my chest, and my father was the only person I knew whom I could trust with this information.

"She's in the kitchen."

"Good, what I have to say is for your ears only. Later you can decide whether to share it with Mom. Could you take me off speaker phone so she doesn't come into the room?"

"Moses, I don't keep secrets from your mother. Secrets are little lies that can ruin a relationship."

"I know, Dad, but can you just indulge me for a moment? I need to speak to you man to man."

"Sure, son, but I must say you have me concerned."

I waited while he took me off speaker and left whatever room he was in.

"Okay, son, go ahead. Your mother can't hear anything we say."

I released a sigh of relief. I didn't want to have to explain this shit to my mother and my dad. My mother would make a big deal about it.

"Dad, I fucked up and I could use some advice."

"Fucked up how? And you know I don't like that foul language."

"Sorry, Dad, but there is no other way to say it. I fell in love with a woman who was already married, and she worked for me."

"Son, didn't I tell you never to shit where you work?"

I could tell he was disappointed with me because he almost never cursed. It didn't take many words from my father to make me feel like a child all over again. "Yeah, you told me… but in the heat of the moment, I wasn't thinking straight. She was so beautiful I couldn't help myself. If it makes you feel better, she actually came on to me. I didn't have the willpower to turn her down."

"Better? How is that supposed to make me feel better? I thought I taught you better than to let your dick do the thinking for you."

I knew I would have to eat a slice of humble pie, but I wasn't prepared to eat the whole damn thing. I didn't call him for a lecture. I needed advice on how I was going to deal with a wife, and a baby who most certainly wasn't mine.

"Dad, I know I messed up. I didn't call you to confirm it for me. I need your help, so can you please hold your opinions to yourself until I tell you the rest of the story?"

"I'm sorry. You know I only want the best for you. Your mother and I are worried about your being in Atlanta by yourself."

"I got that, Dad. After this is over I may even move back home, but I've got to get through this."

"Damn, sounds serious."

"It is. The woman I am involved with is Latino." I wanted to let this information settle in before I continued. My parents were very proud of their heritage and did not condone interracial relationships.

"Shit," my dad said. His outburst caused my heart rate to accelerate.

I didn't mean to ever hurt my parents, and judging by the way he was cussing, I could tell he was broken hearted. "Dad, I'm sorry. I didn't choose to love her, it just happened."

"Son, your mother is going to have a duck-plucking fit."

"I know. That's why I haven't told her. There's more."

"Oh shit."

"She got pregnant. At the time I believed the child was mine. Remember when I called and told Mom I was having a baby?"

"Yeah, your mother and I argued about that for two days! I told her she was only hearing things she wanted to hear. Because of you, I couldn't get any for over a week."

"I wasn't lying. Her name is Ariana, she said I was the father. Dad, she changed my life, and I wanted to be that child's father. I was trying to persuade her to leave her husband and marry me."

"Oh Jesus." He blew out a deep breath. I could tell he was outside smoking, which was something my mother forbade him to do in the house.

"She said she loved me, Dad, and I loved her. To me it was simple, but she said it was more complicated."

"Okay, I got all that, what happened?"

"Dad, I have to tell this my way. I need for you to understand that I wanted to be there for my child just like you were there for me. But she was committed to someone else and it was driving me nuts."

"Father God! Don't tell me you did something stupid and had him killed."

"No, I said I was in love, not psychotic."

"Thank God."

"I'm sorry, Dad. I haven't done things the way you wanted me to but at least now you know I'm not gay."

"Under normal circumstances, I would've been happy to hear that you weren't, but this mess you've gotten yourself involved in—"

"Have you ever had a woman in your face, who did it for you on every level, every day? I couldn't help myself when she came on to me. Shit, what was I supposed to do?"

He said, "Things have changed since I was a young man. When I met your mother, she wouldn't let me get with her until I married her. I realize things have changed, but why a Latino woman? Why not a black queen?"

"Dad, you know as well as I do that you can't control who you love. It was just something about her; it wasn't meant as a slight to black women."

"Okay, I can respect that. So what's the problem? Her husband found out and he wants to kill your dumb ass?"

I didn't appreciate the way he was making light of the situation. I needed him to care about it as much as I did. "It's a long story, but her husband was murdered."

"Whoa, you said you didn't kill him. Should I be worried?"

He didn't know the half of it.

"It was pretty intense at the time. I will go into it in more detail the next time I see you, but I have to get the rest of the story out before Mom comes looking for you."

"You got that right. I'd better put out this cigar."

"Ariana told me the whole time she was carrying the baby it was mine. I believed her, Dad."

"Wait, hold up. You said she was married, son, so how in the hell could this child be yours?"

My dad was irritated. I heard it in his voice.

"Dad, I know you're upset, but hear me out, please. She said she wasn't having sex with her husband and that he was incapable of having children."

"Son, that's the oldest line in the book. I can't believe you fell for it."

"I did, hook, line, and sinker, and to make matters worse, I married her."

I heard his phone hit the floor. "Holy Mother of God," he shouted.

I could hear the pain in his voice. I was his only child, and I hated being a disappointment to him.

"She lied to me, Dad. The baby is white. I feel like such a fool for believing her."

"Whether the baby is white or purple, if you love this woman it shouldn't make a difference."

"But what about the lies she told me?"

"Your whole relationship was built on a lie. So now the only question that really remains is, what are you going to do about it? Her husband is gone. Are you ready to abandon her?"

My father had a good point. While I was still hurt that the baby wasn't mine, a part of me still loved Ariana.

"I guess I'm going to make a go of this marriage."

"Good, and you're going to have to make an effort not to hold the sins of the mother against your child."

"I'm going to work on it. I really love her. Thanks for hearing me out, Dad."

"So are you trying to tell me we are grandparents?" my mother asked.

"Mom, how long have you been on the phone?" My stomach sunk. If she didn't hear the whole conversation, I was going to have to start all over again. Once was enough. If she did hear the conversation, I knew she was going to want to see the baby and see him quickly.

"I picked up as soon as your father left the room. He's no good at keeping secrets from me and he knows it."

My dad laughed. When I realized that she wasn't mad, I started laughing as well.

Mom said, "So when can I see my grandchild?"

CHAPTER TWELVE
ARIANA RAMSEY

Moses came into the kitchen and tossed his key on the counter. "Hey, sweetheart, did you have a good day?"

I stopped stirring the tuna salad I was making and looked around to see who Moses was talking to. I assumed he was on the phone because he hadn't called me sweetheart in months. "Uh... actually I did. The baby slept well today. Hopefully, he'll sleep through the night. How was your day?"

Moses gave me a happy-meal smile and it made me nervous. "It was very enlightening."

I didn't know what he meant by that, and I was afraid to ask. He was in a rare mood for whatever reason and I didn't want to ruin it. He leaned over and gave me a gentle kiss on the lips. An electric shock passed between us, which made us both jump.

"Ouch, hot stuff coming through." I pressed a finger to my top lip.

He kissed me again and this time I felt no pain, only passion. "Sorry I shocked you. Was that better?"

"Mmm, I'll say it was." I closed my eyes and savored the moment.

We didn't share moments like this often. His kiss was tender. I could actually feel the love it represented. As he moved away, I felt his absence. He was still smiling at me, and it was kind of creepy as if he knew something I didn't. He reminded me of the man I fell in love with.

I said, "Moses, what's going on? I'm not complaining, but you have me confused. When you left this morning you barely looked at me, and tonight I get not one kiss but three."

"Can't a man kiss his wife?" His smile lingered on his face, but I was still uneasy.

"I wasn't complaining. I just wanted to know what happened so I could make it happen more often." I laughed it off, but I'd never been so serious in my life. I was sick of all the fussing and arguing we'd been doing. It wasn't good for me and it damn sure wasn't good for the baby.

"Where's your father?"

I froze. Something was definitely wrong. "Who are you?" I grabbed a knife from the countertop. I'd been through that subterfuge bullshit before, and I was not about to go through it again.

"Sweetheart, put down the knife. Everything is okay. I just came to some conclusions today and they have changed my outlook on this." He reached for the knife and I allowed him to take it from my hand, but I still wasn't sure things were on the up and up.

I frowned. "What kind of conclusions?"

"Don't you worry your pretty little head. Just know that things are going to be different around here—starting tonight."

He unknotted his tie and left the room. I sunk down on the closest chair. Despite Moses' assurances, I did not feel relieved. I felt like I did when my uncle entered our house and pretended to be my father. It was already five and I hadn't started preparing dinner.

"Where did my day go?" I jumped up, dismissing my insecurities about Moses, and put some effort into dinner. As I opened the refrigerator, I heard LM whimpering through the child monitoring system we'd installed throughout the house.

I grabbed a bottle of breast milk from the refrigerator. From under the sink, I got a small pan to heat his bottle. Although Moses had purchased a top-of-the-line bottle warmer, it took more time than it was worth trying to figure out how to use the damn thing. Some things didn't need modernization. I placed the bottle in a little water and turned on the burner of the stove.

LM's whimpers were gathering intensity, so I turned up the heat being careful to shake it every few seconds so it wouldn't have any hot pockets. The water had just started to simmer as LM began to cry in earnest.

"Hey, big guy. What's all the noise for?"

I heard Moses talking to his son. LM immediately quieted. I froze.

"What the hell is going on here?" I mumbled to myself as I edged closer to the monitor.

"Let's go see what's taking your momma so long with your milk."

I broke out of my trance, but I still felt like I was walking through a cloud as I walked around the kitchen in circles. Moses met me halfway and took the bottle from me. He gave me a sexy smile, which almost made my knees buckle, and he winked at me. He turned around and went back upstairs. I watched them until they disappeared at the top of the steps. Something very strange was happening in my own house and I didn't know what it was. I had prayed that Moses would take an interest in my child, but I never thought God would've moved so quickly.

When Moses returned to the kitchen, he had changed into some jeans and a T-shirt that showed off his muscles. My heart swelled with love, but I was still concerned.

"Where's the baby?"

"After I burped him, he went right to sleep. I changed his diaper too, so he should be good for another few hours." He took the paper off the kitchen table and winked at me again.

I gave him an uncertain nod as he walked into the family room.

"Where did you say your father was?" Moses asked again.

"Uh, he said he had some errands to run. He's been gone all day."

"Come here for a minute."

Nervously, I walked into the room expecting the worst. He was lying on the sofa. The paper was on the coffee table. Untouched.

"Come sit your sweet pussy on my face," he commanded.

I did a double take. "What did you say?"

He laughed. "You heard me." His baritone voice sent a ripple down my back straight to my pussy.

"What about my father? He might come back."

"Then I guess you had better hurry up."

It drove me crazy when he spoke dirty to me. I still had on my panties, but Moses took care of that. He roughly pulled them to the side and buried his face between my thighs. I exhaled. He pushed his tongue into my pussy. I was thirsty for his love. I wanted to come deep in his mouth.

"Ah… that shit feels good." I ground my pussy against his face without a care in the world. He fondled my breasts. He stuck his finger in my pussy as he gently sucked on my clit. I was close to a climax and we'd just started.

"That's it, baby, that's my spot."

He didn't respond because his mouth was full, but he heard me because he increased the pressure on my clit. His arms were wrapped tightly around my thighs, holding me in place. But he really didn't have to hold me, I wasn't going anywhere.

I said desperately, "Fuck me, baby." I had a lot of regrets in my life, but loving Moses wasn't one of them. This man took me to heights that I didn't even know existed.

He pushed me away long enough to breath, my juices dripping off his face. "You like that?" he asked as he drove his face back into my pussy.

How did he expect me to answer when he was pleasing me like this? "Ah," I moaned. If he was trying to drive me fucking crazy, it was working. All my insecurities were forgotten. "I'm cumming!" I squirted in his mouth.

My entire body shook with an intensity I forgot existed. He pulled my body down and rammed his dick into my pussy. My walls wrapped around his dick like a snug glove. He was such an energetic lover. I grunted when I felt his dick hit my wall.

"Oh my God," I moaned. "Oh Lord," I shouted.

"Damn, baby, this shit is good. I've been dreaming about your pussy all day long." He rammed his dick inside me again. His brow was creased and his lips were pulled back. His eyes were wide open like windows to his soul.

"Don't stop." Technically, we should've waited. I had a difficult delivery and the doctor advised us to wait on sex for two more weeks, but I couldn't tell this man no. He just turned me on.

"Back that shit up for me then." He was asking me to back my ass up so he would fuck me doggie style and he only had to say it once.

"I got you, give it to me." I bent over and looked at him over my shoulder.

That was all he needed to hear. He pushed his dick so far up in my shit, I had no choice but to come on it. His weight fell on me as he came; it was cool, I needed the rest.

"Damn," he said.

"You got that right. That was awesome." If not for the threat of my father coming in and catching us snoozing, we both would have basked in the bliss, but a crying baby shut down all that.

CHAPTER THIRTEEN
TILO ADAMS

I scowled at my reflection in the mirror. "I should have never left that house without killing Moses. What the fuck was I thinking?" I brought my hand down hard on the countertop. When he comes for me, and I had no doubt that he would, it would be my own fault. I shouldn't have taunted him, but every time I closed my eyes I saw his face. I didn't want to spend the rest of my life running from that motherfucker when he should've been planting food. If he didn't give up the chase, I was going to make it happen.

If he had shown half the balls I'd given him credit for when we were plotting to steal the money, I might've brought him along with me. "Naw, bitch, who you fooling? You never learned to share as a child, and you're too damn old to learn how to do it now. He can kiss my black ass. That's what he can do for me." It didn't bother me at all that I was having a conversation with myself.

Ever since I pulled that trigger which killed everyone in my life who mattered to me, I heard voices inside my head. They started yapping the moment I used my gun for greed instead of serving and protecting. Some might call it a conscience, but to me it was just another fucking pain in the ass that I cared not to deal with. "Shut the fuck up," I shouted.

I took one last look around my apartment, then I placed my final items in my suitcase. With my new look, I was finally confident enough to chance leaving the country. I was blond now. The dreads I'd spent so much time grooming were a thing of the past. I had a new identity and with it a new life. I actually looked like the name on my identification, Bianca. My decision not to leave town was risky. At the time, I believed it was my best move, however, now I regretted that decision. Historically, most criminals were caught after or during their travels. They were most exposed because they could not control things and the people around them. I didn't want to make the same mistake. I wanted to find a locale where I could grow old, fat and happy.

In order to do this, I had to find out if anyone other than Moses was searching for me. The last thing I needed was to show up at the airport and get arrested. Hence, my call to Moses. He didn't appear surprised to hear from me, so I concluded he hadn't given up and would be a major thorn in my side until I found a way to eradicate him. I already knew money wasn't the answer, or, at this point, an option. I was gonna have to either kill the motherfucker or make him wish I had. Didn't much matter to me, whichever way it went down.

As I gazed into the mirror, I didn't recognize myself. It wasn't just the hair, it was in my eyes. They were blank and no longer filled with light. Without warning, tears flowed out of my eyes, and I realized my life as I knew it was over. I'd killed two innocent people and stolen their inheritance. I bought myself a front-seat ticket on a one-way, custom-painted rollercoaster ride straight to hell.

CHAPTER FOURTEEN
ARIANA RAMSEY

"Dad, when Moses gets in from work, I'll run you over to the hospital. They won't let me bring the baby and I don't want him exposed to all those germs." I put LM back in his crib after I changed him and sighed. If I didn't need to go to the hospital, I would've gotten into the bed myself.

"Why can't we get a babysitter?"

I looked at my father like he had lost his damn mind. What did he mean, we? I wasn't sure about letting him go to the hospital. Gabriela had only been awake a few days and I didn't want to upset her. He was reading the paper, but put it down as he watched me.

"Babysitter? That's not about to happen. Moses and I haven't even broached the subject of babysitters yet. I'm terrified about leaving my baby with strangers. You never know what they could be doing while you aren't there to protect them."

"When will he be back? I really want to see Gabriela."

For some reason his statement angered me. I felt like he was getting comfortable with a very uncomfortable situation. Most days I could catch myself before I went off on him, but those days were getting harder and harder. I swung back and forth between loving and hating him. If he was so eager to see us, why did it take the death of our mother to bring him home? I spoke before I could get a hold of my thoughts. "Why the rush now? You missed most of our lives. You missed all of Ramón's." I shocked both of us with the brutal truth. I promised myself I would keep my negative feelings within, but all the anger I felt rolled out of my mouth unchecked. Before I knew what was happening, I had assumed the ghetto chick, neck-rolling posture of someone about to kick ass in the streets. He didn't know nothing about that shit and something deep inside of me wanted to be the one to show him.

"He will be home when he finishes taking care of his business because, unlike you, he supports his family. He doesn't just send money. He's here for his son." I didn't have to finish the rest of my statement because he knew what I was going to say. I slumped down on a chair, ashamed of myself.

He said, "Your words hurt, but nothing you can say can hurt me more than my own inaction. I know I have my shortcomings, but there are a lot of things you don't understand. I've always provided for this family."

I shook my head because he still didn't get it. Being a father wasn't about the money. We needed him, but that time had come and gone. I wasn't feeling well and I was taking it out on my father.

"Padre, I'm sorry. I wasn't trying to start an argument with you. A lot of things have gone on over the past few months and my body is playing tricks with me. I want to make sure Gabriela is okay, and then we can deal with all this other stuff later." I felt defeated.

"Ariana, I spoke to Moses about this and he made a very valid point. He said I should be the one to explain myself to both you and Gabriela. He, uh—"

"When did you get to speak with Moses? He didn't say anything about it to me."

Padre turned red and looked very uncomfortable, but I was not about to let him off the hook.

"Well, I, uh, I...uh—"

"What are you not telling me?" I was imagining all kinds of things, so I needed him to tell me what really went down so I could stop coming to my own conclusions. Moses was different yesterday, and I needed to know if my father had something to do with it.

"It's nothing really. I didn't realize your husband didn't mention it to you." I followed him into the kitchen.

I was really getting mad. The way he said it, his tone, implied there was something wrong with my marriage.

"It must have slipped Moses' mind. He normally tells me everything."

My father stared at me like he didn't believe a damn thing I said. Of course it could have been my hormones making me act all crazy and shit.

"Have you said anything to Gabriela about me?"

I paused, distracted. I wanted to know why Moses didn't tell me about speaking to my father. I also wanted to know what else he was hiding from me.

He said, "Ariana."

My father brought me back to the present.

"Huh?"

"Have you told Gabriela anything about me?"

"I haven't told her that you are here. She's still getting herself together, so I don't want to bombard her with too much information at one time." I started to get nervous. The truth was that I hadn't told Gabriela anything, not even about our brother Ramón. I was waiting for her to ask me what happened.

"She hasn't asked any questions?"

I fidgeted. "Well… she's curious about what happened to her."

"She doesn't remember anything?" He pulled a glass from the cabinet and poured some water in it.

"Uh, she believes you have something to do with her being in the hospital."

A vein in his neck stuck out; he stopped moving, glass halfway to his mouth.

"Me? Are you serious? And you're okay with allowing her to believe this when you know I had nothing to do with it?" He slammed his glass down on the counter and started pacing back and forth.

"Padre, I don't know what I'm doing right now. She looks so fragile, I don't know how much she can take. Hell, what do you think we should do?"

He didn't hesitate. "I think we should tell her right now! There's been too much deception as it is."

"I'm not the one who started this shit." I followed him into the living room.

He put me on the defensive. Were it not for him, none of this would have happened.

"It doesn't matter who started it, Ariana. It has to end. I can't have Gabriela thinking I harmed her or her brother." His voice was more subdued and authentic.

"She doesn't know about Ramón, either. I don't know how to tell her."

"That's it! I'm going to the hospital now." He rushed toward the door.

"Padre, wait, at least let me go with you. She doesn't know you."

He looked like he was about to refuse, but he lowered his hand.

"Fine, hurry up. This shit has gone on long enough." Tears rolled down his cheeks as I reached for the phone to call Moses to see if he could come home.

I had mixed emotions about his tears. While I understood he wasn't responsible for the actions of his brother, he created the circumstances that allowed the situation to happen. And I was not about to let him go to the hospital and upset my sister's recovery. That was not about to happen if I had anything to do with it.

Padre stumbled, falling back onto the couch, clutching his heart. His face turned blue. He looked like a Smurf. I immediately regretted lashing out at him.

"Padre!" I screamed, running toward him. "What's the matter? Are you okay?" I knelt in front of him, uncertain of what I needed to do. The last thing I needed was another parent dying right before my eyes.

"I need to see Gabriela," he said, gasping for breath. Padre seemed to transform right before my eyes, suddenly looking old and sickly.

He's faking. There's nothing wrong with him, I thought.

"Padre, are you ill?" Even though I didn't believe his little act, my heart started beating a little faster. What if he wasn't faking? I didn't think I could stand to lose both my parents, even though he'd been absent most of my life.

"I need my pills. They are in the side pocket of my suitcase," he moaned and rolled over on his side. His tongue hung from the side of his mouth. He appeared to struggle for air.

Faking or not, I rushed to his room and grabbed his suitcase and brought it back to the living room. I beat myself up for being so mean and hateful. As much as I wanted to hate him, I still loved him. My hands shook as I dug into his case. I kept looking over at him to see how he was doing. "Should I call for an ambulance?" I was getting nervous.

He shook his head and I continued to search.

"Do you have them?" he asked as my fingers closed around a small prescription bottle.

"Yes, here they are. How many do you need?" The directions were on the front of the bottle, but the words would not come into focus.

"One."

The fucking bottle wouldn't open. It had one of those child-safety caps on it, which were designed in my opinion to piss folks the fuck off. A few seconds later, I opened the bottle and shook out a single tablet into his hand. He held it, his eyes beseeching me for assistance. I raised his arm, guiding his hand to his mouth. He placed the pill under his tongue. He leaned back against the couch and closed his eyes. I was scared.

"Are you okay?" My face was inches away from his nose.

He didn't answer, just nodded his head. I sat down next to him and watched him like a hawk. His color slowly started to return. I wondered what was wrong with him that he could have an attack so quickly and recover seemingly in minutes. However, those minutes seemed like hours. Slowly, he opened his eyes. His breathing had slowed down as well.

"That was a big one," Padre replied as he struggled to sit up straight.

"How long has this been going on?"

His eyes didn't meet mine.

He said, "About five years, but there's nothing to worry about. It's all under control."

It didn't appear to be under control to me. What if I wasn't there and he couldn't reach his pills? What would have happened then? Would he have died?

"How come—" I didn't have to finish my statement. My parents were the masters of deception.

"It's not so bad...as long as...I keep my medicine close...no stress."

He was in the wrong house for that shit. Part of me wanted him to go to a hotel, but the daughter in me wanted to keep him close so I could look after him.

He looked at me. Sadness filled his eyes. "So much wasted time." Another tear slid out of his right eye.

I reached up and wiped it away. It was a tender moment, filled with forgiveness and remorse. We both turned when we heard a key in the door.

CHAPTER FIFTEEN
TILO ADAMS

I leaped up out of the bed drenched in sweat. I was convinced someone was in the room. I grabbed my gun from underneath my pillow, ready to shoot whoever had managed to get into my hotel room.

"Who's there?" I whispered, afraid of the answer. My heart slammed against my chest, its vibration pounding in my head. My arms shook as I tried to hold my gun steady. I slid my legs over the side of the bed and crouched into position. If someone was going to attack me, I preferred them to do it while I was standing.

My eyes struggled to see in the dark, but the sweat in my eyes made it difficult to see clearly. I pivoted around in a circle but nothing jumped out at me. This was the third time tonight I'd awoken from the same dream.

"It was the dream again, you idiot." I slowly lowered my arm and exhaled. Even if I was dreaming, it was very vivid. I would be lying if I said it didn't have me all shook up.

I went into the bathroom and ran some water in the sink. Part of me wanted to jump into the shower to wash off some of the sweat. The other part of me just wanted to get back in the bed and pretend it never happened. Again.

I allowed the water to get hot and grabbed a washcloth from the stack on the counter and rubbed it over my face. I refused to look into the mirror because I didn't want to see what my face looked like. There was nothing cute about being scared half to death.

The recurring dreams were getting on my fucking nerves. They started the day I shot my former lover, Gabriela. In my dreams, her eyes beseeched me to help her However, each time I walked toward her she disappeared before I could reach her. I turned off the light and made my way back to the bed. The sheets on the side of the bed I'd been sleeping on were soaking wet. It looked as if I had peed on myself. If I had, it wouldn't have been the first time. I turned down the comforter on the other side of the king-sized bed and climbed in. I pulled the covers up under my chin and tried to pretend the dream never happened.

"Shit," I said aloud to the empty room. I hadn't slept for more than four hours in over two months. I checked under my pillow to make sure I'd put my gun back within easy reach. I sighed when I felt the cold, hard steel against my fingertips. My dream was always the same. It started out so beautifully and ended so terribly wrong. I wanted to forget the details of my nightmare, but my thoughts had a mind of their own and took me right back to where I'd left off. I was scared to close my eyes, fearing the images would flash once again through my mind. The shit was getting old. I knew I would feel some remorse for my actions, but I had no idea it was going to be like this.

"This is some bullshit!" I exclaimed. I was exhausted and had not anticipated all the guilt I'd feel while I was planning the caper. Obviously, I didn't know myself as well as I thought I did. When all else was said and done, I found out I too had a heart, and I broke it the day I pulled the trigger.

"You pussy," I said, beating my pillows to get comfortable. I was mad at myself for being so weak. This wasn't my first kill, so I couldn't understand why I couldn't shake it and it be done. Having sex with Gabriela may have contributed to my discomfort, but enough was enough.

However, I could not get her face out of my mind. It was in her eyes. I didn't think she believed I would pull the trigger. Truth be told, I didn't believe it either. I thought I was going to punk out at the last minute, but I didn't. I shot her in cold blood like I had her brother. In my dream, her eyes blazed with love and forgiveness. They begged me to save her, but I didn't.

She would never understand. Her brother had to die because he knew everything. He worked for Moses, and he knew the operations of the family business. He also harbored hatred in his heart, and it wouldn't take much for him to transfer that energy to me. He was a liability I couldn't afford to have hanging around. I shot Gabriela because I knew that she'd hunt for me for the rest of my life for killing her brother.

I allowed Ariana to live for two reasons: one, I didn't want her son to grow up without his mother; and two, I wanted to piss Moses off. He was already mad that the child she bore belonged to another man. He would be equally pissed when he realized his fake wedding was actually real. "I wish I could've seen Moses' face when he realized his wife wasn't dead." I laughed out loud.

Laughter always came before the tears.

CHAPTER SIXTEEN
CARLOS MENDOZA

I got up off the sofa a tad bit too fast. My head was a little woozy, but I refused to succumb to the dizziness. I stumbled a little bit, but, otherwise, I remained on my feet. "Can we go now?" I was anxious to see my daughter and to clear my name.

"Padre, don't you think you should rest some more?"

"I'm fine, let's go." I shot Ariana a warning look. I didn't need her telling Moses about my little episode. Even though I made a deal with him to find Tilo, he still hadn't earned my trust. I was going to be watching him as much as, if not more than, he was watching me.

Moses walked through the front door. "What's going on?" Moses put down his briefcase and gave Ariana a kiss on the cheek.

I shot Ariana another warning look, but she either completely missed my warning or I sucked at it and she ignored it.

"Padre isn't feeling well. He wants to go to the hospital, but I think he should lie down and take a nap," Ariana insisted as she slung her purse over her shoulder.

"I said I'm fine." I didn't want to get into a fight, but I would if I had to. I was going to the hospital either with Ariana or without her.

Moses said, "How long has my little man been asleep?"

If Moses felt the tension in the air, he kept it to himself.

"Actually, I just put him down. We shouldn't be gone long. If Padre wants to stay longer, he can get someone to bring him back."

Perfect. I would have suggested the same thing because I didn't want to have the discussion about my health with her right now.

I was tense as we approached my youngest daughter's hospital room. Never in a million years would I have believed that our lives would come down to this.

"Brace yourself, she looks much worse than she is," Ariana said before she pushed open the door to room 521.

I paused for a few seconds to get myself together. Even though Ariana tried to prepare me, I wasn't ready for the sight of my little girl lying in a hospital bed. Everything else in the room disappeared as I looked at her. "Sweet Jesus." I rushed forward and touched Gabriela's arm.

Ariana came up on the other side of me and placed her hand on my shoulder. I made no attempt to stop the tears that washed my face. I felt like God was punishing me for every mistake I'd ever made, and He was doing it all at once. I closed my eyes for a brief moment and when I opened them, Gabriela was staring back at me.

"You're awake," I said as relief flooded through my body, but I was also scared.

Gabriela didn't know me and her distrust showed in her eyes. She didn't have old memories to fall back on. She was so young when they moved, four, maybe five, and I wasn't around much. To her I was just a voice on the phone. She had no real memories of me. I wanted—no, scratch that—I needed to hear her voice.

Gabriela gave me, but a moment's glance. This hurt my feelings, but I tried not to let it show. I gained solace when she didn't flinch from my touch. My children had reason to hate me. I needed for them to give me another chance to make things right. Her eyes connected longer with Ariana's than they did with mine. She never spoke; I was worried that she wouldn't. I felt like I shouldn't even have been in the room. Her look confirmed those feelings.

Ariana said, "Hey, sweetie, how are you feeling today?"

Gabriela looked at me again. She didn't seem to care one way or another about me.

"Ramón? Where is he?" Her voice was hoarse and we could barely hear her.

Ariana shook her head and sat down on the bed with Gabriela. I didn't know what to do. I wasn't sure if I should move closer to the bed or leave the room. Gabriela didn't help me because she never acknowledged me. I tried not to take it personally.

I said, "There's something that I—no, we—need to tell you, and it's not going to be easy."

Gabriela looked at me again. Her eyes became hard like two small pebbles. Ariana caught the exchange.

"I know you don't remember him and I'm sure this is going to come as a surprise, but this is our real father."

If Gabriela was shocked by this bit of information, she didn't let it show. She continued to stare at Ariana like she was the only person in the room.

I said, "Hi, I...uh—"

Gabriela help up a hand in front of my face. "Where's Ramón?" she asked again.

"I think you should call the nurse...." My heart was beating faster.

"Good idea." Ariana jumped off the bed and practically ran out of the room.

"Sweetheart, I'm so happy to see that you are doing better."

She continued to stare at me as she tried to pull away from my touch. I refused to let go. I knew this was going to be my only chance to win her over. If I didn't do it now, I might never get another opportunity.

"Where's my brother?" She stretched her words, showing anger with each syllable. Her lips were clenched as she looked straight ahead, refusing to meet my eyes.

"Gabriela, I don't think you should be getting upset."

She pushed my hand off her arm with an energy and strength I didn't know she possessed. I didn't know what to do. As much as I wanted to hug and hold her, I was sure it wouldn't be a good idea. I frantically looked around, wishing Ariana would come back.

"Don't you dare tell me what I should and shouldn't do. Who the fuck are you?" she screamed at the top of her lungs.

I never meant to inflict such pain on my children. What bothered me more than anything was the fact that I'd probably never get them to understand what motivated their mother and me to make the decisions we made. "Gabriela," I said a little more sternly.

She turned to me with a look that could only be described as hatred. "Where's my fucking brother, and who the fuck said you could come in my room?"

I couldn't take it anymore. I started backing out. The nurse burst in and immediately took control. She told me to step out into the hallway while she examined Gabriela. I was grateful for a reason to escape. I was shaken to the core and felt powerless to do anything.

"Are you okay?" Ariana asked as she placed a hand on my shoulder.

Right then, I needed her touch. "Oh God, I'm so sorry for everything."

"Do you need to sit down?"

"Stop fussing over me. I'm fine." I immediately regretted taking my frustration out on Ariana. Obviously hurt, she withdrew her hand.

"Sweetheart, no, I'm sorry. That didn't sound quite the way I intended it to. I just meant I don't want you making a big deal about what you saw earlier. I'm fine ... really I am. It doesn't happen often. I am stressed and it doesn't help my condition. You have to understand—"

"You can go in now. I've given her a shot so she can rest. Please don't stay long," the nurse instructed as she exited the room.

I understood the warning in her voice. Ariana went in first and I reluctantly followed. I knew it wasn't going to be easy coming back into their lives, but damn, I never expected this.

CHAPTER SEVENTEEN
MOSES RAMSEY

The baby and I were in the living room when Ariana came home from the hospital. I could tell she'd been crying so I assumed it had something to do with her sister. I had not gotten the chance to go to the hospital to visit Gabriela yet. It was something I needed to do, but I wanted my visit to be kept a secret.

"Hey." She put her purse down on the sofa and stared at the television.

I was surprised she didn't make a beeline for the baby, but I didn't think she even realized that I was holding him. "Where's your father?"

"Said he wanted to be by himself." Ariana wasn't being very talkative, which was highly unusual for her.

"How did it go?"

"Bad."

I waited for her to elaborate, but she just stared at the television as if she were actually interested in it. I might have thought so, too, if it weren't football. Ariana hated football.

"Is your sister okay?"

She tore her eyes from the television and stared at me like I'd said the dumbest shit on the planet. "Would you be okay if you found out that everything your parents had ever told you in life was a fucking lie?"

"Is that a rhetorical question?" I could have confessed to my own deception while the door was wide open, but I punked out.

"Seriously, they lied about everything."

What was I to say? I was just as guilty. "Stay here, we need to talk." I went upstairs and put Moses down for what I hoped to be the night. It felt good taking care of him, watching our first game together, and being responsible. I hoped that what I was about to tell Ariana wouldn't change our future together. I poured both of us a double shot of rum on the rocks before I returned to the living room. Ariana was still staring at the TV.

I turned it off. "Here, you're going to need this."

"Oh shit. If this is more true confessions, I've had enough today."

"I understand. But there is something I need to get off my chest, and it's best you hear it now rather than later."

"Is it going to be bad?"

I nodded. I didn't want to hurt her, but I was ready to start the healing process. "Your meeting me wasn't by chance."

"Excuse me?" She put her drink down on the table untouched.

I drained my glass and reached for hers. If she wasn't going to drink it, there was no sense in letting aged rum go to waste. "Now before you get all upset, it's not as bad as it sounds. Your Uncle Monte, posing as your father, hired me to follow your mother. He believed she was having an affair, but I never confirmed it. The only reason I am telling you this now is because I'm tired of keeping it inside. I want us to build a solid foundation together, and it can't be done if it starts out on a broken slab."

She sat back, despondent. I could tell she was a little leery. She looked like she was about to bolt from the room at any moment.

"One day I followed you."

She gasped and started to get up, but I stopped her.

"Honey, wait, please let me finish."

She sat back down with her arms folded across her chest.

"You were looking for a job and I created one just for you." I hung my head. This conversation was going to go one way or the other. She was either going to be flattered that I put so much energy into meeting her, or she was going to flip the fuck out about the invasion of her privacy. I braced myself for her reaction.

She started watching the television again. Only problem, was… it wasn't on. I didn't anticipate this reaction. Silence was a motherfucker because folks started confessing to stuff they didn't even do just to fill the void. I was not about to get tricked into that shit, so I waited her out.

"Can you fix me another drink?" she said as she nibbled on her bottom lip.

Perfect. She must have read my mind. I went to the bar and grabbed the entire bottle, hoping we didn't need it. After Ariana drank what I would have easily called a triple, she was ready to start talking.

"So, was my mother cheating?" She filled her glass again.

I was relieved she wasn't focused on my deception. I wiped my sweaty brow and tried to keep the smile of satisfaction off my face. "Not that I could tell. Whenever she left the house, she was with Ramón."

Ariana nodded her head, but she wasn't finished. "What else?"

"Huh?" If she was requesting something specific, she was going to have to spell it out for me because I was not about to start admitting things all willy-nilly.

She poured another drink, and I began to worry things wouldn't turn out as planned. Even though this marriage started out fraudulently, I really did want my marriage to work. I only had to remind myself of how I felt the day I found out she was having a baby, and I knew that I wanted what my mother and father had, and I believed I could get it with Ariana. I reached out to put my arm around her shoulders, but she pulled away.

"Were you a part of the scam my uncle pulled on my family?"

I was appalled by the suggestion. I did some fucked up shit... but that stuff with her uncle, I didn't even see it coming. "Hell no! I didn't know the man like that. He fooled all of us."

"How am I supposed to believe you?" She was on a slow boil—the alcohol contributed to the heat.

"Are you kidding me? I thought you would be flattered I went the extra mile just to meet you." I attempted a smile.

"Flattered? Are you high?" Her voice reached a high-pitched squeal, which grated on my nerves.

"Honey, calm down. You will wake the baby."

She jerked away from me again.

"Don't be mad. I couldn't say anything to you because I was working for who I thought was your dad. So I kept watching the house—and you—while collecting a check, until I decided I had enough of the charade. Instead of watching out for Mrs. Mendoza, I followed you to the unemployment office."

She still didn't say anything, so my stupid ass kept on talking falling into the same trap I was trying to avoid. "I went back to my office feeling excited. I was about to take matters into my own hands. I sat down at my desk and composed an ad to appear in the paper for an office assistant. See, I had no idea what your skill level was and, to be honest, I didn't give a damn. It took a month before you finally took the bait and came in for an interview." I sat back, confidently smug about the way I explained my actions.

"Is any of that supposed to make me feel better? I feel violated."

"Honey, don't... I'll admit it was a fucked-up situation. But when I saw you, I was already in. There was no way I could change it, and I didn't want to lose the opportunity to get to know you. I'm a private investigator. It's what I do, but I never expected to fall in love with you. That was never part of my plan." I reached for her again, but she still moved away from me.

She poured herself another drink, and I was still working on mine.

"Are you finished with true confessions?" She was mean-spirited and sarcastic, but I could understand it.

I ignored her apparent attitude. I'd probably feel the same way, if the shoe were on the other foot. "I turned down so many applicants waiting for you to come through the door. I didn't even care if you knew how to turn a computer on, let alone use it." I started laughing, but she didn't join in. "I wanted to get to know you. My heart practically skipped a beat when you walked into the office. Remember, I didn't have a receptionist, so you walked up to my door and knocked. This was the closest I'd been to you, and you were even more beautiful up close than you were from a distance.

"My dick was hard as a rock, just smelling your perfume. You broke my heart when you told me you were married. It felt like you'd thrown a bucket of ice-cold water on me. I felt so dumb. I'd spent so much time watching the family, it never even dawned on me to follow you home. I just assumed you were single."

"So why did you give me the job?"

"I convinced myself that you were off-limits and therefore were untouchable."

Ariana shot me a dirty look, shaking her head, but she didn't look as mad as she originally had. "You should have told me the truth."

"You're right and I have to admit it was hard. When you told me you were married, I almost told you the job was filled but I was caught. If I said no, you could have sued the shit out of me for marital discrimination or something stupid like that." I was lying through my teeth, and I was mad at myself for not being more thorough in my investigation. I began to second-guess myself as to what else I'd missed.

"So, no regrets?" She was clearly drunk, swaying as if she was listening to music.

"Uh...of course not." In reality, I was full of regrets, but I was stuck like chuck. I was going to have to spend at least eight hours a day with a woman who I was deeply attracted to. My gut told me that this was going to be very hard to deal with. Despite my fears, I was still excited about getting to know this exotic creature who stood before me. Perhaps if I listened more to my gut instinct instead of my dick, things wouldn't have turned out as badly as they had.

"Hey, I wasn't going to sleep with you. That's not why I hired you. I just wanted to be around you. I promise."

"But you slept with me anyway."

"That was your idea, remember? You came on to me."

"Ouch, I thought we came on to each other."

I'd hurt her feelings. Shit, I didn't want to waste time talking. Between the baby and her father, Ariana and I had so little time alone. I was missing my wife. "Damn, baby, I didn't mean it like that. All I'm trying to tell you is that I fell in love with you the moment I saw you. I had to have you, and I'm so happy to have you as my wife."

She looked as if she didn't believe me, but one kiss ended any further discussion.

CHAPTER EIGHTEEN
GABRIELA MENDOZA

One Month Later
Maylor Institute for Rehabilitation – Augusta GA

Ariana walked into my hospital room with a bundle of flowers.

"What the fuck is going on, Ariana? I feel like I've been on some other planet and the whole world has marched forward without me."

"Please don't get upset, sweetie. I know I haven't been by to see you as much as I would have liked too, but the doctors thought it was best for your rehabilitation for you to focus on getting better."

I turned my head. I was so mad at my sister, the sight of her made me feel physically ill. If situations were reversed, I wouldn't have abandoned her like she did me. "What are you doing here?" I tried to keep the animosity I felt out of my voice. With nothing but time on my hands, my mind had created all types of scenarios for why my sister always changed the subject when I asked about the night I got hurt and why she had sent me to this God awful place for rehabilitation.

"What do you mean? You know I couldn't come every day with the baby and all that."

"I hate this place." I was not to be consoled.

"This is the best hospital for rehabilitation in the state. And it's over now, the doctors say you can go home tomorrow."

"I don't need you making decisions for me."

"Gabriela, stop being a baby. You needed help to recover and I couldn't be there for you, so we made the best decision for you. You know I love you, right?"

"We, who the fuck is we? And who is footing the bill for this torture chamber?"

"Uh," Ariana fidgeted in the chair.

"Please tell me that man is not covering the bill. I don't want to owe him anything when I walk out of this bitch."

"What did you want me to do? This place is very expensive. We wanted you to have the best care and your insurance wouldn't cover it."

"My care at Emory was fine. You could have let me go home and I would have learned to walk and care for myself."

"You couldn't have gone home alone. You could barely stand, let alone take care of yourself. Even if you came home with me, I wouldn't have been able to take care of you and the baby."

Although my sister spoke the truth, I still didn't like it. When we relied on my father before, it almost cost us our lives. "What makes you so sure that it's him this time and not another stranger?"

"It's him Gabriela. He's very sorry for what was done to us and he wants to make it up."

"How is he going to do that? Is he going to bring momma back from the dead?"

"He's our father, not God. We were quick to blame him for her death, but who is to say that she wouldn't have died anyway without all that happened?"

"Momma was fine before she got the phone call and you know it."

"I would like to think she was but we didn't know them very well. They both lied to us our entire lives."

"Well, what about Ramón? If he hadn't been hanging around with those awful friends of Carlos, Ramón would be here right now."

"Sweetie, they didn't have anything to do with what happened to Ramón."

"He had something to do with it. Those men would have never been in our house had it not been for him." I couldn't believe my sister was taking his side.

"They were friends of Monte not Padre's."

"Obviously he has you brainwashed. Where is he? Is he still staying with you?"

"No, he moved out. He is staying in our old house."

"I thought Monte sold it."

"He tried, but Padre was able to stop the sale."

"Humph. What did he do, shoot the buyer?"

"No, he was able to prove he was the legal owner. I'm telling you, Padre's not a bad guy and he's really sorry he wasn't there to protect us."

I was getting extremely annoyed. "Don't you get it? I didn't want to talk about Padre. If you want to talk about something, tell me what happened to Ramón. Every time I mention him you want to run off. Is he really dead? I see his face in my dreams and there is so much blood."

Ariana nodded her head as tears welled in her eyes. "Tilo shot both of you. Ramón wasn't as lucky as you were."

"Huh? What?" I couldn't breathe. I felt like someone was standing on my chest. As hard as it was to accept, I did not doubt my sister's account.

"What else do you remember?" She set the flowers she had been holding on my bedside table.

I couldn't concentrate on what Ariana was saying to me. I didn't want to believe that Tilo tried to kill me…I thought she loved me. My head thrashed back and forth as I was assaulted with memories.

"Gabriela, should I get the nurse? Are you in pain?"

I was hurt, but not from my injuries. My heart was breaking in half, but I couldn't speak about it now. I needed time to wrap my arms around what Ariana had just said. "My head hurts." I didn't want to talk anymore. I turned over on my side, hoping she would get the hint and leave me alone.

"Okay. I will be back in the morning to take you home."

Home, what did I have to go home to? Everything I cared about was gone.

"It's going to be okay," Ariana chanted.

She lied. How was anything ever going to be okay? Ramón hadn't even had a chance to live his life and he was dead because of me. I wanted to be alone. I needed to be alone. "Leave." My voice was muffled against my sheets.

"What did you say?"

"Leave. Please." I understood her desire to comfort me, but I couldn't handle it right now. I needed to be by myself.

"I don't think I should—"

"Go, dammit!" I tried it the nice way, but it didn't work. If yelling at her was the only way that I could get her the fuck out of my room, so be it. "Go now, please," I whispered.

"If you need anything before tomorrow, call me," she said as she quietly closed the door behind her.

I summoned the nurse.

"Yes, may I help you?" the nurse said through an intercom.

"My head is hurting. Can you give me something for the pain so I can sleep?"

"Sure, let me check your chart and someone will be there shortly."

My head was hurting, but not enough to require drugs. I wanted them to escape reality. I didn't want to think about what my sister told me. It was hard enough thinking about Tilo trying to kill me, but she took things to another level when she killed my brother.

"That bitch had better run 'cause when I find her, her ass is mine!" I meant that shit. I was going to find that lying bitch and when I did, it was not going to be pretty.

CHAPTER NINETEEN
ARIANA MENDOZA

I cried all the way back to the hotel room I booked for the night. Gabriella's hospital was over two hours from Atlanta so to drive home only to come back the next day, would've been stupid. While I was gone, Moses watched LM. It was hard being away from my child.

I couldn't shake feeling like I had failed my younger sister and brother. Even though I had nothing to do with the madness that caused Ramón's demise and her attempted murder, I still felt responsible because I was the eldest. I called Padre when I got back in my room.

"How is she?" Padre asked.

"Physically she was okay, but I'm not so sure how she's doing mentally. I keep waiting for her to show some sign of emotion, but every time she gets to that point, she sends me away."

"She was always a willful child."

His comment surprised me since he was not around much when we were children. "I told Gabriela about Ramón."

"I wanted to be there when you did. Is she okay?"

"She's as okay as she can be under the circumstances. I wanted to wait until you were around, but the timing was right. She said she dreamed of him covered in blood. So I told her."

"Do you think she remembers anything?"

"She might. It's so hard trying to read her mind."

"Your mother was just like that."

"She was? She didn't seem to have a problem expressing her emotions to me." I laughed as I rubbed my butt. I had my share of whippings, so if she held something back, I would have hated to see it.

"Trust me, she held a lot back. I see your mother in both of you."

"Oh yeah? What do you see in me?" I was enjoying this conversation. This was the first time I'd spoken to him and didn't feel like pointing fingers.

"You got her diplomatic side. She was about harmony and balance."

The line went quiet for a few seconds as I absorbed his words.

"I knew she needed help, but I was too selfish to come."

I was surprised by the way the conversation changed. "Padre, I was with her most of my life; she never said she was unhappy."

"Don't you see, that's how she was. I knew her well enough to know what she wasn't saying."

"Moses said Monte hired him because he thought Madre was having an affair."

Padre quickly inhaled, but he blew the air out just as rapidly. "To be honest, in all the years we were together, I never entertained that thought."

"Did you care?"

He didn't answer. For a moment, I thought he was going to ignore the question.

"Our relationship was complicated. Your mother didn't love me. She respected me, but she didn't love me. There is a big difference."

"Why did y'all stay together so long?"

"We didn't know any better. Things were different when we were coming up. Our marriage was arranged…and for me, I never thought about doing anything other than what I was told to do."

I wasn't expecting this type of honesty from him. I expected him to paint this rosy picture, especially since my mother wasn't there to dispute anything he said.

"Regrets?"

He didn't hesitate to answer this one. "Plenty. My biggest regret is that I didn't come home sooner. I could've, there was nothing holding me in Colombia. My parents were gone. I think I was afraid; too much time had passed."

"Did Uncle Monte have a family?" I was curious about the man who lived in our house, but rarely showed any kindness toward me.

"His wife died before they had children, so no. I was his only family."

"Wow, maybe he was jealous of you. You had five children. You had sons."

He sighed again. "We'll never know."

He was right, we wouldn't.

"In case you're wondering, Moses said he never found any evidence of an affair."

"That's good to know. Get some rest and I'll come see you when you get back tomorrow."

"Good night, Padre."

"Good night, my child."

CHAPTER TWENTY
GABRIELA MENDOZA

I was facing the door when it opened. I was relieved he got there in time. "Thanks for coming on such short notice." I attempted to sit up straight as I raised my bed.

"I'm glad you called. I was never sure when was the right time to come." Moses stood at the foot of my bed.

"Where's my sister?"

"At the hotel with the baby. She was really surprised when I knocked on her door."

"Good." I nodded my head. I wasn't sure how to start this conversation with my sister's husband. He was a virtual stranger to me. The only things I knew about him were the things my sister told me. My brother Ramón worked for Moses for a while and idolized him, and this meant a lot to me.

"How much do you remember?" Moses made it easy on me by cutting directly to the chase.

"Pretty much everything, I think. I needed to speak with you to help me fill in the gaps." I was partially truthful. I did have a few holes in my memory, but more than anything, I wanted to know if he knew Tilo and I were lovers. If he didn't know, it was a secret I was prepared to take to my grave.

He took a seat in the only chair in the room and pulled it up close to my bed. He really was a handsome man. He reminded me of LL Cool J, only younger.

I said, "How is it that you came to know Tilo? I remember her saying something about your being her boss."

"It's kind of a long story. The short version is, she was looking for you. Apparently you hadn't shown up for work for several days and would not answer your phone. I was dropping off Ramón and she followed me. I busted her following me and she started filling me in on what she thought was going on in the house."

"Is that all?"

"She thought all of you were in danger. Ramón confirmed it, so I got involved."

He still wasn't answering my question.

"So you hired her? I still don't understand how all that came about."

"Like I said, it's complicated, but our relationship was strictly professional."

He knew, I could tell by the way he answered the question. Now I needed to find out if he had shared that information with my sister. I took a moment to think about how to phrase my next question.

"I think you should know that your father has asked me to find Tilo; however, your sister is totally against it."

"And?" I was nervous, but I tried not to let it show.

"Between you and me, I'm gonna find the bitch."

"Perfect. I want in for personal reasons."

"I was hoping you would say that. So far I haven't been able to find out anything else about her. Her FBI records are sealed. They believe she's dead. They wouldn't even tell me what she was working on."

"I still can't believe she was an FBI agent. If she was working on a case, it was obviously dealing with my family. My guess is that she wanted the bonds Ramón got from Madre's safe-deposit box."

"That's a safe assumption, but I don't think that was the reason. Call it intuition, but I think it goes deeper than the bonds. If you want my opinion, the bonds were an added bonus. I think she was looking for something else," he said.

"This shit is crazy. Tilo never appeared to be that type of person. She wasn't Rambo. She was scared of her own shadow." My heart felt like it was breaking into little pieces. Tilo was the only person I'd allowed into my personal space, into my heart, and she deceived me. Suddenly, I didn't want to talk anymore. I didn't want to know any more details of what had happened to me. "Moses, I think you should get back to the hotel before my sister gets suspicious. We will talk later?" I still had questions, but I wasn't ready to deal with the answers.

"Sure. I'll see you later at the house when Ariana brings you home."

"No offense, I don't want to come to your house. I'm not going to feel comfortable, and I honestly ain't ready to play aunty."

"I can understand that. Sometimes LM makes so much noise, I want to leave too, but I love my little man. Where do you want to go?"

"My apartment. The rent is paid up for the year."

"What are you going to tell Ariana? You know her feelings will be hurt if you don't come home with her."

I allowed my head to sink down to my chest as I thought of a solution. "I'll make her understand. Trust me."

"Okay. Call me when you're ready to work."

"Moses, this one is personal. Can we keep things between us?"

"I'm good with that, but I've already told you your dad wants in. It's personal to him too! Are you cool with him being involved?"

"Honestly, I don't know. I have to wait and see. For now, don't tell him I'm on board. There are a few things that I don't want to explain to him, or even my sister, for that matter."

"Gotcha. I think I can handle that."

CHAPTER TWENTY-ONE
CARLOS MENDOZA

Moving into my old house was easy. All I had to do was flash around some money and threaten to tie the property up in court for years. The buyer snatched it up. The money I paid out to get it back, was nothing compared to what I believed was hidden in the house.

Over the years, not only was I sending the bearer bonds to my wife, Alelina, I also sent cash the likes of which had not turned up yet. She told me it was in the house, and I was fairly certain where to find it. No one knew of this stash so I was fairly confident it was still there. I intended to use a good portion of the money to find Tilo. She killed my son and harmed my daughter. I was looking forward to teaching her a lesson about messing with my family.

I didn't feel any connection with my old house because none of our old things were in it. The walls were painted white and barren. The rugs that used to cover the hardwood floors had been removed. Everything that made it a home was gone.

Therefore, I wasn't prepared for the emotional rush I felt as I stepped into our kitchen. All of our old appliances had been replaced with the latest technology. I knew my wife didn't commission the work. She claimed the old stuff worked just fine for her. She was a frugal woman by nature; it was one of the things I loved about her. For a moment I was overwhelmed with sadness for my family.

My footsteps echoed across the hardwood floors as I walked from the kitchen back to the living room. It wasn't a bad house. It was old, but it was built during an era when builders actually cared about what they were creating. This house had character. Funny, I didn't realized it until I saw it empty. In fact, if things worked out with my family, I would consider staying in Atlanta and making this house into a home.

As I entered the living room, I realized this was the room where my son was taken from me. I walked around to see if I could detect where he had actually fallen. Just thinking about Ramón lying in a pool of his own blood was enough to make my legs wobble. I knew my youngest son resented me. I would have done anything to have been able to go back through time and undo the hurt and pain I caused him.

I left the living room and went to the bedroom I once shared with my wife. The time passed so quickly, it was hard to believe I hadn't been there in over ten years. I paused for a second at the door to get my emotions in check. I wasn't big on displaying my feelings, but since I was alone, I allowed myself to let go of the pain I felt. As I pushed open the door, I pretended things were as they should have been and waited for my wife to greet me. But of course they weren't—and never would be again. The thought tugged at my heart and I lost my composure completely.

I sank to my knees as my sobs overwhelmed me. The force of my tears was so hard I rolled onto my side and brought my knees to my chest and rocked from side to side. A lot of plans for our future were made in this room. This was the only place in the house where I freely spoke to my wife and she talked back to me. It was the only room where we shed our façades we were forced to wear and rejoiced in a love we weren't allowed to nurture.

I continued to rock until my sobs became muted whimpers. It was a good cry, long overdue. I continued to cry, but my tears weren't just for the death of my wife and son. It was the end of my vision and my dreams. Things would never be the same and there was nothing I could do about it. It was a bitter pill for me to swallow since I always prided myself on being in control. But someone I didn't even know had taken the power from me and I wanted it back.

I indulged myself for more than an hour. It was an hour that I didn't have to spare, but I didn't have much choice—my grief knew no bounds. As I wiped away the last tear I struggled to my feet. I wasn't as young as I used to be, and getting my legs up under me was harder than I thought it would be. If my brother was still alive, I would have shot him myself. I ultimately felt it was because of him that my life was ruined.

I turned on the light to the stairs leading down to the basement. The bulb that normally lit the top of the stairs had obviously blown out, but there was enough light coming from the window at the bottom of the steps for me to see my way. I carefully walked down the stairs. The last thing I needed to do was to fall and break a hip or something.

Like the rest of the house it was empty of furnishings with the exception of a washer and a dryer. I guessed the new owners decided to keep them, even though they were old as hell. For the first time since I entered the house, I smiled.

CHAPTER TWENTY-TWO
GABRIELA MENDOZA

I was all packed and sitting on the side of the bed when Ariana pushed open the door. The nurse had already removed my IV and had given me my discharge papers.

"Hey you. Are you ready to go?" she said with a gorgeous smile on her face.

"I'll say. I didn't sleep at all last night. My physical therapist tried to work me to death after you left."

"They are just making sure you're ready to go home."

"I guess I shouldn't complain because they obviously did something right, and at least I get the chance to leave."

"That's so true. There were times when I thought you weren't going to make it," Ariana said.

The nurses all told me how lucky I was to be alive. I knew that I should be thankful, but I wasn't there yet.

"Let me get that for you," Ariana said as she attempted to grab my bag.

I stepped back, surprised. I wasn't used to having her waiting on me. It was usually the other way around, especially when she was pregnant with LM. She had me doing everything, and I do mean everything. This was like poetic justice.

"It's not heavy, I can carry it," I protested mildly for appearances.

"Girl, it ain't often that I get to wait on you, so you'd better enjoy it while it lasts. Trust and believe as soon as we get to the house, you're on your own."

I cringed when she mentioned going to her house. Not only did I not want to go there because of Moses, I also didn't want to be up half the night because of a crying child, nephew or not. "Where's Moses?" I asked as we walked through the door.

"Girl, you know that fool drove all the way down just so I could nurse the baby. He had bottles of milk at the house. He should be on his way home now."

I could not help but to laugh at the way she turned up her lips when she said it. "Why you say it like that? He wanted his child to have some fresh milk."

"I know you're right, but my boobs needed this break. That boy wants to eat all the time. When I get you home, I'm going to wean him off the breasts."

I missed a step and stumbled when she said that. I didn't want to burst her bubble or anything, but I wasn't feeling that at all. "Uh, Ariana...I'm not so sure that going home with you is a good idea. I mean, you and Moses are still honeymooners. I don't want to be like a third wheel. Plus, we've got a good relationship; I'm not trying to ruin shit by moving in with you." I hoped my explanation and misgivings were enough to make her change her mind.

"Girl, Little Moses is a third wheel. You would be more like an intervention. We've lived together most of our lives. It won't be anything different, so stop tripping."

Damn, she was making me feel like shit. We'd just passed the nurse's station when the head nurse looked up and saw me.

The nurse said, "Hey, wait, you can't just walk out of here. Let me get someone to assist you."

"Nurse Walker, that won't be necessary. My sister will help me if I need it."

"It's hospital policy." She put down her pen and called someone over her radio to assist.

"For crying out loud. Can't I walk out with my dignity?" I whined.

"Calm down, sis. It will only take a minute and we will be on our way."

I leaned up against the station and tried to hide my irritation. It took another ten minutes before we were finally able to leave the hospital, but this time I was fit to be tied. I just wanted to go someplace and be by myself.

"You comfortable? We should be at the house in no time. I can't wait for you to meet LM." Ariana said as she pulled out of the hospital parking lot.

"You really are going to have to think of another name for your child. You can't keep calling him LM, he'll get a complex. I can understand how it would be confusing calling him Moses. And you sure can't call him little. The little girls will have my poor nephew traumatized by second grade."

We both laughed.

She said, "I see it's going to take more than one to the head to change that wacked sense of humor you have."

"I'm just saying, Li'l? Even after he explains why y'all call him that, kids are still going to be curious. You're going to have folks following him to the urinal to find out what's really going on. God forbid his dick…" I held up my pointer finger and thumb, squinting as I looked between my parted fingers. "Lawd, you should start working on this right away before the name sticks. I'm not calling him that. I just won't be party to that nonsense, and you can best believe I'm going to tell him just as soon as he's old enough to understand."

We couldn't stop laughing.

Ariana said, "His middle name is Ramón."

The car became so quiet I could hear the crickets chirping outside the window. "Damn, I ain't ready to call him that either." I looked out the window, trying to think of how to get back to the happy wave we were just riding.

"It's all good. We'll think of something. I don't want my baby traumatized."

"Can we stop by my old apartment before we go to your house? I want to see what Tilo did with my things."

"Gabriela, don't you think you should rest first? Ain't no telling what you are going to find when you do go by there. Hell, she might have thrown your stuff out on the streets."

"Can you just humor me?" I said quietly, but my mind was made up. I was moving home. "Wait, where is my car?"

"Moses drove it over to our house. But I'm not about to let you drive. You just got out of the hospital. You should be thinking about getting in bed, not riding all around town and shit."

"Ariana, we can do this the easy way or the hard way." I was done discussing it. I just needed my keys so I could be on my way. "So what's it like having Padre around?" I was trying to change the subject to avoid an argument.

"He is not the same man I remember. He's more…mellow and relaxed," Ariana answered.

"Are you sure that it's him?" I asked. We had been duped once and I for one wasn't ready to be duped again.

"I'm pretty sure. He's very remorseful for staying away so long, and that's more than I can say for his brother who pretended to be him."

"Shit, that wouldn't be hard to do. The fucker didn't show one ounce of compassion when Madre died."

We sat in silence for a while as Ariana drove. I was still going through it and trying to come to grips with the fact that my brother Ramón was dead and was never coming back. We both started speaking at the same time.

"I was thinking about Ramón," Ariana said.

"I know. I was thinking about him too, and our mother."

Ariana said, "Don't you start crying because that will make me cry too."

She was right. We had had enough pain over the last six months. It was time to heal. "You're right. I'm sorry. So, how are things going with you and Moses?"

Ariana wiggled in her seat. I was trying to read her body language to see what that meant, but I was clueless. I wasn't sure if she was wiggling because she was uncomfortable speaking about him or because she had a hot, freaky flashback and had to fan the coochie.

"It's going good, I guess. When I first came home from the hospital, he was very standoffish, but he's warming back up to me now. I think we are going to make it."

"You were worried?" I was surprised. I knew Ariana loved Moses. She risked her first marriage on him, and he appeared to love her as well. But who was I to judge? I thought Tilo loved me.

"I hate to say it, but yeah, it was rough at first. We argued all the time, especially about his obsession with Tilo. Her name came up a lot, and I finally had to check him about it. I don't even want her name mentioned in my house."

My hands started sweating. Tilo wasn't my favorite person these days either, but it would really fuck me up if I found out that she was screwing Moses too. I tried to play off my concerns. "Are you serious? Why? She didn't even know either of you until all this shit went down, right?" A forgotten memory bounced around in my head. Tilo did know of Ariana. I told her about the affair, her marriage, everything. Damn.

"She may not have known me personally, but I think it's mighty strange she was the one who found me and took me to the hospital after I got away from Monte's madness."

"Honey hush. I could tell the moment I saw Moses that he was in love with you." Even as I said it, I began to doubt the validity of my words.

Ramón said the same thing to me when he saw the way Tilo looked at me. I was learning a valuable lesson: looks could be deceiving.

"You're right. Things are better now. We've gotten past the bad stuff," Ariana said.

"So how does he do with the baby?"

"Girl, at first he wouldn't go near him. If LM was crying, Moses would walk right on by him like he didn't even hear him. I swear I cried myself to sleep every night for a solid month."

"Obviously that has changed since he brought the baby down here to get fed," I said laughing.

"Oh yeah. It's better now. He's come around."

"So, what prompted the change?"

"To be honest, I don't know. But I am glad it happened because I don't think I would have been able to continue down the same road we were going."

"Well, for your sake, I'm glad."

We arrived at Ariana's house. I was eager to get going, so I immediately gathered my things.

"Wait, give me a minute to check on the baby, and I'll ride over there with you."

"No, I need to do this by myself. If I have any trouble, I promise I will call you to come get me." I didn't want to argue with her about it, but I would if I had to.

"Gabriela, I don't have a good feeling about this. I bet if I look through your discharge papers it probably says you shouldn't drive."

"Whatever. I'm going. I'll call you after I get settled in." I left her sitting in the car.

CHAPTER TWENTY-THREE
TILO ADAMS

I woke up in a cold sweat once again. I pushed back the heavy covers—damp with my sweat—and rushed to the bathroom. I was shaking from head to toe. My eyes swung around the room, frantically looking to see who or what had scared me so badly. I held my hands in front of my face and they looked like they didn't even belong to me. I didn't want to admit it, but I was losing touch with reality. My life had become a series of bad dreams and sullen memories. More than anything, I wished I could have a do-over. If God granted me one, I was certain I would do things differently.

"This shit has got to stop," I said out loud. Every time I closed my eyes it was the same damn thing and the shit was old, but I didn't know how to make it stop. The sleep that I managed to get was sporadic at best. It took me hours to fall asleep, but when I did I was tormented by dreams, visions, and other unspeakable horrors.

I never imagined life as a criminal would be so hard. Now I understood what it meant to be on the lam and it was not a pleasant feeling. My cell phone sat on the vanity, but it was just a paperweight because there wasn't a single person in it who I could call just to get me through times like these. My mom thought I was dead. With the exception of Moses, everyone else did too.

"I need to get away." It was time to make a move. I had been saying this every morning for the last three months, but I had yet to act on it. I was still holed up at the Omni Hotel in Atlanta. Fear kept me there. I was afraid to trust the fake ID and passport which I obtained, even though I'd gotten it from a reliable source. "Bitch, stop talking about going away and do something about it." Talking to myself had become second nature. It didn't bother me that I was having a full-blown conversation with myself. With the nightmares I was having, it was a miracle I wasn't walking down the street babbling like an idiot.

I was so exhausted. I flopped down on the toilet seat and rested my forearms on my thighs. I peed like I hadn't used the toilet in a month. I didn't have the strength to stand up. As I rested my head on my knees, I drifted off to sleep. My nap, however, was cut short by another scary image of Gabriela's face after I had shot her brother.

"Shit." I went over to the sink to wash my hands. As the water got hot, I grabbed a washcloth from behind the door. The water felt good on my face and soothing to my eyes. For a moment, I considered using it as a compress and crawling back to bed. I was sick of the nightmares and I was truly ready for a change in scenery. It was time that I did something about it. It didn't make sense to have all this money and be afraid to leave the hotel. I tried to leave the bathroom without looking at my reflection, but my eyes had a mind of their own. The vision before me repulsed me. My eyes were bloodshot as if I'd been crying, and the dark circles underneath my eyes looked like I'd been in a fight and lost.

"Damn, girl, you've got to pull your shit together." I threw the washcloth in the basin and left the room. Before those stupid dreams, I had a plan. It was time I started acting on it.

I had always wanted to go on a cruise. Now that I had money, I was going to treat myself to one. I booted up my laptop and did a Google search for "cruises." The list was seemingly endless, and I was about to give up my search. I didn't want just any old cruise. I needed to get away and anonymity was key. I refined my search to "celebrity cruises" because I knew they weren't traveling on the average cruise ship. Bingo!

"'Aw, sookie sookie now." I clapped my hands with enthusiasm. Suddenly things were looking brighter. I looked at the different videos and decided I was going to take a world cruise. Mapping out the different cities I wanted to visit, Cunard Cruise vacations, based out of England, seemed like a great choice. I saved the trip to my Yahoo! Trip Planner and looked at the logistics of getting there.

"This bitch is going to set me back about thirty stacks, but it will be worth it. At least I won't have to worry about running into anybody I know. Hell, I might even see Oprah on the ship." I was giddy with the possibilities, but I was also grateful for the break from my reality. Planning the cruise allowed me time to plan for a future and to forget the past. I double-clicked on the *Queen Mary 2* and pulled up the 2014 itinerary.

"Oh shit, they have a cruise leaving on April thirteenth from New York." I pulled out my BlackBerry and checked the date. Being locked up in this hotel room, I'd lost all concept of time.

It was March 25 so it only gave me a few weeks to get to New York and purchase some clothes for my upcoming trip. I spun around in my chair and started to check out flights to New York. If I could get out of Atlanta today, I was going for it. I'd been pushing my luck by staying in the city anyway. It was time for this eagle to spread her wings and fly.

CHAPTER TWENTY-FOUR
MOSES RAMSEY

I heard Ariana enter the house, but I did not go into the kitchen to greet her. Instead, I waited for her to come find me.

"Hello."

"Huh?" My eyes were glued to the television, and I acted like I wasn't paying attention to her.

"I said hello."

She sounded annoyed as I knew she would be.

"Wait." I pulled her down in my lap. "I just want to hear the rest of this story."

She turned toward the television. A commercial was playing so she didn't know what had captured my attention.

I started leaving a trail of kisses from her cheek to collarbone. "Mmm, you smell so good."

"Ah," I murmured.

I pumped the brakes when Barbara Walters came back on for her special report. *Thirty Days and Thirty Nights* was the name of the special I had been waiting on. However, Ariana wasn't feeling it as much as me.

"Have you been following these stories?"

"No." She was pouting.

"It's crazy. The violence in Mexico is out of control. Ever since the raid on the Cali Cartel happened here, the drug violence over there has gone through the roof. They are cutting off people's heads and leaving them in the streets with notes on them and shit."

Apparently, her interest was piqued as she slid off my lap. "How long has it been on? Did you record it on the DVR? I think my sister will want to see it too."

"It just came on when you came in."

She got the remote off the table and started recording the show.

The TV anchorwoman said:

"The bodies of eighteen men were found in a mass grave in South Acapulco. Authorities suspect the bodies to be those of the missing members of a group of men who vanished while vacationing on September thirtieth—"

The TV screen went to an emergency test broadcast.

"Nah, are they serious? I wanted more information."

"Yo, this is crazy. What the fuck were eighteen men doing together on vacation? That's what I want to know."

"Eww, Moses, that's just nasty."

"I'm just saying. I don't know ten motherfuckers willing to go on vacation together, let alone eighteen."

The show came back on.

"Gunman kills fifteen men at a car wash. Thirteen of the men worked at the car wash, but they also were clients of a drug rehab center. Mexican authorities have apprehended a single gunman responsible for this latest massacre."

Ariana chuckled, "Damn, sounds like a pissed-off woman to me."

I didn't say anything as I tried to figure out a way to tie this into my case with Tilo.

The anchorwoman continued.

"The case of the eighteen dead men doesn't add up. Authorities say relatives of the men insist they were ordinary guys with no affiliation to the bloody drug wars plaguing Mexican cities. Police are skeptical about what the travelers were up to."

"Babe, it's more than that, boo. Mexico is showing its ass. Let me show you a chart I'm working on." I got up to retrieve my briefcase, but Ariana was engulfed in the show. I completely understood her fascination.

As a nation we did not act like the people I saw looting and protesting in the streets. I could not imagine what could have happened to push them to the streets. I grabbed her hand and pulled her away from the set.

"What does this mean? I don't understand." Tears rolled down her cheeks as she looked at the face of her people.

"Honey, don't cry. I probably shouldn't have even let you see that with all that we've been through. Things are definitely getting out of hand over there."

As we sat down at the kitchen table, we could hear LM begins to stir around through our monitor.

"I'll get him," I offered as I handed her the chart that extrapolated five years of violence and what appeared to be six months and counting of retaliation. The citizens of Mexico were fighting back, which made sense since her father said the leaders of the cartel were leaving Mexico in droves.

"Do you see a trend to the violence?" I asked when I got back with LM.

"I see that the citizens are angry about the violence and they are fighting back. What do you see?"

I nodded. "So much of the violence is centered around the police. Yeah, there are some random shootings, but most of it is stemming from the people being tired of a corrupted government."

"This is about Tilo, isn't it?" I wanted him to tell me that I was wrong. I was praying that he would say I was tripping, but his brilliant smile confirmed what I feared the most. My heart felt like it was skipping a beat.

"Yeah, I think so," I whispered.

"I have a headache and I'm going to take a shower." Ariana left the room in a huff as if nothing she had seen on the television mattered. I sighed as I went into the kitchen to warm up a bottle.

♠ ♠ ♠

Ariana wasn't exactly thrilled to hear Tilo's name mentioned in our house. She forbade me to mention her, but I led her to cross the line with my painstakingly staged evidentiary trail. I really had no conclusive evidence that Tilo was involved in the upheaval in Mexico, but I played my long shot so I could work the case without ending up in divorce court.

I felt bad about deceiving Ariana; however, I could not think of any other way. Now that Gabriela was home from the hospital, Ariana was going to rely more and more on me to care for our son, so I had to make a way to bring my work home without any unnecessary cloak-and-dagger bullshit. I wanted to believe that Ariana would respect the privacy of my office when I was not there. But since she used to work for me, she might not believe in the same sanctity.

I pulled my phone from my hip as I came back from putting the baby to bed. I quickly dialed the last number on my phone. Putting the phone up to my ear, I waited for it to be answered.

"Did you do it?" a man said.

"Yes, it's done." I peered upstairs to make sure that I was still alone.

"Good. Any problems?"

"No. Everything went fine." I kept a close lookout for Ariana. I couldn't let her sneak up on me.

"Okay. Now just try to relax and wait," the man said.

My palms and armpits started to sweat. "That's so much easier to say than do."

"Well, you're going to have to do the best that you can. You've waited this long, a few more weeks won't hurt you."

"I hear ya. Look, I've gotta go. Ariana is upstairs taking a shower.

"All right son, I'll talk to you later." I closed my phone and went into the kitchen and pulled out a bottle of Absolut and two glasses from the cabinet. I carried the glasses into the living room.

When Ariana came back into the living room looking sexy as ever, I had already had a few drinks.

"Are you feeling better?"

"My headache is gone. What are you doing other than getting tipsy?"

"Waiting on you to join me." I patted the couch for her to sit down.

Ariana went into the kitchen and grabbed her own glass and joined me. "You know we don't have long before little man gets back up, right? Even though he's not actually sucking my tit, my boobs start to get tight and feel real heavy right before it's time to feed him. I guess they know it's time to get the pump."

"You want me to rub them for you?" I was only playing, but if she wanted to put her titty in my hand, I damn sure was gonna handle them. When she didn't take me up on my offer, I went in the kitchen to get her pump and an empty bottle.

"Hey, what are you going to do with those?" She had a sexy smile on her face. For a minute it was almost the way it was in the beginning when we had fun and played with each other.

"I was hungry," I jokingly replied. I missed those days of fun and flirtation before we became man and wife and I desperately wanted them back.

"Oh really? Well, that bottle is reserved for the baby, but if you play your cards right, mister, I'll let you taste the milk from the sprout! Fresh, not that bottled shit."

"Oh, I love it when you cuss. You're so sexy with it." All of a sudden, I was in a playful mood, and I wanted to recapture the passion that used to flow between us.

"Oh, daddy, I like when you talk to me like that, but it's going to have to wait 'cause LM's alarm is about to go off any minute." She walked up close to me and gave me a deep, soul-searching kiss. I wrapped my arms around her and tried to hold on to the feeling. This was my biggest problem these days—holding on to the love that drew me to Ariana in the first place. It wasn't another woman who drove a wedge between us, it was the fatherhood of our son. I couldn't help but to feel cheated, even though I knew she was married when we first started dating.

I stepped away as soon as I heard LM wailing in the speaker. It seemed like I had just put him to sleep. I tried not to look at it as a buzz kill, but my dick wasn't listening. I pushed away from her as Ariana took the bottle and went upstairs. While I waited for her to return, I went through the mail stacked on the kitchen table. The stack, mainly bills, had been sitting on the table all day, but this was the first time that I'd bothered to look through them. One letter, the size of a postcard, stood out. The envelope had no discernable postmark, which meant it was hand delivered. I opened the letter and written on it were the words:

Wish you were here—not! LOL.

I didn't need a psychic to know who the card was from. The bitch was taunting me and it was pissing me the fuck off. It was bad enough she lied and got away with the money. Now she wanted to play games.

"Why is this bitch still fucking with me?" I slammed my fist into my hand. If Ariana had opened this note instead of me my gig would be done. Obviously Tilo needed to be caught as much as I wanted to catch her.

CHAPTER TWENTY-FIVE
GABRIELA MENDOZA

I parked in front of our building with the engine idling. Part of me felt sure Tilo would be inside with an explanation on her lips. If she was, I honestly didn't know what I would do.

Our subdivision was quiet, but this afternoon it was almost too quiet. It seemed like the entire building was in mourning with me. Even though my brother had been dead for three months, to me it was still fresh. It was warm in the car so I rolled down the window, but it was still too quiet and the silence was torturing me. I turned on the radio, but the music sounded foreign. I was trying to get up the nerve to go inside, but my feet would not cooperate.

The buildings adjacent to mine had plenty of people going in and out or lounging outside on the benches soaking up the afternoon sun. Our building was strangely void of human activity. Rather than going into our apartment, I decided to visit the rental office instead. When we first got the apartment, Tilo insisted we pay the rent for the entire year. At the time, I thought she was nuts, but now I'm glad we did.

Lucky for me, the rental office wasn't crowded like it normally was. Vacancies in our complex were highly sought after due to location and the size of the units.

"I'd like to speak to the manager please," I said to an attractive receptionist.

"Are you looking for an apartment?" She handed me a brochure with the different floor plans that they had.

"No, but I still would like to speak with the manager."

"He's on the phone right now. If you would like to have a seat, I will let him know that you are here."

"Will he be long?"

"Uh, I'm not sure."

"Thanks." It was a dumb question and I realized it as soon as I had said it. I sat down on the sofa feeling nervous, but I wasn't sure why. Thankfully, I didn't have to wait long. The manager came out of the office. I could tell by the look on his face he recognized me.

"Ms. Mendoza, wow! It's Ms. Mendoza." He looked at the receptionist and bobbed his head excitedly.

We stood there staring at each other for a few uncomfortable seconds.

"Can I speak with you in your office?" I felt like a lab rat under observation. So naturally, I wanted to get out of there as soon as I could.

"Absolutely. I am so glad to see you," he said as we walked into his office. We weren't close friends, so I didn't know why he was feeling all giddy and shit.

He closed the door behind us and took a seat at his desk.

"Uh…" I searched his desk for a nameplate but there wasn't one. "Sorry, I've forgotten your name." The sad part about it was that his face didn't even look remotely familiar, but it could have had something to do with my partial loss of memory.

"Not to worry. My name is Richard Peyton. I'm so sorry about what happened to your family." He paused. "I followed the news."

"Wow, really? I wasn't aware that it was on television." I was going to have to speak to Ariana so she could fill me in on exactly how much of our business was public knowledge.

"Yeah, it was the number one story for days. The most excitement we've seen around here in years, no disrespect."

I didn't even know what to say. He was talking about my life like it was some soap opera on television.

"I'm glad you survived. The news didn't say a lot about how you were doing, so I'm glad to see you."

His concern might have meant something to me if I knew who the hell he was. "It's my apartment that I want to speak to you about. It's a two bedroom and I won't be needing the second room. Can I switch to a one bedroom, and what would that entail?"

Richard didn't appear to be surprised by my request.

"That's not a problem. We've been holding your things in storage waiting for someone to come and claim them."

I was confused. Why would my things be in storage? "Storage? Someone moved my things?" I felt violated. I couldn't believe that someone had actually touched my stuff. It was a weird feeling. It was bad enough that it felt like someone was stomping around in my head. I was relying on being able to go home and try to piece together the puzzle my life had become. I never contemplated anyone moving those pieces around. It was a bit disheartening, to say the least.

"Um, yeah. Uh, someone vandalized your apartment and the entire building had to be cleared. We are in the process of remodeling the entire building. Whoever did it poured gasoline throughout the apartment. A resident smelled the fumes and reported it before any permanent damage was done. Since we didn't know how you were doing, I had your things put in storage."

I was speechless, but there was no doubt in my mind of who attempted to torch the building. Richard confirmed my suspicions that Tilo was not dead.

"...police but they never came."

My mind was spinning and I wasn't really paying Richard any attention until I heard him say "police."

"What? Excuse me?"

He looked flustered and uncomfortable, but I didn't care about that.

"I said I was surprised the police weren't interested in searching your apartment with all the other stuff that was going on."

I wanted to slap the fat, pompous fuck right in the face, but he wasn't worth the time or the trouble. He was a mini-drama queen, and I didn't have time for that shit.

"Okay, whatever." I wasn't about to go into my personal business with him. I rolled my eyes, letting him know exactly how I felt about the situation. "So what now? I really want to get settled."

He logged on to the computer and found me another apartment, then handed me the keys. "I will have your things moved within the hour. You will need to switch the utilities over to your name. I believe we were able to save everything except the bed and the sofa. You might also want to get your clothes cleaned just in case they still smell from the gas."

"Thanks for your help." Even though I was mad about the violation and destruction of my property, I took it as proof that Tilo was still alive. I didn't know how I was going to do it, but I was going to find that bitch and make her pay! I was sure of that much.

CHAPTER TWENTY-SIX
MOSES RAMSEY

I sat down at my desk and pulled a cigar from the humidor. "Ah." I exhaled. I missed smoking my cigars. Ever since the baby, I hadn't been able to smoke in the house. I didn't want to smoke in my truck either because there would be times that they would be in the vehicle with me, and I didn't want the baby to smell the fumes. I wasn't worried about Ariana so much; she claimed to enjoy the smell. So rather than feel guilty about lighting up at work, I cherished the stolen moment.

I studied my cigar as I blew smoke rings at the ceiling. Tilo enjoyed a good cigar as well. I had already contacted the local cigar shops and left pictures of her and asked them to contact me if she came to their stores. It was a wild shot, but I was trying to think of every angle to get some type of lead on her whereabouts.

Every time that I thought about that bitch beating me at my own game, I wanted to hurt someone. I wasn't used to losing. It was a bitter pill for me to swallow.

I swung around in my chair and focused my attention on the scenery outside my window. I needed to relax and get my mind off the case.

The case was only one of the reasons that I came into the office early. I was supposed to hear from the doctor today about the DNA test that I'd had performed on LM. My mother insisted I test the baby after I sent her a photo. She claimed that I used to look exactly like LM when I was his age. I didn't pay much attention to what she said. Frankly, I thought it was wishful thinking on her part, but I indulged her nevertheless. I wasn't holding my breath, but I was spending more time with LM and I was enjoying it. I'd already forgiven Ariana for letting me believe she wasn't sleeping with her husband. I even accepted her baby as my own, but in the back of my mind, he would always be her child. I had been fooled once before and I had no intention of getting fooled again. I blew another plume of smoke into the air as I reached for my coffee.

"Yuck." I spat the coffee on my desk. I expected the coffee to be warm, but it was downright frigid and it left a nasty taste in my mouth. I slammed the cup on the desk, causing the coffee to slosh over the side of the cup.

"Shit." As I scrambled to grab a napkin out of the center drawer of my desk to wipe up the mess, the phone rang. "Not now, dammit," I yelled at the phone as if it would hear me and stop ringing.

"Hello," I barked into the receiver.

"Uh…may I speak with Moses Ramsey please."

"This is he." I didn't recognize the voice, and this only added to my irritation.

"Oh, okay. Is this a bad time?"

"No, of course not. Who is this?"

"Uh, I'm sorry, this is Dr. Richmond's office. I have some test results for you, and I was trying to schedule a time for you to come into the office to discuss them."

"Is that really necessary? I mean, can't you tell me over the phone?"

"No, sir. Dr. Richmond will not allow us to read the results over the phone. You understand confidentiality and all..." Her voice trailed off, leaving me to fill in my own blanks.

"Fine, what time do you want me to be there?" I was beyond pissed at this point. Part of me understood the need to deliver the news in person, but the other part of me was irritated and eager to hear the results.

She said, "We have a ten o'clock and a two o'clock available today."

I glanced at the clock. It was nine and their office was only twenty minutes away. "I'll see you at ten." I hung up the phone without waiting for her to confirm. When I got to the office, I would apologize to her for my rudeness. I took my cup over to the little wet bar and rinsed it out. I didn't want to admit it, but suddenly I was nervous.

"Nigga, don't let this get you all twisted in the head." Even though I knew that LM wasn't mine, my heart wanted to believe there was a chance. I tried not to get emotionally attached, but I couldn't help myself. I turned off my computer and grabbed my suit jacket from behind the door. I also grabbed my overcoat and slung it over my arm. I was feeling a little warm. I knew it had everything to do with the news I was about to receive and nothing about the weather.

CHAPTER TWENTY-SEVEN
CARLOS MENDOZA

The washer and dryer that I had purchased from a second hand store when we first moved to Georgia was still there. I breathed a sigh of relief. If someone had disposed of them as well, I don't know what I would have done.

I probably would have dug up my brother, the son of a bitch, and shot him again. I laughed, but I was dead serious. I pushed a button, hidden from view, which lifted the appliances off the floor and slid them away from the wall. I entered the combination that would unlock the door to the secret room hidden beneath the appliances. I held my breath as I walked down the stairs. I hadn't been in the room in years, so I wasn't sure what to expect. I was fairly certain it hadn't been detected, but I was still nervous.

Secrets of our past and the hopes for our future were in this room. The books lining the walls would be a gift to my daughters. In them were first hand accounts of what we were forced to do to ensure their safety. Perhaps if they read the journals, they would find it in their hearts to forgive us for the deceptions we perpetrated.

I turned away from the books. I didn't come for them. I came to make sure the money my wife hoarded was still safe. This money was going to be the means of our escape from the grips of the Cali Cartel, but unfortunately we waited too long. Another tear slid down my cheek. I thought I'd left all my tears upstairs in the bedroom, but I was wrong.

Greed kept us in the game, and I knew that I would pay for that sin for the rest of my life. My brother Monte sucked me into his world and used the threat of my family's safety to keep me in it.

I pushed back the wall of books and stared at the stacks of money. I had no idea how much was there, but I was sure it was more than we could spend in a lifetime. The realization should have comforted me, but it only made me sadder.

"Why didn't we get out sooner?" Weeping again, I fell to my knees.

"I'm so sorry, Alelina…so sorry. I really did love you…I thought I knew what I was doing." The walls of our makeshift safe seemed to shake as my wails shook the rafters of the seven-by-eight-foot room that I was in. I stayed on the floor until I was ready to lift my head without sorrow.

"Ariana, have you spoken to your sister today?" I said into the phone.

"Uh…actually she's here."

I could tell that she was uncomfortable speaking with me. "Is she okay?"

"Yeah, she's fine."

She wasn't offering any additional information, which really bothered me. Something was wrong, but it was obvious she wasn't going to tell me about it.

"Is she looking down your throat?"

"Sure is."

"I know that she is going to fight you on this, but I really need to show both of you something. Can you both come over to our old house?"

She hesitated before she responded. She let out a loud sigh. "Padre, I'm not sure I—"

"Will you come over?" I tried not to sound overly eager. They had been through so much, and I didn't know how much more they could take.

"Now?"

I could feel her irritation even through the phone line. As much as I wanted to push, I knew I couldn't. "I'd really appreciate it. But if you think Gabriela is not up to it, we can do it later." I tried to prepare myself for the rejection I was sure was coming.

"I'll have to ask her, hold on."

I held my breath as she muted the phone. "God, please." I prayed like I had never prayed before. It felt like an eternity before she came back on the line, even though it was only a few seconds.

"We're on our way."

I let out a huge sigh of relief. "Okay, I will see you when you get here. Thanks."

CHAPTER TWENTY-EIGHT
GABRIELA MENDOZA

"What is this about?" I had so many other things that I could have been doing, so I didn't feel like participating in this little outing with my dad.

Ariana said, "Your guess is as good as mine. He didn't offer any explanation when he asked us to come." She held my adorable nephew in a baby carrier.

We were standing outside of our old home, but I didn't feel anything. I'd already said my good-byes, so I wasn't feeling this reunion at all.

I turned up my nose. "This is some bullshit. You may have accepted him into your life, but I don't give a rat's ass about him."

"It's not about accepting him into my life. He's still our father; you can't change that. You haven't spent any time with him. He's really not that bad." She pushed a pacifier in LM's mouth.

My sister was always the gullible one, but this time I thought she went too far. We went through hell, and I wasn't the forgive-and-forget type of person. "Whatever." I wasn't up to debating with her at the moment. I wanted to get back to my apartment to see if I could learn something that would help me to find that lying-ass Tilo. Once someone wronged me, I was all about payback being a motherfucker. As far as I was concerned, Tilo won round one, but I intended to take home the prize and hang that bitch out to dry.

"Do you want to leave?" Ariana asked as I paced back and forth on the curb.

Part of me wanted to leave, but the other part wanted to know why he wanted us to come. If he was going to provide any answers, I was willing to stay. "Naw, we're here now. Let's see what that motherfucker wants."

"Gabriela, quit it. He's still our father," Ariana said firmly as she smiled at LM.

"Well, the jury is still out on that as far as I'm concerned. Being a father is more than donating sperm, and that's all he ever did for me." I opened the door and led the way into the house. If I was going to do this, I wanted to get it over with so I could get back to my business back at the house. "Hello?" I yelled. I refused to call this man Padre until he showed me he was worthy of the title. I tapped my foot as I impatiently waited for his response.

"Padre, it's Ariana and Gabriela," my sister yelled.

We walked into the empty living room. This was the first time that I'd been in the house since the night I was shot and Ramón was killed. A flashback of the night he died almost brought me to my knees.

"Gabriela, are you all right?" Ariana gripped my arm, but it felt like she was a million miles away.

"Yeah." I pulled my arm away from Ariana. "He needs to hurry the fuck up. I can't be in this house too long. Too many memories." I had no idea I would feel this way. I wanted to get out of there so I could grieve again in private. I looked toward the stairs expecting our mother to come down them, but that wasn't going to happen. "Where the fuck is he? Call him, I don't have all day," I barked at my sister like she was to blame for my feelings. She wasn't in the house that night, so she couldn't possibly be feeling the same emotions I was feeling.

Ariana whipped out her phone. "Padre, where are you? We are here." She nodded her head and closed her phone. "He's coming."

I heard footsteps, but they didn't appear to be coming down the stairs. I looked around in confusion. "Where the fuck was he?"

"Gabriela, your mouth is filthy," Padre announced as he slowly came into view.

I wanted to tell him to kiss my ass, but I held the words inside. My sister said he used to have a fiery temper and I didn't want to experience it.

"Padre, what are we doing here? Gabriela needs her rest." Ariana said.

"Gabriela, I know this is hard for you, and I sincerely apologize, but I need you to see this."

My father sounded humble. A part of me hoped that I could feel love for him again.

"What is it? I need to get back home to rest." I was lying my ass off. I just wanted to get out of there.

"Of course, I understand and I thank you both for coming. Will you follow me?" He was being so formal, I was scared to follow as he turned and walked out the same doorway that he had come from.

Ariana said, "Give him a chance, Gabriela. He's trying."

I could not ignore the pleading in my sister's voice. I would indulge her; but if I smelled bullshit, I was out—even if it meant turning my back on the only family I had left. "I just want you to know, I ain't feeling this."

LM started to get fidgety.

"I know. But please indulge him."

We followed my father through the kitchen and into the basement. The urge to run out of the house was overwhelming.

"Where are we going?" I demanded as I stopped midway down the stairs. If this was some dog-and-pony shit, I'd have rather he tell us about it before I walked down the stairs. For all I knew, it could be another trap we were walking into blindly.

Ariana said, "Gabriela, please, this won't take long." She tried to calm LM.

How the hell does she know how long this shit is going to take? I let loose a loud sigh as I counted backward. Ariana grabbed my hand and practically dragged me down the rest of the stairs.

Padre stopped at the bottom of the steps, causing us to bump into him. This just irritated me even more.

"Dumb fucker," I mumbled as Ariana jabbed me in my stomach.

She was lucky I wasn't feeling all that strong or we would have been fighting all over the basement.

"Ouch, bitch," I said, ready to let her have it, wishing she weren't holding my nephew.

"Gabriela…enough."

My father didn't have to raise his voice to let me know he was serious. It was a tone I wasn't familiar with but it brought tears to my eyes. I felt like I'd been transported in time and I was a little girl again. I was going to play his little game—one last time—and I was done. Padre led us to where the washer and dryer normally sat but they were pushed off to the side.

"What's going on here?" I asked as I peeked down twelve steps to what appeared to be a sub-basement. I turned to my sister. "Did you know this room was here?"

"No, I didn't. Padre, what is this?" Ariana asked. Her voice was gentler and less accusatory than mine. She was working hard to keep the peace.

"I can show you better than I can tell you," my father replied.

CHAPTER TWENTY-NINE
ARIANA RAMSEY

My cell phone scared the shit out of me when it rang. I whipped it out of my holder and placed it up to my ear. "Hello?"

"Hey, baby, where are you?" Moses asked.

"I'm over at my old house. My father wanted us to meet him here. He wanted to show us something."

"Oh really, what?"

"Don't know yet. What's up?" I could feel all eyes on me as I tried to get off the phone with my husband.

"I called the house and you weren't home and I got worried. You didn't mention going anywhere today."

"It just came up. Padre says it won't take long, so I'll be there as soon as we're done."

"Oh, one more thing, my mother and father are coming to visit."

My heart skipped a beat, but I tried to sound calm. "Oh really? What's the occasion?"

He said, "It's no occasion. It's just time they met their daughter-in-law."

He had a point. It was time, but I could not help but to wonder, why now? We'd been married for months and I hadn't heard boo from them.

"Wow, when are they getting here?" I was in panic mode. There were so many things I wanted to do before I met my in-laws. I needed to get my hair and nails done; the house could have used a thorough cleaning.

"They will be here at four."

If he said anything else after that, I didn't hear it because my mind was working overtime.

"Let me get off the phone, I have a lot to do. I'll see you at the house." I closed the phone. "Gabriela, we have to get going, I have to get home."

"What's wrong?" She looked alarmed.

"I need to get home. My in-laws are coming and I've got to prepare."

"Wow, did you know they were coming?"

"No, Moses just sprang it on me."

Gabriela cringed. "Ouch. I've never met in-laws before, but I think I would prefer advance notice."

"Tell me about it. Padre, what's this shit about!" With one phone call, I'd forgotten about being the peacemaker. My ass needed to get home with a quickness.

CHAPTER THIRTY
TILO ADAMS

Fucking with Moses was probably not a good idea. My stomach was so queasy, I felt like I was about to throw up, but nothing would come out. I felt hungry all the time, but every time I tried to eat, I threw up.

"This shit is getting old," I mumbled to my reflection. I looked like hell, but I felt even worse, if that was possible. The nightmares were driving me fucking crazy. I couldn't sleep because I felt like someone was chasing me all the time. I thought my conscience died with my former lover, but I was obviously wrong. I was disgusted with the weakness I was showing. I had dark circles under my eyes and my whole face appeared sunken in.

I pushed away from the mirror. I refused to spend another second looking at my tired reflection. I couldn't wait for my cruise to start. I needed the fresh start so I could get my head on straight and get back to the business of making money. I was scheduled to leave in a few days for New York, and I had yet to buy a suitcase.

The honest truth of the matter was I was afraid to leave my hotel room. I was sure most of my fears were related to guilt. Killing random people was a piece of cake. Had I known I would feel differently when I killed someone I knew, I would have hired someone else to do for me. Like it or not, I had to face my fears.

I got dressed so I could do some shopping. I didn't need much, but I needed something to go with my new look. I planned on doing my major shopping on the cruise. I grabbed my key card and purse and headed out the door.

I was good until I reached the lobby. I broke out in a sweat when I saw all the people rushing around. I thought they were all looking for me and my heart started thumping inside my chest. I could feel my blood rushing from my head. I was feeling faint.

"Are you all right, miss?"

I leaned against the wall. I was trying to balance my weight without appearing drunk. This was totally unexpected. The feeling unnerved me so much, I couldn't answer right away. I stumbled over to one of the sofas in the lobby and lowered my head between my legs. I tried to control my breathing and my nerves. Slowly my heart rate became normal. I lifted my head and realized that no one except for the bellhop was paying me any attention.

"Can you get me a cab please?" I said.

"Sure, it would be my pleasure."

I watched him go out the door to hail a cab. I should have followed him but my legs were shaking. I waited until he started waving at me before I got up and tried to make my way to the door. I was halfway to the door before my legs gave out on me and I crumpled to the floor. It wasn't a blackout. I was totally aware of what was going on around me, but I didn't have the strength to do anything about it. However, by the time the ambulance arrived, I had gotten a second wind.

A female paramedic said, "We just want to examine you, miss."

"I'm fine. I told the bellhop not to dial 911 but he was insistent upon doing so." My eyes locked with the bellhop's. If eyes could communicate, mine were begging him to corroborate my story.

The bellhop said, "She did tell me not to call, but the hotel requires we do it for insurance purposes and for the safety of our guests."

I was relieved. He was going to get a big, fat tip.

"I understand, but since we're here, why not let us take your blood pressure?" she said, preparing to examine me.

I wanted to choke the fuck out of this preppy bitch who just wouldn't go away. I hated to get ugly, but I was about to show my ass for real. "If my blood pressure goes up, it will because you won't leave me the hell alone. Now go somewhere and save someone who really needs your help."

I wanted to end my sentence by calling her a bitch, but I held it back. However, if she came at me again with the cuff, it was on. I definitely didn't want them to take my pressure because I hadn't been taking my medicine. I left my pills at the apartment, and since dead people couldn't fill prescriptions, I was out of luck.

"We can't force you to accept treatment, but we can advise you that refusing our assistance may have dire consequences, which we will not be held responsible for."

"Whatever," I mumbled as I stumbled back to the elevator.

≈≈

"Rome, don't tell me to calm down. Those idiots you are dealing with have just cost me a million dollars," I yelled into the phone. I knew my pressure was through the roof, but I couldn't pull back. I despised incompetence. Since I couldn't be seen, I was forced to allow others to handle my business for me—for a small fee of course.

"We have no way of knowing how the Mexican officials learned of the new shipment. It could have been a fluke," Rome said, sounding irritated.

"Fluke, my ass. Perhaps you don't understand how this shit works. If I lose money, you don't get paid."

"Tilo—"

"Don't call me that again—ever. The person you are referring to is dead, got it?"

"Yeah, I got it, but what do I call you?"

I thought about it for a few seconds, but since my head was hurting so badly, it was difficult to think. "Call me...Boss. Yeah, that's it, call me Ms. Boss. I kinda like that shit 'cause if the boss ain't happy, nobody is happy. You feel me?"

"Yeah, I feel you."

I knew I rankled Rome's feathers, but I didn't care. I owned him. He had a gambling problem, which kept him out of the FBI. It wasn't big enough to keep him out of civil service. At least, it wasn't at the time he applied for a job with the Atlanta Police Department. If I found out that he was the reason my guns had been hood-jacked, I was going to kill him.

"I want some answers."

"Ms. Boss," Rome practically choked over the words. "It's not my fault. Everything on our end was on point. Shit got fucked up over the border somewhere," Rome whined.

"I don't give a flying fuck where it happened. It happened! And as a result, I don't fucking get paid," I shouted into the phone. If I could've done everything myself, I would have. But I needed to rely on Rome to do at least 95 percent of the things I asked him to do right. If his percentage dropped, so did he.

"What do you want me to do?"

"Get my fucking guns back or be prepared for the consequences. And you might start thinking about ways to take out that mayor too. He's messing with my money and I don't appreciate that shit."

"But this is the second mayor we've handled since the election."

"And your point would be?" I wasn't trying to hear that shit. I was done talking to Rome. I didn't care how he made it happen, I just wanted it to happen. I had one more call to make before I left the country.

I hung up on him and dialed another number. "Yeah, it's me. I just got off the phone with Rome. The motherfucker is scared. I need for you to sell that stupid ass the same shit you took from him, but double the price."

"He can't afford it."

"You idiot, tell me something I don't know. I need that nigga dirty."

"Okay, all right then."

"Wait a week and leak another story saying the guns were jacked. This gets Obama and his administration off my ass and you move up again. You feel me? Obama's team will think they are doing a good job and move their nosey asses out of Mexico so we continue to get rich." I was feeling pretty good because everything seemed to be going as planned.

"What about the kidnappings?" my anonymous malefactor said.

"Damn, man, do I have to tell you everything? You've got to keep things poppin', keep the violence spread out. Don't do too much in any one area or we'll have more attention than a little bit. Get creative. Do something to surprise me for a change. Shit! If I have to tell you how to do everything, what do I need you for?" I slammed down the phone. "I ain't trying to change the name of the game, I'm just trying to be the winner." I rolled over for a few hours to get some much needed rest. When I woke up, I promised to try, once again, to eat something and hold it down.

CHAPTER THIRTY-ONE
MOSES RAMSEY

My stomach was filled with butterflies. I had never been so nervous in my entire life. I didn't know what scared me most, the fact that I'd actually fathered a child, or Ariana's reaction when she found out I had a paternity test done without her knowledge.

Mom and Dad were excited about meeting my wife and their first grandchild. I was still trying to digest the fact that LM was actually my son. Part of me was beaming with pride, and the other half hated the way I treated him when he was born. I despised myself for allowing Tilo to fill my head with nonsense that almost made me kill his mother. This made finding Tilo a number one priority because I could not ever let it be known what I'd planned to do.

Planning this dinner party was my mother's idea. Since I didn't have much time to cook, I stopped by Ariana's favorite restaurant, Olive Garden, and placed an order to go. On a whim, I also stopped by the liquor store and bought some wine and their best champagne. I wanted everything to be perfect. While I never intended to tell Ariana about the DNA test that I secretly performed, I was hoping the baby pictures my mother had brought would convince her who LM's real father was.

Finding out he was my son was a real eye opener. With it came a newfound commitment to the love I had for Ariana. I wanted and needed for us to grow as a family. Tonight, I was going to tell her that. The fact that my mother and father would be there to witness it was a bonus.

I quickly set up the table with candles and flowers after I called Ariana to make sure she was on the way. Mom and Dad were resting in the guest room and eager to meet their first and only grandchild. As I lit the last candle my mother came down the stairs.

"Sweetie, do you need any help?"

"Mom, I thought I told you to get some rest." I wasn't surprised she didn't pay me any attention. Hell, my dad had been complaining about her being hardheaded for years.

"Who can rest at a time like this? Do you know how long I've waited for this moment? Your father and I aren't getting any younger. Well, your father is getting older, I'm just getting better."

I couldn't hold back the laughter. My mother was a piece of work.

"Mom, you haven't changed one bit."

"Why should I mess with perfection?"

We laughed again.

"Is Dad still resting?" I was fussing with the table settings because I was nervous. I wanted my parents to love Ariana the way I did. I had a lot of making up to do with her, and I planned to start tonight. I never wanted her to know I'd planned on killing her and running off with Tilo. My hand tightened around the stem of the glass that I was holding. I still had a hard-on for that bitch and couldn't wait to get my hands on her skinny neck.

"He's snoring, so I guess you could say he's resting. I don't understand how he can sleep with all the racket he's making."

"You love it because you've been sleeping with the racket for over forty years."

It was her turn to chuckle now. "Boy, get away from the table and sit down somewhere. I don't know why you didn't let me cook."

I pulled out a chair at the kitchen counter and sat down. "I couldn't ask you to fly here and then put you to work as soon as you got here."

"Shoot, I got to eat too."

She had a point, but I wanted to do all of this myself. I wanted everything to be perfect when my wife came in. I even went out and upgraded her wedding ring.

Mom said, "So tell me about your wife, not that stuff you told your father. I want to know what made her special to you?"

"She has a beautiful spirit, Mom. When she is around, all I can see is sunshine and happiness. Please give her a chance," I pleaded.

"Son, she is the mother of my grandson. She already has cool points with me. Try to relax. Everything is going to be okay."

I wished that I could feel as confident as she did, but she didn't know all the details of my relationship with Ariana. I loved my mother, but I couldn't share my deepest deception with her. She would never understand.

"What is it, son? You looked troubled." Worry lines were etched on my mother's forehead.

"It's nothing. I just wish they would get here." I looked at my watch. It had been forty-five minutes since I'd talked to Ariana and I was getting antsy.

"I think you need to have a glass of the wine you bought. While you're at it, pour me one too."

She was right. I was wound tighter than a clock. I went over and grabbed two glasses off the dining room table and poured some wine into both glasses. I handed one to my mother and we clicked together in a toast. "To the good life," I whispered.

CHAPTER THIRTY-TWO
CARLOS MENDOZA

I could not bring my family back, but I could try to repair some of the damage I had done. Not that I believe money cured all that ailed you, but it might help. I held my breath. In my heart, I knew this was my last chance to prove to them that their mother and I really did want a better life for them.

I never thought all our secrets would come to light, but the only way I was going to regain their trust, was to be honest about my mistakes. My biggest regret was that Alelina wasn't there with me while I did it. The only thing I could do was pray they would learn to love me after the deception was revealed. I had to make them understand that we did what we thought we had to do in order to survive.

"Why are we here, Padre?" Ariana demanded again.

I was taken aback by her tone, and I almost snapped on her. However, I waited until they were fully in the basement before I turned on the auxiliary lighting. They say a picture is worth a thousand words. The walls of the subbasement were bloated with one hundred dollar bills. I watched their faces with great anticipation.

"Oh my God. Are you serious?" the girls cried in unison.

"Is this shit real?" Gabriela whispered.

I knew this was going to be a big shock to them because it blew me away too. I was surprised by the amount of money tucked inside the walls. It seemed like my wife held on to every penny I sent her. "I told you we had money," I boasted.

"Is this blood money?" Gabriela demanded.

"It's your money. It represents everything your mother and I worked for over the years. It's the least I can do to gain forgiveness." I looked at LM, who was all eyes.

"You can't put a price tag on forgiveness. We survived without money. We needed a father in our life," Gabriela shouted. She was clearly agitated while Ariana walked around, apparently in a daze.

"I can't change the past, as ugly as it is, but I would like to change the future." My heart was pounding as I waited for their response.

Ariana and Gabriela were grown. I missed the most precious years of their life and no amount of money could change that. I got it, even if they didn't believe it. I only wanted a chance. Not to be their father, I missed that boat, but to be a friend and ultimately someone they looked up to. I wanted the opportunity to be the man I should have been, and I wanted to have an active role in my grandson's life.

I held out two large duffel bags so they could take some of the money with them. It would take many more trips to get it all. I didn't know what I would do if they turned their backs on me and walked out. The waiting was torturous. Ariana was the first one to take the bag from me. I held my breath while I waited to see if Gabriela would as well. After several more seconds, she accepted the bag and I relaxed somewhat.

I watched them fill up the bags. There was more than enough money there for all of us to live extravagantly for the rest of our natural lives. My share would be used to continue the search for the bitch who ended my son's life.

Gabriela stopped packing and startled me with a question. "Are you planning on leaving anytime soon?"

I didn't detect any of the animosity that I earlier felt. "No, Gabriela, I'm going to stay awhile. Maybe even make this my home. And, if Ariana will let me, I want to spend some time with my grandson."

"I'd like that." Gabriela answered.

Ariana seemed oblivious to us all as she continued stuffing her bag.

"I'm sincere. I messed up. I allowed things to keep me away from you both. It was never a case of my not loving either of you."

Gabriela said, "We read some of the letters you sent to Madre."

I was surprised by this information because with the nature of what we were doing for the cartel, I always told her to shred the letters after she read them. "Where did you find the letters?"

"I found them in Madre's desk after she died. We were trying to make sense out of what was happening."

I was not pleased with this turn of events, but it wasn't what I said in those letters, it was more of what I didn't say that mattered. The average person wouldn't have understood. Once again, there was nothing that I could do to change it. I exhaled deeply. Mending our relationship was going to be a lot harder than I had anticipated. Tension in the room was so strong, I felt like it was a tangible thing that I could reach out and touch.

Gabriela looked as if she were about to ask another question. Before she could say anything, Ariana's phone rang. She turned her back to us to answer the call. She spoke a few words in a hushed voice and ended the call.

"When you're ready, everything you want to know is in these journals." I could tell they didn't even notice the journals lining the walls.

"Can we continue this later? I need to get home," Ariana said as she attempted to throw her weighted duffel bag over her shoulder. The bag weighed almost as much as she did.

Gabriela dropped her own bag and attempted to help her sister, but I gently pushed her aside so I could assist.

"I'll help you with your bag, Gabriela, when I return," I said over my shoulder, scooping up LM's carrier in my other hand.

"I'm going to stay for a while if that's okay with you," Gabriela said, surprising the hell out of me.

"I thought you were riding with Ariana?"

"She has plans. Can you drop me off at my house after we're done?"

"Of course. I'll be upstairs if you need me."

This was not the way I wanted this visit to end, but I was powerless to do anything about it. My daughters had gone on with their lives, and it was up to me to catch up. I helped Ariana to her car and waved sadly as she drove away.

CHAPTER THIRTY-THREE
GABRIELA MENDOZA

"So what's your take on this bullshit?" I phoned Ariana as soon as I heard the front door close. I wanted him to think I was staying, but I was testing him to see if he trusted me alone in this room.

"I really don't know what to think. Girl, I thought Tilo took all the money there was."

I couldn't help but laugh, even though it wasn't funny. "Yeah, I bet she thought so too. What she got was chump change compared to what's in that room."

"I know, right."

Just thinking about Tilo's trifling ass pissed me off. I could not believe that she played me like she did.

"I doubt if you will ever find her," Ariana said.

"Oh, I'm gonna find the bitch, trust and believe that. And when I do, I'm gonna do to her what she tried to do to me! Rock-a-bye baby for real."

"Gabriela, you can't mean you would…shoot her?"

Was she serious? "You are kidding, right? I mean, the bitch shot me. She killed our brother! You damn right I'm gonna shoot the bitch." I was done with people trying to do me any way that they thought they could and thinking it would be okay. The incident with Tilo changed me. I was about to be the bad bitch and I had no regrets.

"Sis, you're scaring me. I'm about to turn this car around and come back so I can talk some sense into you."

"Pump your brakes, Ariana. This ain't got nothing to do with you. She didn't shoot your ass, so please save it. I will shoot the bitch even if it means that I'll spend the rest of my life behind bars. You don't understand, she played me big time. She became my friend for a specific reason, and then she tried to kill me. That's something I don't take too lightly."

"I hear ya, sis, but don't do anything foolish. I can't afford to lose my sister too."

"I've got to find the bitch first and when I do, it's on."

"Well, I gotta go. Wish me luck."

"Yeah, go handle your business. I'll give you a call tomorrow and maybe we can get together and read some of these journals. Are you going to tell Moses about the money?" The line was silent and for a minute I thought the call was dropped. "Ariana, you still there?"

"Yeah, I'm here. I was thinking. I will probably show him the money, but it won't be tonight."

"If it was me, I'd keep it to myself for a minute. But you know your man better than I do. I'll speak with you later." I grabbed a few of the books off the shelf and dragged my bag up the stairs. Padre was still an enigma to me. He appeared remorseful, but I felt like he was still hiding something so I wasn't ready to let my guard down with him.

The whole experience with Monte and Tilo had made a cynic out of me. I wasn't the same trusting person anymore and it scared me. I felt like Ariana would be a fool to show Moses all the money she had. I learned the hard way that money made some people do some crazy shit.

♠ ♠ ♠

I had mixed emotions about going back into the apartment that I shared with Tilo, but it was necessary for closure. I had successfully moved into another building and retrieved most of my clothes. The furniture was soiled, but our electronics survived. I needed to walk around the old apartment one last time so I could formally say good-bye to those demons that plagued me at night. Knowing your lover tried to kill you is a bitter pill to swallow, and I hoped by coming to the apartment I would find an adequate chaser. Part of me was surprised the key to the door still worked, but the other half of me wanted to burn the bitch down myself. I put my purse inside the front door and went down the hall to check the mailbox.

I wasn't surprised to find it jam-packed with bills and junk mail. Since no one was taking care of my affairs while I was in the hospital, my credit was going to take a serious hit, but I would deal with it later when things calmed down some.

"Hell, with all the money our father threw at us, who needs credit?" My voice echoed off the walls, sounding distorted and alien to me. The kitchen still had some of our personal items. Magnets were still attached to the refrigerator and our grocery list was still hanging from a hook on the wall. A brown, singed oven mitt and matching pot holder sat on the counter waiting for the next meals to be cooked. Other than the kitchen, no room held memories for me. I looked under the cabinet and got a box of trash bags to put my mail in, and left the bag next to the door as well.

The light on the answering machine caught my attention as I was leaving the room. In my haste to leave, I almost overlooked it. I was scared to listen to it so I unplugged the machine and stuffed it in the bag as well. I would listen to it later when I was more comfortable in my new apartment. This place, without Tilo, was giving me the creeps. I walked through the other rooms but didn't see anything that I wanted to take with me. I was officially done with this part of my life.

I was about to leave when my front door was kicked in and I was roughly pushed back. My head smashed against the wall, and for the second time in my life, I had a gun pointed at me. I didn't know what to do as warm piss flowed down my leg. I stood in place—too scared to move—with my hands framing my face against the wall.

"What...what do you want?" I whispered. I assumed it was about the money, but I'd left it in the car. The keys were on the floor. They could have it if they would just let me live.

"Shut up and face the wall."

I didn't have to be told twice. I wouldn't say another fucking thing if it would keep me from going through the same shit I just went through. I heard additional footsteps behind me. A second person entered my apartment, closing the door behind him.

"If you scream, I will shoot you. Do you understand?"

I couldn't answer him if I wanted to. I was trembling so badly my lips were shaking. I nodded my head in acknowledgment.

"That ain't her," the second man said.

I needed him to shut the fuck up because he obviously made the first guy mad, judging by the way he was pushing my ass into the wall.

"Where's Tilo?" the man holding me demanded.

The only thing I could tell was that he was light skinned with a slim build. I could tell this because he had thrust his leg between mine as he did a slow grind on my ass. His movements could have been sexual if he wasn't holding a fucking gun.

"I have no idea. The bitch shot me and left me for dead." If these were friends of Tilo, they could kiss my ass too.

"Bitch fucked you too?" The guy holding me relaxed his grip somewhat.

The other guy said, "How do we know she's telling the truth?"

If I had a gun, I would have shot that motherfucker myself. I wanted to turn around so bad so I could see his face. I wanted to remember him.

"Look at her. She done pissed herself." He shoved me, but I had no place to go.

"Sounds like Tilo hasn't changed. What did she clip you for?"

I started to relax a little bit. I wiped the tears and saliva off my face as I told them how she killed my brother. I also showed them what she did to me. "What did she do to you?" *Bitch, is you crazy? This ain't no social gathering and these motherfuckers ain't your friends. How you gonna start asking questions and shit?*

"Come on, man, let's go. It stinks in here." His heavy footfall signaled his retreat.

A tiny spark of hope started to flicker in my body. The guy holding me turned around to leave, but as much as I wanted them gone, I wanted some more information about the woman I used to love. "Please, what did she do? I need to find the bitch and make her pay." I didn't turn around because I was afraid if I looked at him, he would have no choice but to shoot me.

His silence was tormenting me, but he finally spoke. "The less you know about this lady, the better off you are. Stay out of it. We are going to find her."

This chilled me because I knew he was going to kill her. As much as I hated Tilo, I didn't want her dead unless I was the one to pull the trigger. "Real talk, I don't know if I can do that." I was being honest with him and myself. Tilo tried to kill me, and I won't let it go as long as I have breath in my body.

"Stay out of our way or next time you won't be so lucky."

With that he was gone, and I didn't even know what he looked like. I waited with my hands up just in case they decided to come back. My legs were still shaking, but my heart was slowly coming back to normal. I couldn't get the voices out of my head, and I knew I was going to have to share this information with someone soon to help me sort it out. I got my things and left.

♠ ♠ ♠

I threw the mail on the kitchen table in my new apartment and carried my bags into my bedroom. I was tired and wanted nothing more than to climb into the bed and go to sleep, but I needed a shower. I took off my clothes and tossed them in the corner. I ran the shower and pulled a nightgown from my dresser. Although I normally didn't sleep with anything on, I didn't feel comfortable being naked in the new apartment alone. I paused in front of the mirror before I stepped in the shower. Despite the fact that I'd been in a coma, my body still looked good. Exercise was a part of my normal routine so the momentary break didn't do too much damage. My hair had grown longer than I was used to having it, but overall, I still looked good.

"So what are you going to do with yourself?" I asked my reflection in the mirror. I was hoping the mirror held an answer because I had no clue. I was even questioning my sexuality. Since the only people who knew about my sexuality were either missing or dead, I could honestly go either way. Tilo was my first and I responded willingly. I never gave myself a chance to know how I would have responded if I was approached by a man. Shaking those thoughts from my head, I stepped into the shower and allowed the hot water to wash away my stress and my pain. My body was healing, but I had no idea how to heal my heart.

CHAPTER THIRTY-FOUR
MOSES RAMSEY

"She should be here by now." I was trying to keep the food warm without burning or overcooking it. I paced back and forth while anxiously watching the clock. I wanted things to be perfect. When we got married, it was rushed. I didn't have time for all the pomp and circumstance, but now I wanted to rectify it. My plan was to get down on one knee and propose to her in front of my parents and my child.

"My child," I whispered. I couldn't stop saying it, and each time I did, I smiled.

Mom said, "Relax, son, all this pacing back and forth is making me nervous. Get out of the kitchen and go keep your father company. I got this." My mother was right. I was driving myself nuts.

I was acting like a teenager meeting my girl for the first time instead of a married man. "I don't know, Mom, but ever since I found out LM was my son, I feel different inside. Is that normal?" My heart was hurting because I was carrying around a lot of guilt. I actually wanted this marriage to work, and I was ready to put in the effort.

"Of course it's normal, son. But it usually happens before the baby comes." My mother started laughing, but I was too tense to join in. She knew some of the circumstances surrounding my sudden marriage, but she didn't know everything and I planned to keep it that way.

"You got jokes. Today is the most important day of my life and you want to be a comedian."

"I'm not making jokes. It's the truth, but you've never done things the way you were supposed to, even as a child. You probably got that from your father's side of the family, but you obviously did something right because otherwise Ariana wouldn't have agreed to marry you in the first place."

"I hope so, Mom. I really was an ass those first couple of months."

"It's never too late to show Ariana how you feel, but you have to mean it, son. You can't just go changing your mind." She gave me one of her momma looks that let me know she meant business. She grabbed my hand and pulled me over to the kitchen table.

"Sit," my mother instructed. She had her hand on her hip.

I could tell she was about to read me the riot act. My dad, who was about to enter the kitchen, turned around and walked back out. He must have known things had taken a serious turn and decided to run while he had the opportunity.

"Mom, I don't want to burn dinner." I started to get up, but she pushed me back and turned off the low flames.

She took a seat across from me. "Son, I got that your marriage didn't start off in the conventional way, but the good thing about this old thing called life, is that as long as you have breath in your body, you get to try again to do the right thing?"

"Yeah, but—"

"But is for assholes and I didn't raise an asshole." Her analogy was so bizarre and out of the blue, I wanted to laugh. One look at the serious expression on her face stopped me. My father cleared his throat, letting us know he was ear hustling in the other room and having a difficult time trying to remain serious as well.

"I understand, Mom...but, Mom, I've made some major mistakes in my marriage. Things you don't know about. Part of me wants to tell her, but I'm sure if I do she'll leave me in a New York minute." This was as close to asking for advice as I was going to get.

"Then don't tell her," my father spoke from the other room.

"Shut up, Ricardo. You ain't in this conversation."

"And you shouldn't be either. That boy knows what he got to do, and if what he did was so damn serious and he wants to keep that woman happy, then he should shut the hell up and keep it moving." He came back into the kitchen.

"Ricardo, now is not the—"

"Hush, woman, this is between me and my son. Now you know I ain't much for getting into other folks' business—especially grown folks—but you 'bout to fuck up. Do not—let me repeat this—do not tell your wife anything that you know is going to hurt her unless it's a matter of life or death. If you are truly sorry and it's never going to happen again, and—let me repeat this—and if it won't affect her health or welfare, keep your damn mouth shut."

"Ricardo, don't tell this boy to go into his marriage lying."

"First of all, he's not a boy, and second, he's already married. There is no logical reason to stir up some shit if you don't have to, that's all I'm saying."

Mom said, "If she loves you, all things are possible."

I understood where both of them were coming from. The guilt was killing me, though, and I had to tell somebody. "I tried to kill her." Tears flooded my eyes when I thought about how far I was willing to go for the almighty dollar.

"Son, like your father was saying, ain't no sense in stirring up some shit if you don't have to. All that matters now is whether or not you love her." She got up from the table and took over tending to the food.

I sat at the table stunned and confused. "I do love her." I wiped the tears from my eyes. I wanted to look at my mother, but shame prevented me from doing so.

Dad said, "People make mistakes every day. If Jesus can forgive you, why can't you forgive yourself?"

"I'm trying, but every time I think about what could've happened, I feel like I should tell."

"And who would benefit from that?"

I knew she was speaking the truth, but she didn't understand how heavy the guilt was. My dad said what he had to say and went back into the living room. I thought he was finished dishing out advice, but he wasn't.

"Son, your mother is right. If you tell Ariana the truth, there is a good possibility she will walk out on your ass and we'll never get to see our grandson. And let me just say this, if that happens and I have to live with your evil-ass mother for the rest of my life because of it, I'm not going to be happy about that. You feel me?" He flipped the paper for emphasis.

"I beg your pardon, Ricardo. I'm not evil," my mother huffed.

"You are when you don't get your way. I can't blame you. I spoiled your ass so it's my fault. Besides, she needs someone else to love besides me." He was grinning from ear to ear when he said this, and I couldn't keep a smile off my face even though my heart was still heavy.

My mother shared a look with my dad. I could feel the love radiating from them. I wanted the same relationship with my wife.

"You are right, Mom. I'm going to take that secret to the grave."

"What secret?" Ariana asked as she stepped in the room, carrying my son.

CHAPTER THIRTY-FIVE
GABRIELA MENDOZA

"I need some answers and I think you're the only one who is going to give it to me straight." I walked into Moses' office without stopping to knock.

He seemed surprised to see me. However, before I could say anything else, he grabbed me by the arm and dragged me out into the outer office.

"Shush." He pointed to the walls and pointed to his ears.

"What?" I whispered.

He put his finger to his lips and shook his head angrily. I tried to yank my arm from him. I didn't know Moses well, so he certainly didn't have permission to put his hands on me. Once we were in the hallway, he let go of me.

"I think my office is bugged. Until I find out who is listening, I don't want to talk in there."

I was skeptical. If he were such a hot shot detective, why couldn't he find a damn bug. However, if there was any validity to his concerns, I didn't want my business put out on Front Street.

"What are you suggesting then?"

He looked worried as he peered back at his closed office door. He drew some keys out of his pocket and locked the door.

"Come on." Moses turned and walked toward the elevator with me following close behind.

I was still trying to decide if I liked my sister's husband. He was fine and funny. Did I mention fine? But I wasn't sure I trusted him.

"Does this type of shit happen to you often?" I asked when we were in the elevator. No wonder my sister was fascinated with him. Life with him would certainly be interesting.

"Actually, this is a first time, but I'm pretty sure I know who planted the device."

We walked the rest of the way in silence to a small coffee house on Peachtree Street. He walked in front of me, and I got a chance to admire his broad shoulders and his tight ass. I could also see the imprint of his hamstrings as they pushed against the fabric of his pants. I had to admit, he was a well put together package. He held open the door of the coffee shop, and I chose a table near the window so I could look out to the street as we talked.

"Coffee?" he said.

"Please, cream and sugar."

He walked toward the counter and pulled out his wallet. I looked away as I felt a familiar twinge in my panties. The last thing I needed was to become attracted to my sister's husband. I was, however, excited to know I was capable of being turned on by a man. Maybe once this mess settled, I could speak to Moses about hooking me up with one of his friends.

He came back to the table with about ten packages of sugar and a handful of cream. "I didn't know how sweet you liked it."

He drank his coffee black. I grabbed some cream and three sugars and fixed my cup. He sat back in his chair and watched me until I started to feel uncomfortable.

"What?" I asked defensively.

"I didn't say anything. I was waiting for you to tell me why you wanted to see me."

"Oh." I felt embarrassed, and I was sure it showed all over my face.

"You blush just like your sister," he said with a chuckle in his voice.

I took a sip of my coffee and burned my damn tongue. "Shit."

He burst out laughing and I laughed with him. I sat back in my chair and relaxed. He was not the enemy and, even though I didn't agree with the way that he came into my sister's life, he was here now and I had to deal with it.

"Sorry about not visiting you in the hospital. Time kind of got away from me."

"Damn, you should have lied and said you came. I wouldn't have known."

"True, but I don't believe in unnecessary lies."

"Hmm, interesting."

He raised an eyebrow. If he wanted to know what I meant, he didn't ask.

"So let's get back to the business at hand. What can I do for you?"

"Did you see the news this morning? They said they found a body in the woods that they believe could be Tilo."

Moses nodded as he took a sip from his coffee cup and sat back in his chair. "Yeah, I saw it."

"Well? That's good news ain't it?"

He frowned and suddenly looked uncomfortable. "Gabriela, I don't think it's her. We will have to wait and see."

"You seem mighty calm about this. I'm freaking out."

"My gut tells me it's not her. It would be too simple. Until we know for sure, there's no point in getting all riled up."

"That's easy for you to say. She didn't shoot your ass and leave you for dead. I see this woman's face almost every time I close my eyes."

"That's understandable. But I told you before, finding her is a priority for me too. We will just have to wait for the autopsy report."

"Those tests can take weeks! What am I supposed to do in the meantime?"

"Did Tilo have any new piercings or tattoos?"

"Uh," I didn't want to answer his questions.

"Let me put it this way. If you know of anything that wouldn't be in her medical record, then we can use that information to prove the body they found isn't her."

"She has a small infinity tattoo on the small of her back. It's relatively new so I doubt anyone else knows about it." Tilo had insisted we both get matching tattoos. Getting rid of mine was now a priority for me.

"That's great. As soon as I get the autopsy report, I'll check for it. Is there anything else I can do for you?"

"You can tell my sister to lighten up. Ariana is spoon-feeding me information. She is treating me like a cripple."

He nodded his head as if he understood where I was coming from. "I don't necessarily agree with that, but I'm not ready to fight my wife on this one. You've heard the saying: happy wife, happy life haven't you?"

I shook my head. "I just need to know what happened that night."

"I don't know what else I can tell you. Tilo and I arrived at the same time, but if you recall, I went downstairs with your uncle, so I don't know what transpired. The only person who can answer your questions is Tilo, because she was the only one, other than you, who walked away. Do you remember anything?"

"Not really. I have little flashes when I sleep, but when I wake up it's all gone."

"You know Tilo shot Ramón, right?"

I felt like someone had reached inside my chest and pulled out my heart. I clutched my chest in pain. No matter how many times I heard the same thing, it still felt the same. "She told me, but it's so hard for me to believe. She just wasn't like that with me. I mean, how can you be so sure that Tilo did this to us?"

"I can't say with a hundred percent certainty, but my gut tells me she did it."

"What if some other members of the cartel stormed the house and shot us and took Tilo as a hostage?"

"That theory doesn't make sense because the cartel had issues with your family and not Tilo. If anything, they would have shot Tilo and taken you and your brother hostage."

This made sense to me. Getting my mind to accept it was a different matter. The part of me that still loved her wouldn't let me accept it. "Please don't treat me like a child. I get enough of that from Ariana," I snapped. I was taking my frustration out on him and I knew it.

"I'm sorry. That wasn't my intent, but you're grasping at straws. If a member of the cartel actually stormed the house, which I doubt, they would not have missed. I believe Tilo shot Ramón without blinking an eye, but when it came time to shoot you, it wasn't as easy and she didn't bother to check to see if she actually killed you. That's the only explanation that makes sense to me. My only question is why?"

"Yeah, you're right. I was just hoping that it wasn't true. I keep thinking she is going to put her key in the door and come back."

Moses passed the test. I remembered the envelopes of money that Ramón had given me before he was killed. If Moses mentioned the money, then it would mean he was in on it too.

"I don't believe that is going to happen. Everything Tilo did, with the exception of her botched job on you, was planned to perfection."

I frowned. "Why do you say that?"

"Well...I know she faked her death. I know she's somewhere alive and well, and I also believe she has the bearer bonds that Ramón told me about."

"I didn't know you knew about them." A warning flag went up in my head.

"That has to be it, nothing else makes any sense. She really exposed herself when she left me a voice message. If I thought it would do any good, I'd take it to the FBI and try to convince them to reopen the case."

"What! She called? Why didn't you tell me that sooner? What did she say?" I actually felt tingles down my spine as I jumped up and rushed over to him.

"Hey, hold up now." He was on his feet and trying to get me to sit back down before everybody in the coffee shop was all up in our business.

I stopped shouting when I realized how crazy I sounded. I backed up a few paces, but I didn't sit back down. "I'm sorry. I'm good now." I took a few deep breaths to calm my nerves, but it was not working.

"I didn't tell you because I didn't want you to think I was a nut. First she sent me a postcard at the house, today she called and left the message." He took his seat, but I was ready to run to his office to listen to the tape.

"Why is she contacting you?" I snapped at him, feeling jealous.

"You are in a coma, remember?"

"I'm in a coma? What do you mean, I'm in a coma?"

"Your father and I thought it would be a good idea not to let anyone, with the exception of your family, know about you coming out of the coma. You're old news now so it doesn't matter."

"My father? What's he got to do with anything?" My second red flag went up.

"I know how you must feel, but he's as determined to find Tilo as I am."

"Moses, you couldn't possibly know how I feel. Hell, most days, I don't know myself." I was conflicted. I still wasn't sure how much he knew about my relationship with Tilo. "Can I listen to the message?"

Moses studied me for several minutes before he dialed his voice mail. He passed me the phone when he got to Tilo's message, and I confirmed that it was indeed Tilo's voice. My heart felt like it was about to bust out of my chest.

"Did you know Tilo tried to burn down our apartment?" This time Moses was the one jumping out of his chair.

"Shit, when?"

"I think I need something stronger than coffee. What about you?"

"Fine. Do you want to come by the house?"

"No, meet me at my place in an hour." I turned to leave.

"Where do you live?"

I smiled. If he didn't ask for directions, then it meant he already knew. I hated to be so suspicious of people, but until my full memory returned, I was being extra observant about the people around me.

The reason why I wanted Moses to come to my apartment was so that we could compare the voice on his answering machine to the taped greeting on my answering machine. If it was her voice, I would have no choice but to get with the program. Why else would she call Moses? As I waited for him, I decided to go through the stacks of mail from the mailbox.

I sorted the mail into two piles: hers and mine. Hers was mainly junk mail since all of the bills were in my name. At the time, Tilo told me her credit was jacked up so she asked me to put them in my name. In hindsight, she probably did this so no one would know where she lived. I didn't think about it at the time because I thought of it as additional security. She couldn't get tired of me one day and kick my ass out without notice. On one hand, my theory worked since she didn't kick me out. Instead, she fucked me on a whole other level I didn't even think was possible.

I shook my head as I went through the mail. I was going to have to spend the better part of the day paying the overdue bills. Thank God I had a boatload of cash to do it with. I wondered if Ariana told Moses about the money, so I called her up.

"Hey, what's up?" I said.

"We're about to go shopping."

I could hear the happiness in my sister's voice.

"We?" Damn, she wasn't wasting any time spending her money.

"Yeah, didn't I tell you Moses' parents were coming to visit? His mother and I are going to hit the malls to get some things for LM."

"Oh yeah, I forgot." I was disappointed that she didn't invite me to come along.

"I was going to call you later to see if you and Padre wanted to come over to dinner. Are you feeling up to it?"

"Huh?" I was jealous because her life didn't miss a beat. Even though she lost her husband, she continued to march forward with a new band. I wanted to get on with my life, but I had to find all the pieces to put my puzzle back together.

"Dinner? Where is your mind, child?" Ariana said.

"Sorry, I completely blanked out. Uh, I'll get back to you about dinner. Have fun on your shopping trip."

"Cool, thanks."

"Hey, did you, uh, tell Moses about the money?"

There was a long pause.

"No, I haven't had time. When I got home, girl, Moses had this romantic dinner and shit all laid out and everything. It was so nice. And, of course, his parents were here. They were fussing over the baby, so it really slipped my mind."

"Oh, okay. I was just checking."

"Why?" she said.

"I don't know, I just wanted to know."

"All right…I guess I'll talk to you later."

I said, "Yeah, I'll call you if I can make it over later."

"Fine. Get some rest. You don't sound all that hot to me."

As I hung up the phone, I never felt so lonely in my life. I never had a lot of friends, but I did have family. Right now, I didn't feel a part of Ariana's family. She had moved on with her life while I was still circling like a plane in a holding pattern.

"I need to put my hands on this bitch who ruined my life." I crushed a bill in my hand without even realizing it.

Someone knocked on the door. I tossed my MasterCard bill on the table and went to answer the door. It was Moses. "I just got off the phone with your wife."

Moses stopped like a deer caught in headlights.

"Relax, I didn't tell her you were coming over."

He came in and closed the door behind him. "Don't get me wrong, I'm not in the habit of hiding things from my wife, but she really doesn't want me involved in chasing Tilo. As far as she's concerned, Tilo is dead. Until I can prove otherwise, I'm not saying anything to her."

Prior to Tilo's deception, I might have busted Moses for lying to my sister, but I understood where he was coming from. My sister could be a royal pain in the ass. "What do you want to drink?"

"Actually, I stopped by the store before I came over. Do you like Moscato?" He pulled the bottle out of a brown bag and set it on the table.

I went to get glasses and placed the answering machine in the center of the table.

He said, "What's this?"

I pressed play and Tilo's greeting filled my apartment. "You've reached 678-555-5555. We can't come to the phone right now, so you know what to do—"

I pressed stop on the machine as the greeting finished.

Moses practically choked. "Damn, that's her. She sounds just like the voice on my answering machine. She didn't even attempt to disguise her voice. Were there any other messages?"

"No, I guess we weren't that popular. Where do you think she is?" I said.

"I honestly believe she's still in town."

"What about the postcard? Do you have it? Can I see it?"

He pulled the postcard out of his briefcase, which I hadn't even noticed when he came in. "Is this her handwriting?"

I studied the short note as tiny hairs stood up on the back of my neck. I read her words. *Wish you were here. What the fuck does that mean?* I was angry. Tilo was flirting with him.

He said, "So is this her handwriting? If not, somebody is fucking with me."

I studied his face before I answered. I had so many questions but very few answers. "Yeah, it's her handwriting," I grudgingly admitted while the wheels turned in my head. "Moses, I'm still not clear as to how you even know Tilo."

He sat back in his chair and took a sip of wine. "I really don't *know* her, know her, if that's what you're thinking."

"Well, it did cross my mind." I put it out there for him to explain.

He sighed. "One night I was bringing your brother home. It was late and I didn't want him to catch the bus. When I dropped him off, a car followed me. I led the car down a one-way street and I cornered Tilo before she could get away."

"Why would she follow you? I don't understand."

"She said she was checking up on you. We went to get some coffee and she told me the whole story once she found out that Ramón worked for me."

"What do you mean the whole story?" I started sweating. Strange because it was cool in my apartment. I fidgeted and squirmed in my seat as I gulped my wine.

Moses continued to stare at me, which only heightened my feelings of discomfort. He said, "Uh…she told me you didn't come to work and she was concerned. And she told me about the letters your mom wrote."

"Damn, she told you all our business and she didn't even know you. That's strange, don't you think?" I was watching Moses like a hawk. He appeared as uncomfortable as I felt.

"In hindsight, yeah, it's strange. But there was a lot of things going on at the time, so I didn't pay attention. I was more concerned about Ariana and the baby." He had a point. Who had time to pay attention to details?

"Did Tilo tell you about us?" Since she had blabbed about everything else, it only stood to reason that she told him about me.

"She said you were lovers and that you lived together. If you're worried about me saying anything, don't. What you do behind closed doors is none of my business."

"Um, wow." I sighed. I felt dirty and I wanted to take a bath.

"Gabriela, don't go there. She fooled all of us. I'm just telling you this so you know it's just part of the game."

"She was my first." I don't know why I told him that. It was none of his business. He didn't ask, but I needed to tell someone. I was so confused about everything. I felt so exposed and I didn't like the feeling one bit.

"Gabriela, one experience does not define who you are. You're young and you have a whole lot of life to live. You're going to make mistakes, but you have to brush yourself off and keep it moving." He didn't reach out to comfort me and I appreciated it. At that moment I didn't think I could have stood to be touched. We sat quietly for a few more moments.

"When I went by our other apartment," I said between sniffles, "some guys busted in the door asking for Tilo. I didn't get to see their faces, but I'm positive one of them was black. They must have been watching the apartment, so we're not the only ones who know she's still alive."

"What did they want?" Moses' voice rose with alarm.

"I don't know. They asked for Tilo. I told them I was trying to find her myself, and they basically told me to stay out of their way."

"Shit, who were they?" Moses started pacing.

"I have no idea. We never had people over. Our life was very private. My sister didn't even know where I lived. Ramón knew, but that's it, as far as I know."

"It doesn't matter. I'm finding Tilo. Period."

"If you don't, I will."

After Moses left, I went to several banks and got safe-deposit boxes in each one, which I stuffed with money. Since I couldn't account for where the money came from, I couldn't put it into my account. I was tired by the time I got back home, but I wanted to pay the bills that had accumulated while I was in the hospital. My MasterCard statement was the last one I opened. I was actually surprised to see the bill because, unlike my other cards, this one should have been current because I rarely used it. I kept this card for emergencies such as car repairs and to build my credit.

"Shit, this is a joint account." My hands started shaking as I opened the bill. I dialed Moses as I read the charges.

"Moses, oh my God, Tilo used my credit card. There's a charge on my card for AirTran Airways and I didn't make it."

"Damn, I need to see that bill. Can you bring it by in the morning. I'm going to ask your dad to come as well."

"Your office? I thought you said it wasn't safe."

"It's clean now."

"I'll see you tomorrow."

CHAPTER THIRTY-SIX
CARLOS MENDOZA

I really didn't have time to stop by Moses' office. I went anyway, especially when he said Gabriela would be there.

"Hello, Moses, how are you?" I looked around the office. To my dismay Gabriela was not there.

"I'm well. Where have you been? We haven't seen you around the house."

I took a seat in a soft leather chair. "I'm sorry, I've been so busy lately. Tell Ariana I will be by before the week is out."

"Perhaps you should tell her yourself. She is going to wonder when I saw you, and that's going to open up a whole dialogue that I don't think you or I want to have."

"You've got a good point. I forgot myself for a moment. Is there anything new going on that I should know about?" I was ready to get this meeting under way with or without Gabriela.

"I hope you don't mind, but I'd really—"

We both looked up when Gabriela came into the office. There were a few uncomfortable seconds as she came in and took a seat.

"Hello, Gabriela." I felt awkward because I wanted to hug her and I didn't know how she would react if I did. I certainly didn't want to do it in front of Moses and risk the embarrassment of her pushing me away.

"Padre." She stared at me as if she wanted to say more.

I longed for the day when we were more than just civil to each other. Until that day came, I would take what I could get.

"Carlos, just to bring you up to speed, I met with Gabriela yesterday and we discussed our mutual desire to find Tilo. I told her that you also wanted to find her. So we asked you here so we could all be on the same page, working together."

I nodded. "Okay, that's good to know."

Moses said, "Gabriela, did you bring the bill?"

She handed him an envelope. "I was paying some bills when I noticed two charges on my credit card that I couldn't possibly have made. They both were made while I was in the hospital so I called Moses."

"Did someone steal your identity?" I asked.

"No, I don't think so," Moses answered for her. He handed me the envelope, but I missed any correlation I was supposed to get.

Moses said, "It means she's on the move. These charges to the airline look like luggage fees to me. It's too small to be actual airfare tickets. If I'm right, she's been in Atlanta up until two weeks ago. Gabriela, can I hold on to this statement for a few days while I check them out?"

"Yeah, I don't need that part. Should I cancel the card?"

"No," Moses and I said together.

Moses elaborated, "She might not ever use the card again, but if she does, we'll know."

Gabriela nodded as she sank back in her chair. "Moses, don't forget to let Padre hear the message from Tilo?"

"Dag, I almost forgot."

I was getting excited because I felt like we were finally doing something to bring this matter to a close. Moses started dialing what I assumed to be his number on the phone. We all sat in silence as the office greeting came over the speaker. He pressed a few more buttons and finally the message played. We sat in silence until it was finished, but I was chilled to the bone.

I jumped up from my chair, outraged. "I know this voice." I was so angry just thinking about the implications.

"You should. Didn't she call you and tell you to come home?" Gabriela looked at me strangely, but she couldn't possibly understand where I was coming from.

"Carlos, what's going on?" Moses looked at me.

I heard Moses talking to me. So many thoughts were going through my head. However, I couldn't process them all. I was getting angrier by the second. More important, my chest started pounding. I realized I was losing control as I clutched my chest and fell to the floor. Gabriela screamed as she fell to her knees beside me. I tried to get my pills, but Gabriela's hands were in the way.

"I need an ambulance at 435 Peachtree Street. Hurry, it may be a heart attack." Moses slammed down the phone. "Gabriela, do you know CPR?"

"Uh—"

"My pills," I whispered through parched lips.

"What did he say?" Gabriela shouted.

"Move," Moses said as he took command.

I was grateful he was there.

"My pills," I said again.

He pushed my hands away and found my pills. "How many?" He had the bottle open and poured them in my hand.

I blinked once. The pain in my chest was so tight I couldn't even talk. I was afraid to move.

"I'm going to assume you mean one." Moses took the pill and placed it in my mouth.

I moved it under my tongue. I tried to smile, but I was still in too much pain.

"What's happening?" Gabriela was losing it. She was crying, but I couldn't help her; not at that moment.

Moses pointed to the phone. "Call your sister. I think she might know what's going on with him. But do us a favor and take the phone outside."

The pill was working, but each episode was worse than the one before and it scared me. As the pain receded, I exhaled. If I wanted to be around to be in my children's lives, I knew it was time I do something about these episodes. I couldn't keep ignoring the pain.

"You good or do you need another pill?" Moses asked.

"Better." I struggled to get up, but he pushed me back to the floor.

He said, "Not so fast. You're going to the hospital to get checked out."

I didn't have any fight in me. I was going to do whatever they told me if it meant an end to the pain. I settled back on the floor and waited.

CHAPTER THIRTY-SEVEN
ARIANA RAMSEY

I wasn't in the best frame of mind when I rushed into the hospital. It seemed as if my family members were being plucked from my life one at a time. "God, please don't take my father away from me again."

Gabriela wouldn't give me much information. She was hysterical. Moses wound up giving me a brief recap of what was going on. However, I could not figure out how or why all three of them were together, in his office, when my father collapsed. I left LM with my in-laws and rushed to the hospital.

Moses and Gabriela were seated in the waiting room when I rushed in. I was out of breath from running from the parking deck. Moses leaned over and gave me a soft peck on the lips. I was embarrassed by his public display of affection since we'd spent most of our relationship hiding behind closed doors.

"What happened?" I said, looking between the two of them. I hugged my sister and sat down next to Moses. "Padre was having chest pains, and Moses told me to call for an ambulance. He didn't want to come to the hospital, but Moses insisted, so I rode over with him."

I said, "That's good. I'm glad you both were with him to make sure he took his pills."

All eyes swiveled to me.

"You knew about this and didn't tell me? I can't believe you," Gabriela said accusingly.

"I wasn't trying to keep it a secret, but I haven't had time to tell you."

"After what happened to Mom? Are you serious?" She walked over to the window, obviously pissed at me.

I walked over to her, but she brushed my hand off her shoulder. "Gabriela, it happened the day I was coming to take you home. Padre wanted to know what I'd told you about him and Ramón. I told him you didn't know anything and he went ballistic." I turned to Moses because Gabriela was ignoring me. "Moses, you came home right after it happened. Don't you remember?"

"I remember something, but I agree with Gabriela. This could have been very bad if he wasn't able to tell us about his pills. We wouldn't have known to check his pockets and he might've died."

I looked around in disbelief. How did I become the bad guy when I just got there? I felt like they were ganging up on me. "Okay, I admit I should have said something. I wasn't trying to hide it, though. Damn, can I get a break?" I was close to breaking down in tears. Everything that had been happening seemed amplified.

Moses came over to me and wrapped me in his arms as I started crying. "Honey, I'm not mad at you and neither is Gabriela. We're all acting on our emotions. Please stop crying." He rained tiny kisses along my hairline and forehead, trying to relax me. Moses might not have been mad, but I still had to fix things with my sister.

Gabriela said, "Ariana, you have to stop babying me. I'm not a child. Believe it or not, I am a strong Latino woman and I can take it."

I swallowed the lump in my throat. "I wasn't trying to baby you, and I know how strong you are. In many ways you're stronger than me. But think about this honestly, you haven't wanted to talk about Padre, so I forgot to mention it."

"So you're going to turn this around on me?" Gabriela was livid.

"Yeah, I am." I was pissed too.

"Wait, hold up. You two are taking this too far." Moses pulled me back in my seat and stood between us.

Gabriela tried to get around him, but he wouldn't let her. I didn't understand what was going on. I wasn't even mad until she said I was babying her. But wasn't that what older sisters were supposed to do? I was confused by my emotions.

Moses said, "Gabriela, your sister's hormones are fucking with her, so please don't take any of this personally."

I pushed away from Moses. He pissed me off for talking about me as if I wasn't there.

"Moses, what are you saying?" I was all over the place and they both were looking at me like I'd lost my damn mind.

Moses fixed me with a stern look. "Stop." As our eyes connected, he brought me back to my senses. Before I could rationalize my feelings any more, a doctor walked into the waiting room. It was a moment I lived through before, and I assumed Gabriela felt it too because she walked over and took my hand.

"Is there anyone here for Mr. Mendoza?"

The only thing I could think about was the last time we were in the hospital and the doctor told us our mother had passed away. I closed my eyes as if it would help stop me from hearing bad news. I leaned into my sister.

"Yes, we're his daughters. How is he?" Gabriela asked.

"He's stable right now. We're going to keep him for a few days to run some more tests."

"Is it his heart?" I knew the answer before I asked the question.

The doctor nodded. "Yes, I'm afraid it is. He told me he knew of his condition for quite some time, but refuses to have the surgery."

"What type of surgery?" Moses asked.

"He needs a bypass. He has severe blockage to the heart and it needs to be removed."

Gabriela asked, "Did he say why he is refusing the surgery?"

"No, but I was hoping one of you could convince him to change his mind. As you know, the heart is a muscle and your father's heart is tired and overworked. Nitroglycerin relaxes the blood vessels and takes the strain off your heart, but you can only do it so many times for it to remain effective. Unless you get your father to change his mind, the next time this happens he might not be so lucky."

Gabriela said, "Thank you, Doctor. We will speak with him. Can we see him?" Just as she did when our mother took sick, Gabriela controlled the situation.

"Actually, I'd prefer it if he was allowed to rest right now. He's heavily sedated."

Gabriela was not to be denied. "With all due respect, Doctor…"

"Sorry, Broomfield."

"…Broomfield. We recently lost our mother to heart failure. She came in and we never got to see her alive again. May we please see him, just for a minute? I promise we won't disturb him. We just need to tell him…" Gabriela's words trailed off, then she started crying.

I knew what she was trying to say. "We need to tell him we love him. Please, he really needs to know." I had to step out of myself on this one. If Padre was attached to a bunch of machines, I really didn't want to see him that way, but I'd never forgive myself if I allowed my discomfort to stand in the way.

"All right, but please don't upset him."

"We won't."

"Why were you and Padre at Moses' office today?" I knew the answer, but I needed to be sure.

Gabriela's face got hard and defensive, but I was determined to find out the truth. "Ariana, Moses told us that you didn't want him going after Tilo. I need his help though. I have to find her."

"Why? What good would it do to find her? Will it change anything?" I was desperately trying to understand what I was obviously missing.

"No, it won't change anything. Then again, she didn't shoot you and leave you for dead, did she? Now you might be able to pick up the pieces and go on with your life, but I can't. Padre feels the same way because Tilo shot Ramón too. All of our lives have been drastically altered. Can't you see that?"

"Okay, I can see your point, but why does Moses need to be involved?" I asked.

She sighed before she answered. "He doesn't. If you feel so strongly about it, I'll get someone else to help. I thought he would be the logical person because he knows Tilo, and he's familiar with everything that went down. But on a more serious tip, I thought you'd want to find the person who has changed our lives forever too."

Gabriela hurt me deeply by insinuating that I didn't care. In my heart, I knew Moses wasn't going to let it go. I was beginning to realize that I was being unfair to him by asking him to step away. My biggest fear was pissing off the cartel. It consumed so much of Padre's life. I didn't want the same thing for me and my family.

I said, "What are you going to do if you find her? Get yourself in trouble?"

"I ain't gonna lie to you. If I find the bitch, I'm going to kill her. Plain and simple. I can't go to jail for killing someone who's already dead. Feel me?"

CHAPTER THIRTY-EIGHT
TILO ADAMS

"Your bag is overweight."

I wasn't paying attention. I'd finally worked up the nerve to leave Atlanta when the news of a body, matching my description, had been found. I was beginning to think they were never going to find it or worse that when they did, it would be more like skeletal remains instead of human. The stress was more than I anticipated. Greg just didn't know how close I came to killing his ass behind this fuck up. But now that they found it and made the correct correlation between the two, I felt more comfortable moving about. Now, I just wanted to get on the plane and go to sleep. I stared at the baggage attendant and wished she'd hurry up. She stared at me as well.

"What?" I snapped as I waited for her to hand me my ticket.

"I said your suitcase is overweight."

"Sorry. I didn't have a scale at the hotel." I shrugged my shoulders thinking it wouldn't be a big deal.

She rolled her eyes. "You need to either take out three pounds worth of stuff or pay a ninety-dollar penalty."

I wanted to reach over the counter and snatch the woman around her neck and punch her.

"Ninety dollars? I'm not paying ninety extra damn dollars. Didn't I just tell you I didn't have a scale?"

"Fine." She stepped over to the scale and placed my suitcase on the floor in front of me. She rolled her eyes again and said, "Next."

I lowered my Gucci shades, looked the attendant straight in her eyes. "What do you mean *next?* You ain't done with me yet."

She looked at me like I was three cards short of a deck and should be riding on a padded bus rather than a plane. "You said you weren't paying the fee so I'm moving on to the next customer. Now if you could kindly step aside, I do have other customers to wait on." She handed me back my license.

Even in my crazed mind, I knew better than to threaten airport personnel. Nevertheless, I was very close to doing it. This woman had plucked my last nerve with her condescending attitude. I grabbed my bag and moved off to the side and thought of my next move. I couldn't believe this was happening, and if my situation was different, I might have waited around for the bitch to get off work and shown her how I felt about it.

I felt like I was teetering on the edge of sanity and a swift breeze could carry me over. My flight was leaving within the hour. I didn't have a lot of time, so I had no choice but to pay. My money was in my carry-on and I didn't want to open it and have a bunch of strangers gawking in my bag.

I approached another check-in counter. "Excuse me, sir. Can I check my luggage here?"

"Where are you headed?" This attendant hardly looked up from their keyboard as I slid him my license. He typed a few things and printed out my boarding pass and gave it to me.

What the fuck has happened to customer service? Would it have hurt the motherfucker to say good morning? I quickly put my fake identification back in my purse.

He said, "Put your bag on the scale."

Using both hands, I lifted the bag onto the scale. I was not feeling this whole airport experience. If I didn't need to get out of town today, I would have caught the damn train.

"Your bag is overweight."

I pressed a credit card into his hand and prayed he didn't notice the difference in names. I tried to act nonchalant while he ran the card and tagged my luggage. I didn't relax until I saw my bag on the conveyor belt. As I walked back through the terminal, it took everything in me not to flip the bird to the bitch behind the Delta counter.

In my frazzled state, I couldn't follow the simple directions to the gates. My thoughts were so jumbled in my head, I could barely read my ticket and I completely forgot the do's and don'ts of airport security screenings. The line was horrendously long, but I was surprised at how quiet the people were. I hated waiting almost as much as I hated idiots and rudeness, and I had encountered all of the above. I was beginning to sweat. I wasn't used to being around so many people.

"I'm sorry, what did you say?"

The lady in front of me practically ignored me as she continued to point at her ear. My mind told me she was being disrespectful I wished I had a gun so I could show her who the fuck she was dealing with.

"But I can't hear what you're saying." I poked her in the back. *How do you expect me to answer you if you've got your back turned to me and I can't hear what you're saying?*

The guy behind me started talking too, but I refused to turn around. I didn't want to speak with him at all. He was wearing torn-up shoes and was probably blowing rent money just to take this trip. Nine times out of ten, he was looking for someone to bail him out of whatever drama he had imposed on his life.

The lady turned around and said, "I'm not speaking to you. I'm on the phone."

Well, damn, how was I supposed to know she was pointing to an earpiece? I saw her lips moving and she was looking at me at one point. "Sorry," I mumbled. As I looked around, everyone appeared to be on the phone talking to someone. I started to feel left out because I didn't have anyone I could call and shoot the shit with. Unwanted tears welled in my eyes. The painful reminder almost brought me to my knees. I stumbled and the man with the fucked-up shoes grabbed my arm.

"I got it," I said as I snatched my arm back. Perhaps I spoke a little too loud from the way people stared. The last thing I wanted was to draw attention to myself, but it seemed like everything I did had the opposite effect. I decided to ignore everyone around me and concentrate on getting through to the gate. "Boarding pass and identification?"

I tried to walk past the lady sitting on the chair. I saw her lips moving. I tuned her out thinking she was also speaking on the phone. She reached out and grabbed me as I was walking past. I snatched away, but was quickly restrained.

"Get your hands off of me, I didn't do anything." I was furious. This whole airport thing was just too much. The people, the pace, protocol, and procedures were all conspiring against me. I was so focused on what I needed to do in New York, I had forgotten what I needed to do to get there.

"You cannot go pass this point without a boarding pass and identification."

I had male guards on each side of me holding my arms. "Okay, I put them in my purse. I didn't want to lose them." I was being pulled over to the side, and I was afraid I would have to go to the back of the line.

"Where are you taking me?" *Do they know who I am?* My thoughts were in hyper drive.

The cute guard said, "We're not taking you anywhere. We just needed to get you out of the way until we got your identification. You're supposed to have them in your hand before you approach a TSA agent. Didn't you see the signs?"

"I'm sorry, I haven't flown in a minute and I keep forgetting all this nonsense we have to endure. My boarding pass is in the side pocket, but I'm afraid I put my identification back in my wallet." I smiled, hoping to take all the testosterone back down a notch or two. Instead of allowing me an opportunity to give them the items myself, one of them retrieved my pass while the other handed me my wallet. I showed him the identification while the other one ran my purse through the x-ray machine.

"Where are you traveling to?"

Was this any of his motherfucking business? Better yet, it was on the ticket. Couldn't he read? I didn't get a chance to answer.

The less attractive one said, "Is this your carry-on?"

The one who had taken my purse had returned it and was looking at my other bag all crazy. Since I didn't see anyone else getting this type of personalized attention, I was getting suspicious. I realized I was probably being paranoid because the bonds I stole from the Mendoza family were in that bag, but I was incapable of stopping myself. Part of me wanted to deny ownership, but—on the off chance everything was on the up and up—I 'fessed up.

"Yeah." I was about to hit the panic button. If the agent even attempted to empty out my bag, I was going to take my chances running. Even though there was nothing illegal about carrying bearer bonds, I had no idea whose blood was on them.

"We need to run your bag through the scanner." The prick didn't even wait to see if I was going to object. He slung the shit on the belt and personally viewed the contents. *Booya!* I felt like I had swished a three-point basket. I could tell the officer was disappointed that he didn't find anything that he could use to detain me. They gave me back my boarding pass and ID.

"You can pick up your bag on the other side once you go through the scan. You won't be needing your identification again, but you might want to keep your boarding pass handy. Have a nice day."

"You have a nice day too," I answered. I farted and I wasn't sure if I'd shit my pants or it was a false alarm. I needed to go to the bathroom and check for skid marks.

Jackasses. I started fussing with myself as I inched my way to the scanner. *Unless you have this secret desire to spend the rest of your life sitting in a six-by-nine cell, I suggest you get your shit together.* People were giving me funny looks. I wanted to yell at them so bad it hurt. Why were people so nosey anyhow? What was going on with me didn't have anything to do with them. I felt myself mentally detach from my body. I allowed the calm me to march ahead of the angry me, so Ms. Angry wouldn't get me into any more trouble.

I stepped around a lady in front of me who I thought was taking too long. Once again, I was stopped.

"What now? Am I supposed to get butt-assed naked now?" I looked around, seeking the support from angry passengers who'd had enough of this fuckery.

The officer said, "No, that won't be necessary, but you do need to remove your shoes, sweater, any electronic devices, any change you may have in your pockets, and a belt if you're wearing one. Place those items in one of these bins. You will be told when to walk through the scanner."

"What? Are we in grade school again? What the fuck do you think I could possibly put in my shoes?" I tried to shut my other half down, but Ms. Angry was pissed off. In my head, I knew what I was supposed to do, but getting my body to do it was the difficult part.

"You'd be surprised." The officer acted like he was used to these types of outbursts and moved on repeating a similar spiel to others in line.

What is he going to do if I refuse? This has to be a violation of my rights. I'm not doing it. We were holding up the line and people behind us started walking around us, shooting us nasty looks as they passed.

"This bitch is nuttier than all outdoors," a passenger said to another.

"Yeah, I just hope she isn't on my flight. I'm not up for any foolishness when we get up in the air."

"I know that's right," chimed a third passenger.

I looked around to see who they were talking about and all eyes were on me. I could only assume I was the nut they were referring to, so I made a conscious effort to ignore the voice raging in my head.

Getting with the program, I took off everything I thought would be a problem: toe ring, watch, bracelet, and earrings. Once I was finished with those items, I reached behind me and undid my bra. I slid the straps down my arms and reached under my shirt and pulled it off. I didn't want the little metal hooks triggering an alarm, which would draw even more attention to me. Satisfied that I had taken off everything that needed to be scanned, I stuffed my bra inside my shoes and put them on the conveyor belt. As I waited on the other side for all of my things, I couldn't help but overhear a rude comment.

"Good thing that scanner doesn't detect crazy," someone said.

If I wasn't so busy trying to collect all my things from the conveyor belt, I might have gone off. It probably was a good thing I didn't, because even though I was trying to be low key, I was still drawing attention. I looked over my shoulder and noticed the same officer who handled my bags was behind me.

"Did I do something else wrong?" It was a struggle not to yell at him and ask that he leave me the fuck alone.

"No, why'd you ask?" He had to be kidding. If he got any closer to me, I would have had to do a pregnancy test.

"Oh, since you were still hanging around I thought—"

"I get paid to hang around." He chuckled, but I didn't find anything funny. His presence was making me nervous.

"Could you possibly hang somewhere else?" I muttered under my breath. This motherfucker had jokes. Before he could respond I grabbed the last of my things and followed the crowd to the terminals.

♣ ♣ ♣

"Miss, you're about to miss your flight." Someone poked me in the arm.

"Huh? What's going on?" I struggled to open my eyes. It felt like someone had tied them down with tiny ropes.

"You are on the flight to New York, aren't you?" Who was this person and why the fuck did they keep poking me?

"Uh, yeah." My eyes finally opened, and I was a little dismayed to see the TSA goon standing in front of me.

"Well, they just made last call," he said. "If you want to get on this flight, I suggest you hurry before they close the doors."

I was shocked. I didn't even remember closing my eyes, and now I was about to miss my flight. I gathered my things and rushed to the gate. "Who would have thought the agent from hell would've been a blessing." I took my seat in first class and promptly went back to sleep. *Damn, bitch, you didn't even say thanks.* "Fuck 'em," I mumbled.

CHAPTER THIRTY-NINE
CARLOS MENDOZA

"How long have I been out? Wait, where am I?"

"Padre, you're in the hospital. You've been here for a few days," Gabriela said.

I sat up. "A few days? Well, I'm ready to go home. I'm feeling better. Get the doctor."

"Padre, they're not going to let you leave. You're very ill. Unless you have this surgery, you're going to die," Gabriela said.

I was surprised to see Gabriela. She was fresh out of the hospital herself and now she was sitting vigil around my bed. And from the looks of things, it appeared as if she had been here for a while.

"Nonsense. I'll be fine. I just got overexcited. It happens from time to time."

"They don't give medication for excitement. Why do you continue to lie to us?"

I was busted. Old habits were hard to break. "I'm sorry. You're right." I felt like our roles were reversed and suddenly I was the child.

Gabriela grabbed my hand. "How long has this been going on?"

"For a few years now. This is the first time I wound up in the hospital, though." I didn't want to alarm Gabriela, but I was actually scared myself. I didn't want to die, not yet anyway.

"Padre, this isn't good. You've got me and Ariana worried sick about you. The doctor said you have to have surgery—this time you're going to get it."

"Nonsense, I'll be fine." I tried to sound confident, but I failed to comfort my own self.

"The doctor said your body is strong enough to recover, but your heart is working overtime to sustain it. If you don't have the surgery, there might not be a next time. You cheated me out of my childhood, are you checking out on me as an adult?"

I was surprised. Gabriela was acting as if she actually cared whether I lived or died. If she hadn't said that, I might have continued fighting her until I'd talked my way out of the hospital. I'd spent so much of my life alone, it was time I started thinking about someone other than myself. If nothing else, I was grateful for her change of heart toward me.

I said, "Fine, I'll have the surgery, but you must promise me that you won't stop looking for Tilo while I recover. She won't stop unless you stop her."

Her eyebrow raised. "Stop what? What more can she do to us?"

"I don't know… but I'm not willing to take any chances. This bitch is evil."

"Padre, she's not even thinking about us. I think I need to call Ariana. You're getting all upset over nothing."

"No, don't call her. There are some things I didn't get a chance to tell you and Moses. After I speak with you both, then you can decide how much to tell your sister."

"Okay. Are you sure I don't need to get the doctor?"

"Really, I'm fine, but I must speak with Moses before this surgery. Could you call him and ask him to stop by?"

She made the call then said, "He's on his way."

"Good. Wake me when he gets here, okay?"

"Okay, Padre. I'll be right here if you need me."

♠ ♠ ♠

I was far from sleepy. I needed time to get my thoughts together. I'd been lying for such a long time, it was difficult to tell the truth. My biggest fear was that my children wouldn't be able to forgive me for a second time. The last thing I wanted to do was bring up the old memories they had just put to rest, but that was exactly what I needed to do to get on to the future. I believed Moses understood the risks we were facing, and I needed his logical mind to make sure Gabriela understood what we were up against.

I didn't immediately open my eyes when my door opened. If it was a nurse coming to check on me, they could do it while I was presumably asleep. However, when no one approached the bed, I took a peek. I smiled weakly when I noticed Moses. For some reason I felt comforted just having him near. "Moses, I didn't hear you come in."

"Afternoon, sir. I didn't want to disturb you."

Gabriela was seated in the chair closest to the window. Her face was strained. I made a mental note to tell Moses to make sure she went home and got some rest. She didn't need to be sitting in the room with me.

"Thank you for coming. Help me sit up some more."

Moses pressed the buttons until I was comfortable. I nodded my head in thanks. He took a seat next to Gabriela.

I decided to get right to the point. "I have two phones. One for my personal use and one is for business. Since the cartel shut down, my business phone has not rung. That is, until the other day. Do you remember when we were in your office, Moses, and I told you I recognized the voice on your answering machine?"

"Yeah," Moses nodded.

"Monte was the only person who had that number, but Tilo called it the other day."

"So Uncle Monte gave the number to Tilo?" Gabriela asked.

"Possible, but not likely," I answered.

Moses said, "Hmm, that doesn't make sense to me either. To my knowledge, Monte didn't know Tilo like that. I'd be willing to bet money on that."

"Okay, you two seem to know something that I don't. Somebody please enlighten me," Gabriela stated.

Moses reached for his briefcase. "Since we are just throwing out theories, here's one I'm working on. I did a Google search on Colombian drug wars and the results were really quite disturbing. I was more interested in drugs and their relation to Atlanta."

I was excited. This was exactly the type of connection I needed Moses to make, but he needed to think on a bigger scale. Drugs were just the tip of the iceberg. Moses inched closer to my bed. Gabriela pulled up her chair beside him. If it weren't for the beeping of the various machines attached to my arms and chest, I would've forgotten I was in the hospital.

"Right, look for a trend in theme or occurrence. This was part of what your mother did, Gabriela, and later Monte took over the job. When the president of Colombia declared war on drugs, he angered many and hurt a lot of families. The cartel struck back with a brutal blow to Colombia, sending a message to the world that the cartel wouldn't be bullied and that Colombia was unsafe," I explained.

"I remember that. In fact, I read about some of it while I was doing my research. People were afraid to travel in fear of being kidnapped or killed," Moses interjected.

"And large groups of tourists came up missing. Mass graves became a familiar sight, and it hit an already poor country right in the pocket. The United States offered its support because American citizens were targeted; and, quite frankly, they still needed the drugs Colombia provided. They didn't want the supply to stop, nor did they want to pay more for the drugs."

Gabriela cringed. "Wait, are you saying my mother was some sort of monster, responsible for the deaths of thousands of innocent people?"

I said with an even tone, "No, Gabriela, please keep your voice down. That's not what I'm saying at all; however, for a moment, don't put people or personalities into this. The bottom line is, it's a business—big business—and the people who got the most money wanted to make sure it continued. The President of Colombia had the right idea but his own people could not be trusted.

"Your mother would leak stories to the press touting the success of various cleanup efforts. But most, if not all, of what she leaked was a lie. Your mother got out years ago and had nothing to do with the current situations." I needed Gabriela to be real clear on that because I didn't want to change the way she felt about her mother or me.

"You're not making any sense, and I don't think I want to hear any more. This is getting too crazy." She stood up, but Moses pulled her back into her seat. She looked like she was about to give him a big piece of her mind, but stopped when a nurse came in to check on me.

"Do we need to leave?" Moses asked. His face was flushed and animated.

"No, you're fine. I'm just checking his vitals and I'll be out of the way," the nurse said.

Conversation didn't immediately resume when the nurse left. I guessed we were all taking a break to absorb what we'd learned and the implications.

"When Monte took over, his approach was more violent. He created such a volatile environment, he had to leave Colombia, but I'm guessing he continued his dirt from here, hence the phone call."

"I don't believe any of this bullshit. Padre, you have all the answers, or speculations, if that's what you're calling them. The people you speak against can't refute what you say because they are all dead or MIA. You're so busy pointing fingers at everyone else, what was your involvement? Huh? Tell us about that shit." She was clearly angry, but it was expected. At least she didn't run from the room.

"I was strictly responsible for transportation and transportation-related details. To my knowledge, I do not have anyone's blood on my hands," I said.

"Oh yeah, right. And they paid you all that money you showed us just for transportation? What do I look like, a fucking fool?"

Moses was watching and not saying anything, but his attention picked up at the mention of money. "Money? What money?"

Shit, he didn't know.

"Uh, um…" Gabriela stuttered. Her face got red.

"Fuck," I mumbled. My mind went into a deep freeze as I tried to think of a good save. It was obvious that Ariana had not told her husband about the money. Although I never told them to keep the money a secret, I understood why she would.

"So what did Tilo say?" Gabriela countered.

I was never so proud of my daughter as I was at that moment. "I think she called me by mistake. She mentioned someone named Rome and told me to sell him back the guns we took from him at double the price."

"I thought you said you only dealt with transportation?"

"I did, I swear to you. Something wasn't right with her. She appeared off, if you know what I mean. That's another reason why I think she called me by mistake."

"Well, who the fuck is Rome?" Gabriela asked.

"I have no idea. I tried keeping her on the phone, so I started throwing out stuff to her that I'd heard on the news. I asked about the mayors who got killed, and she basically said to keep up the good work. She told me to spread out the violence to keep Obama off her back," I said with a shrug.

Moses wasn't participating in the back-and-forth. I was afraid he was still stuck on the money. He appeared to be in deep thought.

"Call me crazy, but none of this makes sense. Why the fuck would she call you of all people if she didn't know who the fuck you are? I've had enough of this foolishness, I'm leaving." She got up again, but this time Moses didn't physically try to stop her.

"I think I know who Rome is," Moses announced.

CHAPTER FORTY
ROME WATSON

"Fuck." I slammed down the phone.

"What happened? Who was that?" my partner, Greg, asked. He was a little pussy.

I wished I could get rid of his whining ass, but I needed someone to watch my back who had as much to lose as I did. "We've got to get some more motherfucking guns, that's what." My mind was racing through the list of possibilities.

"Are you fucking kidding me? How the hell are we going to do that?"

I knew he was going to bitch up on me. He was going to have to grow some balls today because the stakes just got higher.

"Be quiet and let me think."

We were in the evidence room where we'd been assigned to work as punishment of sorts. My supervisor deemed our investigative techniques to be overzealous and ineffective. His words, not mine.

"Your thinking is what got us into trouble in the first place."

"Ain't nobody tell your ass to follow me into the house. You could have stayed your pussy ass on the porch for all I cared."

I was sick of having this conversation with him. There was nothing wrong with my technique. I just chose the wrong time to show it. Two-thirds of the department were on the take, and they believed that we removed more than bullet casings from the Mendoza house. Since they couldn't prove it, we were stuck in the evidence room, which probably wasn't the smartest move my captain made. If they suspected we stole something from the Mendoza house, why on earth would they put us in the evidence room?

"Well, my pussy ass was taught to back up my partner, so that's what the fuck I did."

"Then shut the hell up so I can think of a way to get out of this shit." Frustrated, I paced the room. Ms. Boss, as Tilo wished to be called, was a real bitch over the phone, and I wasn't used to her speaking to me like I was the help. She acted like she owned me and last I checked, slavery was over. My biggest sin was greed. Tilo knew of my sins, but she was also a sinner. We kept each other's secrets, but now the tide had shifted.

Tilo Adams was a snitch turned mole. She worked with the police department providing valuable information on local drug trafficking. After several successful busts, she started working with the FBI to bring down the Cali Cartel. Technically, she didn't exist on either bureaus payroll. The department needed Tilo to go away. Neither department wanted her to expose her true role in the demise of the cartel, therefore, her disappearance was ruled a death. She was like a blight to both departments. I didn't feel that way. Knowing how greedy she was, I knew the only way she would agree to disappear was if she got paid. I believed whatever money was in the Mendoza house, she had it. What surprised me even more was that no one else thought about it.

At first it completely blew my mind. I was surrounded by idiots. Then I started analyzing the people around me and realized our department was as corrupt as the now defunct police department in Colombia who had their guns taken from them and were walking around with sling shots for protection.

"You see this dope in here? We're taking the dope and selling it."

"Rome, are you fucking kidding me? You have lost your damn mind. I'm not no damn drug dealer," Greg shouted. He needed to take it down a notch.

"Keep your motherfucking voice down. Can you think of another way to get the money to buy more guns?"

"What about that bitch from the apartment? Do you think she knows anything?"

I said, "No, I think she got screwed, but it might be a good idea to find out her story."

Greg was thinking for a change. I was surprised.

"I guess I can work on that then." Greg was pouting; not a good look for a grown-ass man.

"We've got to get those guns or we are going to be in some real shit, right in our backyard."

"Rome, your gambling is out of control. It's what got us into this shit in the first place. I didn't sign up for this, and I'm damn sure not going down because of it. You're my boy and all, but damn. You're pushing it. Motherfuckers looking for us on the street and shit; fellow cops acting all shady. This ain't cool, Rome. Work it out because I ain't going to jail for you or any other motherfucker. Real talk. You got me in this shit and I'm counting on you to get me out."

He grabbed his coffee cup and stormed out of the room and I was glad he was gone. Greg and I had been friends since the academy, but his bitching was getting on my damn nerves. Yeah, I fucked up, but at least I had a plan. What did he have? We'd seized over $3 million of heroin and cocaine during the cartel raid. Normally, the drugs would've been destroyed. For some reason, though, we still had them in the evidence room. I took some of it and I planned on taking the rest to get out of the hole I dug for myself. Greg thought things were bad, but he'd flip the fuck out if he knew how deep this shit had become.

CHAPTER FORTY-ONE
ARIANA RAMSEY

"Hey, girl. This is a surprise." I stepped away from the door to allow my sister to come in.

"Where is my nephew? I want to see him."

"Oh really? He's in his playpen." I was surprised but tried not to let it show on my face.

A few minutes later, she came back carrying LM. "He's such a good baby. I've never heard him cry."

"That's because you haven't been around him much. He can go when he wants to, but for the most part, he's a pleasant baby. He kind of reminds me of Ramón when he was little." The smile disappeared off both of our faces.

I said, "I miss Ramón so much. He had so much life left to live, it's unfair."

"I know. I think about it all the time." She coddled and cooed with LM. The mood in the room was melancholic. "Ariana, we haven't had time to talk. Tell me what is going on with you."

I was taken off guard. "Huh? I'm good. You know, just taking care of the baby and my husband."

"How's that going, the husband part?"

Why was she asking me about Moses? I thought it was a little personal and didn't want to discuss it with her. "It's going well, why do you ask?"

"Oh, no reason. I was just wondering. We talked about Mike all the time. You never talk about Moses, so I thought I'd ask."

"Wow, for real? I hadn't noticed."

Gabriela got me to thinking. She was right, I didn't speak of him because in the back of my mind, I still felt guilty about the circumstances of our relationship.

"You are such a horrible liar." She laughed, but she was so right.

I went to sit next to my sister because I needed a hug. "Gabriela, I feel so lost sometimes. I want to be happy. I want to let go and love my husband the way I did when we first met, but I can't. I don't feel like I deserve to be happy. So many people died. Hell, you almost died. How am I supposed to go on and pick up the pieces?"

She pulled my head onto her shoulder as I cried. "Sweetie, I mean this from the bottom of my heart. You've got to get past this. You owe it to LM and Moses. Even if you don't see it, your baby can feel it. And on the real tip, you got a good man and you're tearing him apart."

I pushed away from Gabriela. How could she possibly know how my husband was feeling? "What do you mean?"

"Exactly what I said. Just like you pushed away from me, I see you pushing away from him."

I was afraid to speak and my heart was pounding so hard. "Has he said anything to you?" I practically whispered.

"No, he doesn't have to. It's written all over his face every time your name comes up. You have to remember that even though a lot of shit has gone down with Madre and Padre, you, me, and Padre are still family, and Moses already feels like the odd man out. You've got to show him how important he is in your life."

"You have spoken to him!" I was upset and felt like she was keeping a secret from me.

"No, I haven't. I swear."

LM had fallen asleep in her arms, so I picked him up and carried him back to his bed. Leaving the room, I thought I was going to have an opportunity to think, but that wasn't the case because Gabriela was right behind me. "Are you following me?"

"Uh, no. I thought we were having a conversation. What's wrong with you?"

"Nothing. I just thought you were going to stay in the living room. You didn't walk around the house before."

"And you've never left the room in the middle of a conversation before, either. What's up with that?"

I felt defensive and like she was trying to pull something from me that wasn't there. "Well...um...I've never had a baby to tend to before." I was fidgeting and feeling very uncomfortable. Almost as if I were standing in front of her naked, exposed, with a huge wart on my ass.

Gabriela said, "And you're using the baby as a shield to keep me away. What's really going on?"

"Why are you drilling me?"

"Why are you so defensive? You've always been my best friend and right now I don't feel like I know you at all."

Wow, I felt like she slapped me in the face. Was I losing my mind? I folded on the floor like a balloon without air.

Gabriela dropped to her knees and wrapped her arms around me. "It's going to be okay. I know it is. God didn't bring us this far to leave us."

I tried to pull away because I was seeing my sister in a different light. She always encouraged me, but now it was like she was looking inside my soul and it was a little intimidating.

"I keep trying to escape this depression, but every time I turn the corner, it's right there in my face again."

"I think it's normal—at least from what I've read—for a new mother to feel this way. But your situation is more complicated because of what we've been through. All I'm saying to you is, if you love the man you married, don't shut him out. Let him know what you're feeling. The last thing you want him to do is to turn to someone else because you have no room for him."

I looked at her. "When did you get to be such an authority on relationships? It isn't like we've had the best role models."

"Maybe that's how I got to be such an expert. I've spent so much time watching and listening."

"Point duly noted. So other than offering advice, what brings you around my neck of the woods?"

We had gotten up from the floor and went back downstairs so we could talk without waking LM.

Gabriela flopped down on the sofa. "I just left Padre at the hospital, but I wanted to see you before I went home to get some sleep."

"Fuck, now I feel like the worst daughter in the world. I've been so busy with my own shit, I didn't even remember to ask you about Padre. How is he? God, I feel so bad."

"He's okay. He agreed to have the surgery."

That made me feel better. "Wonderful. What made him change his mind?"

"I think he realized he couldn't keep putting it off."

"I'm so happy. I'm going to ask Moses to watch LM tomorrow so I can go visit Padre. I'm so glad you got to spend some time with him too."

"Padre understands why you haven't been by. However, he did make me promise that we wouldn't stop looking for Tilo no matter what happens to him."

My anger boiled. "I knew it. You didn't come over here to see about me and the baby. It's always been about Tilo. Why the fuck should I put my family on the line to go after this bitch?"

"Because if you don't, she's going to keep coming back. She's not gonna come after me because she thinks I'm as good as dead. But you and Moses aren't, so it's not going to end as long as she knows there is a threat to her safety."

"Oh God, I can't deal with this," I wailed.

Gabriela touched my hand. "Yes, you can, because you don't have a choice. If you tie Moses' hands, you are both sitting ducks, especially if she ever finds out about the money Padre gave us."

"How is she going to find out about the money? I haven't mentioned it to anyone."

"Why haven't you told your husband?"

I gasped. I couldn't tell if her tone was accusatory or if I was just tripping. Either way, I didn't like it. "How do you know I haven't told him?" I bluffed.

"Because you said you haven't told anyone."

She had me cornered. "Oh, um…I, um—"

She laughed. "You aren't just horrible at lying, you suck."

I felt like crying all over again. I didn't even have a good excuse for not telling Moses. It wasn't a conscious decision, I just never got around to it.

Gabriela rolled her eyes. "Don't start up with the waterworks again. Maybe you have your reasons for not telling him. But I'm going to say this and be done with it, our whole life was built on deception. Don't make the same mistake our parents did—whatever the reason."

CHAPTER FORTY-TWO
TILO ADAMS

"Finally." I kicked off my shoes and waited for the bellhop to bring up my bags from the lobby. It was a hair-raising trip, but I was finally settled in a suite at the New Yorker. I couldn't have been happier to be out of Atlanta. I felt trapped in the city, afraid to go out of my own room. In New York, though, the most impersonal city in the world, I was free to be me. I leaped off the chaise and grabbed the hotel phone.

"I'd like to order room service please." I was ready to act an ass because they placed me on hold without even asking me if I minded. *How fucking rude.* The wait wasn't long, but since patience had never been part of my makeup, it was enough to push me into bitch mode again.

"Can you have someone send me up a menu?"

"You should have a copy of the menu in your room," the voice over the phone said.

"Do I sound like I want to fucking look for a menu? Just do your damn job and have someone bring me a friggin' menu, and don't take all damn day doing it." I hung up the phone. Nobody could do bitch better than me. I was in a suite, so they should be used to attitude and an innate sense of entitlement. The doorbell rang before I could continue checking out my rooms.

"About time," I snippily replied when the bellhop brought up my bag. I didn't have many; it was just heavy as hell. He lingered in the doorway for a few seconds. If he thought I was going to give him a handout for doing his job, he was sadly mistaken. I examined my bag to make sure the bonds were still in the false bottom. The doorbell rang again before I could get them out.

"What?" I shouted as I ripped open the door.

A startled Hispanic woman stood there with a full menu in her hands. She appeared to be scared of her own shadow. She handed me the menu and backed away. It was a good thing because, even though I was pretty certain she wouldn't understand a word I said, I would have cussed her out just because. I tossed the menu on the chair and promptly forgot about it.

"What was I doing?" I looked around the room trying to remember what I was doing before I was interrupted. The room was beautiful but distracting because there were too many things to look at.

"That's right. I was about to take a bath." I started taking my clothes off on my way to the bathroom. A nice long bath would help me to relax. Then, maybe, I could finally go out and get some clothes for my trip. A nice white robe was draped across the oversized tub and I put it on while I waited for the tub to fill with scented water. Just as I was about to get in, my cell phone rang.

"Shit, where's my fucking phone?" It shouldn't have been difficult to find, especially since I'd just gotten in the damn room. But my dumb butt was running around the room naked like a crazy person, and I didn't find it until it had stopped ringing.

"Fuck," I shouted. I stood poised to pitch the damn thing against the wall, but stopped at the last minute. *Why the fuck are you throwing the phone?* I checked the last call and dialed it back.

"Hello?" he said after the third ring.

"Greg, what's up?" I switched from bitch mode immediately because he did not play that.

"Yo, I'm done with this shit. Where you at 'cause I need some pussy?"

I did not like his tone. "I'm in New York, boo." I wanted to call him a motherfucker so bad I could taste it, but I knew it would not be a good idea.

"I thought you were going to tell me before you jetted. I'm on my way."

"No. You can't come right now. I need you to keep an eye on Rome for a little bit longer."

"Aw hell no! First, you had me chopping up that body like I was channeling Freddie Krueger. Now you got me babysitting an ass. I told you I'm done with that shit. The mofo gets on my damn nerves, and I'm not no damn babysitter."

"Greg, sweetheart. I've already thanked you for the body. Although you could have done a better job of hiding it in plain sight. It took them over two months to find it."

"I can't help it if these dudes suck. Hell, I did everything but draw a map to it."

"It's okay, they found it now. That's why I need you to stay. We've come too far to fuck up now. Just a little while longer and we'll have the bigger prize."

"Tilo, real talk, I can't do it. If that motherfucker calls me a bitch one more time, I'm gonna bust a cap right in his motherfucking face."

"Think of the prize, boo. You like money. I like money—"

"I like pussy, too, and my pussy is in fucking New York without me. Now, how about that?" He was angry.

I hated to make him mad because his anger could be lethal. I could've used some dick too, but I was thinking long term and he was thinking about a few minutes at best. Good minutes, but not enough to blow several million dollars over.

"Baby, I am starving for some dick. My pussy is acting like I've lost my damn mind, but if you leave now, you're going to leave too much money on the table and you don't want that, do you?" *I will shoot you my damn self if you do that.*

"No, I want it all, but I'm telling you this shit is taking too long. Rome finally said he was taking the dope, and I'm gonna give him subtle hints as to where he should take it, but this shit about taking the money and the guns is a little bit much. You got to make up your mind, which one is more important? 'Cause your greedy ass can't have both."

"Why can't we have both? Think about it, Greg, South America is wide open now and we've got an opportunity to take it." I thought it was important to say *we*, but, in reality, it was all about me. I was tired of taking the back seat in life. I was about to jump in the driver's chair, and anybody in my way, shame on them.

"Because you are relying on a jackass to deliver. Rome is one straw short of a bale. He's a loose cannon, and now that you're putting a foot on his neck, he's acting like he ain't got shit to lose. Now that would be fine if the motherfucker was in this by himself, but you've got me posted next to this motherfucker—all up in the spotlight and shit."

"Calm down, baby. You're just horny."

"You damn right I'm horny. My joint is so hard, it could knock down a wall and shit."

"Aw … If I were there, I'd take care of that for you." I allowed water to splash as I jumped into my tub and turned on the jets.

"What did you say you were doing?"

"Taking a bath. A nice, long, hot bath. Oooh, I wish you were here."

"Fuck, don't go playing with a nigga, 'cause I'll beat the motherfucking jet to New York—that's how much I want to be fucking right now."

"But if you were here, boo, I wouldn't fuck you. Fucking is for kids. I would make love to you like a grown-ass woman. I would pull your long, hot body into the tub and wash every amazing inch of you." I could tell by the way he was breathing that he was getting into my soft words. "I would slide between your thighs and take your big dick into my mouth and suck it as bubbles dance around us, masking our aroma. Have you ever had your dick sucked while underwater?"

"Uh…"

"After I come up for air, I'll wash your balls. One ball at a time. Savoring your sacks and giving them the attention they deserve. One squeeze and I come up again, kissing you. Fucking you with my mouth. That's the only fucking we'll be doing."

"Damn, baby." His voice got deeper.

"What are you doing?" I demanded. My voice was harsh and commanding.

"Rubbing my dick, Ma."

"That's my dick and I didn't tell you to touch it. I want to do it."

He drew in a deep breath. I could feel its vibration over the speaker in the phone. You couldn't tell me he wasn't stroking his dick.

"I just miss you, boo. It's been so long." He moaned.

I felt it reverberate in my pussy. I missed him too, but I couldn't allow my pussy to think for me. I had to be stronger than that. *Girl, maybe some good dick is what you need. You ain't had none in so long, your shit is about to dry up and fall off.*

"Shut up," I snapped.

"Huh?" Greg said.

I could feel his mental wheels screeching to a halt. I had to recover quickly.

"I just want you to feel my body pressed against yours. No words." I sounded lame even to myself, but I said the first thing that came to my mind. These voices speaking to me were becoming rather annoying. I was having a difficult time deciphering what was real or what was only in my head.

"I feel you, baby," Greg said, obviously back in the moment and waiting to shoot his load.

In my sexy voice, I said, "I want you to grab my dick and stroke it."

"Ah shit."

"Don't stroke it too fast, baby. My pussy is tight, waiting for your love."

"What are you doing to me?" His breathing was ragged.

"Just loving you. My pussy is clutching your dick like a tight rubber glove, only softer. Can you feel my heat?"

"Yeah, I, uh…"

I was getting bored and ready to get off the phone. As I sat in the tub, I was making a mental list of all the things I could be doing if I wasn't on the fucking phone.

"You feel that? Umph this shit is good! Now give it to me hard, baby, just like I like it."

"Oh shit. Oh shit, Ma!" His voice rose an octave as he shouted.

I was relieved he didn't take all fucking night to bust a nut. I waited until his breathing got back to normal before I spoke again. "You good?"

"Yeah, I'm good. What do you want me to do?" He was ready to behave like a well-trained puppy.

"Just keep an eye on Rome for a few more days. He's gonna want to find me. Make sure you talk him out of it. If you can't, put his ass to sleep." Satisfied, I hung up the phone.

CHAPTER FORTY-THREE
MOSES RAMSEY

Gabriela knocked on my office door and poked her head in. "Good morning."

She looked different today. She had done her hair and put on makeup. It was the first time her wound wasn't noticeable to me.

"Good morning, you look nice."

She blushed and appeared to have forgotten her reasons for her early morning visit. "Uh, thanks." She placed some papers on my desk and pushed them toward me. "Take a look at these."

"This is very interesting." I slowly perused the papers. All the pieces were starting to come together like a giant puzzle. I was starting to get excited.

"This is becoming so frightfully easy it's scary," Gabriela said. She started pacing back and forth in front of my desk. She appeared to be deep in thought.

"What?" I asked, as I tore my eyes from the pages.

"I don't know. Tilo has been such a precision player all this time. Why is she so sloppy all of a sudden? What if it's a trap?"

I said, "Trap? I don't agree with you. I think the bitch is cracking up if you ask me."

She looked surprised, but that's the way I honestly felt. Tilo was making mistakes, but I doubted it was contrived. The best criminal minds did it all the time or else they'd never get caught.

"Is she? Or is this part of a plan to lure us in so she can finish the job?"

Frustrated, I sat back in my chair and sighed. Gabriela and her sister had a way of sucking the joy right out of a room.

"Y'all must practice this shit," I mumbled.

"Excuse me?"

"Nothing. So what am I missing, since you seem to have this all figured out?"

Gabriela sat down across from me all smug, as if she had all the answers and I was just digging around in my ass looking for shit to play with. "I still don't understand the credit card. Why would she use it?"

"I explained this before. She probably didn't think to apply for credit in her own name to match her ID."

"But she has money. That negates the use of credit," she replied.

"Not really, not when you're trying to sneak around and not draw attention to yourself. Credit cards can be rather impersonal, and it is possible to use one without showing identification. Cash, on the other hand, slows people down because they have to count it, enter it into the system, and possibly give change. Giving change often lends to touching, which makes the encounter more personalized."

She frowned. "Touching? I don't understand."

"If you gave someone cash, and they laid your change out on the counter, how would that make you feel?" I sat back in my chair, satisfied with my analogy.

"I guess it would definitely piss me off."

I grabbed her credit card statement off the desk and headed for the door. "You coming?" I asked, holding the door open.

"Where are we going?"

"To the airport to see if your friend pissed some folks off."

She leaped from the chair as if it was on fire. "Oh yeah, I'm coming. If I know Tilo like I think I do, I can almost guarantee you that she did."

"Have you been to see your father?" I asked while we drove to the airport. I couldn't keep my eyes off Gabriela. I couldn't understand why she took the extra effort this morning to look like a woman.

"Yeah, he's going to be okay. He's strong. The doctors say he has to take it easy, but he should make a full recovery."

I said, "That's good. It hurts Ariana's heart that she can't spend the kind of time she wants to at the hospital because of the baby."

"Padre knows this. She can't afford to take some hospital germs home to my nephew. He's so cute. You must be proud."

I couldn't help the smile that took over my face. Out of all this madness, my son was the best thing to come out of it. "I am. He has stolen both our hearts and now that he's sleeping through the night, I think we're going to keep him."

We both busted out laughing as I dipped through the light post rush hour traffic.

"When this is over, what are you going to do with yourself?" It was not what I really wanted to ask her. She was such a beautiful woman. I wanted to know, even if it wasn't any of my business, if she would seek out another woman or give a man a chance. Not for myself, I was completely in love with her sister, but she needed someone to love too.

"Honestly, I don't know. This thing with Tilo has consumed all my thoughts. I need closure before I can even think about moving on." She spread her arms wide as if she was referring to the all-encompassing world.

I understood so I didn't press the issue. "We've never gotten to know each other, and I'm sorry about that, especially since we're now related. I want you to know I loved your brother and I adore your sister."

"Thanks, you didn't have to say it because I could tell, but I appreciate it just the same. My sister and I had a discussion about you a few days ago. I kind of explained to her why it was important that we continue to search for Tilo, and more importantly, why you should be the one to help us."

She caught me off guard and I temporarily drifted into another lane.

"Hold on now, don't kill us," Gabriela said.

"Right, I'm sorry. You just caught me by surprise. How did that conversation go? Ariana has been adamant about my not getting involved." I was a little uneasy knowing the sisters had been discussing me. I could help but wonder what else they discussed.

"Don't let your butt cheeks clinch up. It was a good conversation. I was telling her about Padre and... oh shit, stop the car!"

"What? What's wrong?" I said as panic settled inside the car. We were traveling in the fast lane of I-285 and she wanted me to stop the fucking car? I eased the car over to the right.

"Get off when you get the chance. I need to think and I can't do it at eighty miles an hour." Gabriela was clearly agitated, but, then again, so was I.

I was also nervous about any connections she could have going through her brain. "You got some kind of death wish or something?"

"No. You said you think you know who Rome is, right? What if he's the same dude who came to my apartment looking for Tilo?"

I pulled the car back into traffic.

"What? You don't think it's plausible?" Gabriela asked.

"It is absolutely plausible. However, I think our greatest concern right now is finding Tilo. Once we do, the rest of the puzzle will come together. Besides, I'm already at work trying to find this Rome guy."

"Really? How?"

"Your father mentioned someone named Rome in his phone conversation with Tilo. I'm almost positive he is talking about a guy who Tilo used to verify some information on those guys that came to your house with Monte. He's working for the

Atlanta Police Department, and he was the first officer on the scene the night Tilo shot you."

"Are you serious? How did you find out this information?"

"Dag, sis, did you forget it's what I do?" I said, laughing.

"My bad. My bad."

"When we get back, I'm waiting for a picture of him. When I get it, I want to see if this is the same guy who paid you a visit."

"Hmm, I wouldn't be surprised. We'll see."

I was a little disturbed by her non-reaction to my lead. If someone had busted up on me, demanding information and threatening me, it would worry the fuck out of me. I would want to know who they were and what they wanted. I felt like she was trying to hold back on me and this made me a little nervous, but I parked those thoughts with the car at the airport.

CHAPTER FORTY-FOUR
ARIANA RAMSEY

"Padre, how are you feeling?" I'd been sitting by his bedside for several hours and was happy that he finally woke up. He gave me a big smile that raised goose bumps on my arms because, even though the doctors told me he was doing fine, I was afraid that he wasn't going to wake up.

"I'm fine. I was just taking a little nap." He fumbled with the buttons on the side of his hospital bed and I took the remote from his hands.

"Nap, hell, you've been out for hours. What are you trying to do?"

"It's the drugs they give me, makes me tired. I would like to sit up please." My heart ached as I watched him wince in pain.

"Do you need for me to call the nurse?" I didn't know what else to say.

"No, the sooner I lick the need for these drugs, the sooner I can get out of this place and go home."

"Good, that's what I like to hear." I felt relieved that he felt strong enough to resist the temptation to drug himself out so he could get out of the hospital.

"Is your husband home with the baby?" Instantly my guard was up. I still didn't know exactly how my father felt about Moses. I didn't want to fight with him, especially since he was recovering from heart surgery.

"No, his mother came down for a few days, so LM's with her."

"Ah, I'm glad you are spending time with them too. I was beginning to worry about it. I want to meet them as well," he replied.

"Why would you be worried?"

"Why are you getting so defensive? I just said I want to meet the parents."

"You're not throwing me shade?" I was confused.

"Huh? I didn't throw anything."

"Shade, it's slang, Padre. I was asking if you were trying to be sarcastic or something?"

"Oh, okay. No, I wasn't. I was just concerned because they weren't around."

There was an awkward silence in the room. I moved closer to the bed and adjusted Padre's blankets.

"Are you cold? I could ask them for another blanket."

"I'm fine, stop fussing over me," he barked at me.

I jumped back, confused. If he wasn't angry with me, why was he fussing? "You are mad. Look, I'm going to go." I turned around and grabbed my jacket and purse as I fought back tears. I didn't know why I was crying because technically my father hadn't been in my life for so long. Why did it feel like I was losing him all over again?

"Ariana, wait. I'm sorry. I hate hospitals and the timing sucks. I resent being here."

"Gabriela told me you wanted her to keep looking for Tilo."

"I did. We have to find her."

"Why? I guess I'm feeling a little like our mother felt. I just want to keep everybody safe."

"I want everyone to be safe too, but sometimes you have to step out of your comfort zone to do it."

"There is still so much I don't understand about all of this. Are you considered to be a good guy or a bad one?"

"I suppose that would depend on who was telling the story."

His words shocked me. I wasn't sure what type of answer I was expecting, but it certainly wasn't this one. "What's that supposed to mean?" My heart was beating very fast as my imagination ran away with me.

"I'm not going to lie to you. Not everything I did was good, but to my knowledge, I was never directly involved with anyone getting killed; but I'm sure I could inadvertently be connected to some very bad things."

"What kind of bad things?"

"Honestly, I don't know the widespread implications, but I'm sure I could be considered guilty by association with a variety of crimes."

"So what are you telling me? Am I going to wake up one day and see your face splattered all over the news?"

"Ariana, calm down."

"Don't tell me to calm down. You just came back in my life and now you're telling me there is a good chance you might be leaving by default!" I was angry and I didn't care who knew it. I was tired of other people controlling my life. I just wanted to lead the normal life I used to live before all this shit started happening.

"I said keep your voice down." Padre gripped his chest, and I was reminded of why we were in the hospital in the first place.

"I'm sorry." I sat back down and tried to get a hold on my raging emotions.

He said, "I'm doing my part to make things right, but it's going to take some time."

If he was trying to make me feel better, it wasn't working. If fact, he was making me even more nervous.

"What does that mean? I feel like you are talking in code or something," I said, exasperated.

"Sweetheart, I will tell you as much as I can, but some things I will keep from you for your protection. Did you see on the news where they arrested this guy at the airport for smuggling guns and money?"

"Yeah, didn't he work at the airport?"

"He not only worked at the airport, he was responsible for exporting guns and drugs south of the border. He was also one of the point people for human smuggling for the cartel."

"How could you possibly know that?" I demanded.

"Unfortunately, it went with the territory. It was part of my job to know these things, but I didn't connect Tilo with any of it until a few days ago. It appears that she was also working with Monte."

"Here we go! Can I have at least one conversation with someone that does not involve Tilo? To hear everyone tell it, she's like some omnipresent being who can do all things! I'm sick of hearing this hussy's name." I really didn't mean to cuss to my father, but I was fed up with hearing about Tilo.

The nurse came in the room. I was happy to see her because I was done with this conversation. I had two names on my list of people I hated and he had mentioned both of them in the same breath.

"Sorry to interrupt, but I need to check Mr. Mendoza's vitals." She brushed past me and began checking his fluids and taking his temperature. "Are you in any pain, Mr. Mendoza?"

"No, I'm fine. I'm ready to go home."

She said, "I know that's right. I suspect if you keep on going the way you are doing, you might be going home soon."

"What's soon?" Padre asked.

"Mr. Mendoza, you know I can't answer that. I'm sure if you ask your doctor, he'll know better than me."

"So he's doing good?" I asked as I packed up my things.

"He's doing fine, and he's the sweetest patient on the ward." She smiled at both of us as she finished up her duties.

I was ready to go and this was the perfect opportunity for me to do so. "Padre, I need to be going anyway. I'll be back to check on you later, and make sure you have the doctor call me." I could tell

Padre wanted to say more to me, but I didn't give him the chance. I kissed him on the forehead and rushed out of the room. I felt like I was being forced into a corner and I didn't like the feeling one bit!

Everyone in my life was consumed with one thing - finding Tilo. I was going to have to find a way to deal with their obsessions or it would certainly drive me insane.

CHAPTER FORTY-FIVE
GABRIELA MENDOZA

I was excited to finally be doing something. After months of inactivity, I was eager to actively look for my ex-lover if only to shoot her ass right in between her eyes. I wanted my face to be the last one she saw on this earth. I wanted this so badly it hurt. As I got out of the car, I had to stop myself from running into the terminal. "So, what is our game plan?"

Moses did this type of shit for a living, so I would have to defer to him when it came to this type of stuff.

"Assuming she bought her ticket online, she probably didn't go to the check-in counter, so let's start with baggage drop off."

The only time I ever flew in my life was when I was a child coming to the United States, so I knew nothing of an airport. I had no choice but to follow Moses' lead.

"Damn, I wish I had a more recent picture. The one I have, I got from her file with the FBI." Moses held the door open for me.

I stopped walking and pulled out my wallet. I had a picture of Tilo that we'd taken in the mall about a month before I got shot. "Here, this one is fairly recent." I was thrilled that I was able to help, and I could not keep from smiling.

"Perfect." Moses took the picture from me and increased his stride. It was hard to tell which one of us wanted to find Tilo the most.

"Hey, slow down. My legs aren't as long as yours are."

"Sorry, force of habit."

I stood behind Moses as we approached the desk.

"Excuse me, miss. I was wondering if you could assist me," Moses said.

"Sure, what can I do for you." She seemed like a pleasant woman.

"I'm trying to find someone and I wanted to show you a picture to see if you remember her."

I stepped from behind Moses and the expression on the woman's face told me she was on guard. I snatched the picture from his hand. "Look, I know you are super busy. And nine times out of ten, with the amount of people that come through this airport, it is very unlikely that you would remember our friend, but we'd really appreciate it if you'd at least look at the photo please." I put the picture on the counter and entwined my fingers in a prayer position. The woman eyed us before she picked up the picture. Her eyes narrowed. I could tell she was actually thinking about her answer.

"Sorry, I don't remember her. Did she come through today?"

"Ah, actually it was last week."

She looked at me like I'd lost my damn mind. Instead of saying it, though, she pushed the picture back at me. "Sorry."

My hope plummeted, but I wasn't ready to give up. I took the picture and continued down the line with Moses following behind me. At the last station, I repeated my spiel and we got our first glimmer of hope from a black woman.

"Um ..." She frowned and pushed the picture away.

"Take your time," Moses said. He gave her back the picture she dropped on the counter.

I wanted to push him away before he ruined the moment but thankfully—if the lady noticed his intrusion—she didn't tear her eyes from photo.

"Honey, I don't need any time. I remember this—" She looked around as if she was afraid.

"Miss, please, we really need to find her. She's bi-polar and is off her medication." I said the first thing that came to my mind.

"Well...her hair is different, but I definitely recognize those eyes."

I was so excited, I almost started jumping up and down at our first lead.

"How is her hair different?" Moses said.

"She is blonde and very, very rude." She turned up her nose again.

I knew the bitchy side she was referring to, and I could not help but smile. "That's my friend. She can be a bitch when she's off her medication."

"You ain't never lied," the lady responded as she looked around again to see if she was being watched.

"Is there anything else that you can tell us about her?" Moses asked.

"I didn't help her. She refused to pay the luggage fee."

My heart sank, but I didn't understand how she could have used the card and not pay the fee. Before I could argue with the lady she pointed us in another direction.

"I think she used curbside check-in. We were busy and she came in here trying to be some sort of drama queen."

I shared a look with Moses because I felt like we were definitely on the right track. "Thanks so much," I gushed barely containing my excitement.

"No problem, I hope you find the —"

"Be nice," Moses warned, but he laughed as well.

I was starting to warm up to him and feel more comfortable. I was also beginning to see why my sister fell in love with him.

"Honey, I'm always nice, but when I'm naughty, I'm better."

If Moses noticed that she was flirting with him, he didn't acknowledge it, and I gave him another five cool points because of it. The last thing I would have wanted to do was go up against his head for disrespecting my sister, but he passed up on the obvious offer.

We were going to the check-in counter when the lady summoned us back.

"Do you want a more recent picture of her? I'm sure we have her on our security cameras because they followed her through the terminal."

"Yes!" I shouted at little bit louder than necessary. This woman was being so helpful. I loved it, but I was also leery because people rarely go out of their way to be helpful.

She gave me a look, which told me to back my shit down a notch.

"Your friend was off the chain. I'll bet you money, if you show her picture at the gate, they will remember her." She spoke with a co-worker and went behind a partition. She came back within minutes with a photograph.

"Wow, that was quick," Moses commented.

"We printed it because we knew she was going to be trouble. At least we know her lack of medication was making her special." She gave the photo to Moses.

I wanted to snatch it from his hands, but once again, I suppressed my impulsiveness. "Thanks," I mumbled.

"Tilo must have really showed her ass 'cause that lady wanted her bad." He chuckled.

"Let me see the picture," I eagerly stated. I was curious to see how Tilo changed her look. I was stunned at the beautiful lady looking back at me. My hands were trembling. She was almost totally unrecognizable. In my opinion, she chose the perfect disguise. Just looking at her hurt me to my heart. I passed the picture back to Moses.

"Damn, I didn't know she had it in her." He stared at the picture, studying the face.

"Yeah, I always thought she was cute, but I never saw her wearing anything other than jeans and a baseball cap. She has on makeup for Christ's sake.

She didn't even own any makeup when we were living together."

"And she got rid of the dreads. Damn."

He didn't have to say anymore. I knew exactly where he was coming from. She was fierce.

"What now?" I asked. Even though everyone told me she was still alive, I was still holding out hope that they were mistaken, but, I could not ignore the proof I had held in my hands, that the bitch was still breathing. I was furious. I got back in line and waited for the lady that waited on us before to handle her customer.

"What are you doing?" Moses asked.

I ignored him. If it were possible to see fumes coming from inside a person's body, mine would be smoking. I walked up to the counter and placed one thousand dollars on it. The woman looked at me in surprise. "I know you can't tell me where my friend went, but could you please issue me a ticket to the same place on the next flight." I knew it was a good chance she was going to turn me down, but it couldn't hurt to ask.

She took the money and folded it up in her hand, sliding it into her pocket. Her fingers got to flying across the keyboard. "Will you be checking any bags with us?" She smiled.

Moses grabbed my arm and tried to get my attention. I shook my head no.

"Gabriela, what are you doing?"

"What does it look like?" I gently removed his fingers from my arm. I wasn't certain what I was going to do when I got to wherever, but I was sure going to figure it out.

"Will this be round trip or one-way?"

"One-way." I had no idea how long it would take me to find Tilo so I thought it would be best to do it this way. I could always get a return ticket once I found her. In my mind, not finding her was not an option.

"One ticket or two?" the lady asked.

"One," I firmly replied as I grabbed my ID from my wallet.

"Two," Moses announced.

He surprised me. He didn't appear to be the impulsive type, and I wondered how all this would play out with my sister.

"Will that be cash or charge?"

I had my card out, but Moses beat me to the punch and gained another five cool points. Later, when he found out how wealthy I was, I would return his money, but for now, I enjoyed his gesture.

"If you're going to catch the next flight, you're going to have to hurry." She took our ID's and presented Moses with the tickets.

"Thanks," he said as he signed for the transaction.

As we walked away from the counter, I started to feel guilty. I was relieved that he was going with me, but I didn't want to cause any problems in his marriage. "Moses, you don't have to go there with me."

"I know, but you may need my help, and I would feel terrible if something happened to you and I didn't do what I could to prevent it."

"Aw, ain't you sweet." I said it jokingly, but I really meant it.

"Shush, don't tell anyone."

I followed him through the airport because I didn't have a clue what to do, and we made it to the departure gate without any problem. "What are you going to tell Ariana?"

Moses took a deep breath and I saw the worry line across his forehead. "I will handle that when I get back. For now, I really just want to ask some questions to see if anyone remembers her and see if we can get a lead on where she is now."

"I got to say this, Moses, I never believed finding Tilo would be so easy."

"We haven't found her yet."

"I know, but we're in a much better position than we were yesterday. I can't believe how she changed her look." I turned away from Moses so he wouldn't see the tears in my eyes. However, he was much more perceptive.

"Don't beat yourself up, Gabriela. She fooled us all. I understand how personal this is for you. But if we do find her, you're going to have to take your emotions out of it or you may wind up getting us killed."

My heart skidded a few feet as I digested what he was saying to me, but he was absolutely right. Tilo had tried to kill me once before so it stood to reason she would try again, and next time she might even be successful. "I wish the bitch would," I replied as anger replaced my pain.

CHAPTER FORTY-SIX
ROME WATSON

"Greg, where you at, nigga?" I said into my cell phone even though I already knew where he was.

"I'm at the house." He yawned loudly.

"Wake your ass up 'cause we got trouble."

"What now?"

I gave him a few seconds to get himself together. My mind was still spinning with all the ramifications from this latest bust, but I was doing my best to hold it together. "You straight? Your ass awake yet?"

"I'm good. What's going on?"

"I'ma need to see you. I got some things to talk to you about, and I don't want to do it over the phone."

"Why, what's going on? Shit, man, it's raining like hell. You coming over here or what?"

"I knew your punk ass would say some shit like that. Open the fucking door. I'm outside." If he was surprised that I came by his house, he didn't admit it. He left me standing there long enough. I was beginning to believe that he had someone else in the house with him. Just as I was about to dial his house again, he answered the door.

"What was so damn important it couldn't wait until tomorrow?" Greg demanded. He was wearing a pair of sweatpants and a loose-fitting T-shirt that had obviously seen better days.

"I see why your ass didn't wanna go outside. You look like something the damn cat dragged in."

"I didn't ask your ass to come over here, so don't come in my house talking shit."

"This ain't really a social call. Shit ain't looking too good for the home team."

"What the hell is that supposed to mean?" He walked to the dining room table and I followed.

"Haven't you been watching the news?"

He looked at me sideways before he switched on the flat-screen television suspended in the corner. "Nigga, didn't I tell you I was asleep?"

I was getting sick of his surly attitude, but I ignored it because I didn't have time for his foolishness. "That fool I was working with done got his ass busted."

"What fool?" Greg looked like he wasn't paying attention and I needed him to get with the program.

"That motherfucker at the airport I was dealing with," I answered.

"I don't have a clue what you're talking about. Can you start from the beginning instead of the middle of the conversation?"

I shot him a questioning look, but he seemed like he was sincere with his request.

"My bad, I might not have told you about this guy. Anyway, I had this guy who works at the airport. He helps me sometimes when I need to get things through that can't go through screening. Most times, it's money or a small shipment of drugs, but every now and then, I'll have him do something major; Especially if I don't have a lot of time to make things happen."

"Okay. I get it. Now would you get to the point where I should give a shit so I can go back to sleep."

"Shit, nigga, you're the one who asked for the whole damn story when I was trying to give you the *Reader's Digest* version. You know I had to replace the guns that got jacked a few weeks ago, so I had to find another way to deliver them."

"Aw shit, don't tell me they jacked the guns again," Greg shouted.

"Not yet, but they are investigating his fool ass because he shot his damn wife. That crazy motherfucker was chasing her up and down the street shooting. He shot and killed her boyfriend and seriously injured his wife. They started investigating his ass and now I don't know what the fuck is going on."

"I seen that shit on television, but I didn't know you knew the cat. But what I want to know is what does all this shit have to do with me?"

"It deals with you because I'm gonna need you to go to the airport and sweet-talk that bitch you used to deal with to find out what is going on with that shipment. We need somebody with inside connections to make sure they are not watching us," I said.

"Us? What the fuck you mean *us?* I don't know that nigga, so I ain't got a damn thing to do with your shit." He put big emphasis on this.

I wanted to whip out my pistol and shoot his ass. "Nigga, what you don't understand is that if I go down, you go down too. So it would be in your best interest to stop giving me a hard time about everything."

"Shit, man, I can't call that girl up. I haven't talked to that bitch in years. I don't even know if she still works there or not."

"She still works there. Trust me on that."

"If you know so motherfucking much, why don't you approach her?"

"'Cause I didn't fuck her, and I wasn't the one she fell in love with."

Greg was really starting to try my patience.

He said, "It doesn't matter if I fucked her or not. She doesn't want to have anything to do with my ass, so I seriously doubt if I can get her to put her ass on the line for me."

"I'm not asking you to ask her to put herself on the line. All I want you to do is go to the airport acting like you forgot she worked there and shit. Hell, buy a ticket if you have to, but get her talking about her co-worker. From there, see if you can get her to tell you what they're talking about in airport security. If she tells you they have turned up the heat at the airport, then we know we got to do things differently. That's all I'm saying."

"Man, you don't know what you're asking me to do. That bitch is crazy, so I'd just as soon pass on this shit and take our chances," Greg said.

"What, you gonna let some bitch punk your ass?" I taunted.

"Fuck you, man. I hope your ass got a plan B 'cause I'm pretty sure this lame-ass one ain't gonna work."

"Whatever, so when are you going to see ol' girl?"

"What? You want me to go now or something?" He acted like he was about to act the fool on me.

"The rain has actually stopped. Ain't no sense in waiting." I sat back in the chair and waited for him to blow up, but he surprised me.

"Fine, let me throw on some clothes."

"Put some water on that ass while you're at it. You want to woo the woman, not run her off," I said, laughing.

CHAPTER FORTY-SEVEN
GREG CARTER

"Nancy, I didn't know you still worked at the airport." I feigned surprise. The years hadn't been kind to her and she looked every bit of fifty rather than thirty.

"I guess you didn't, It's not like you picked up the phone and called me every once and a while."

I suspect bitterness had a hand in her aging because her face had hideous scowl lines that marred any of the beauty I'd once seen in her. She also looked like she had found another lover, one that put on the extra weight she carried on her hips and thighs.

"You still look good, girl." I was lying through my teeth. I prayed that God didn't choose this moment to come back and cast my black ass straight to hell for telling this lie.

"Yeah, right. What, you think I got 'idiot' stamped on my forehead? Are you going somewhere?"

I didn't think blowing smoke up her ass would work, but I had to try. "I was until I saw your pretty face again. Now I'd rather delay my trip and spend some time getting to know you again. What time do you get off?" I could tell I caught her off guard because she knocked over some luggage tags and some ticket jackets. Her bronze face turned a shade deeper. When she bent over, I could see the crack of her ass. However, with her added girth, this was not a very appealing sight. I loved the ladies, but I refused to sleep with anybody I had to throw flour on just to find the wet spot. Fuck that. "Did I embarrass you?" I chuckled as she attempted to act nonchalant.

"No, I'm just a klutz sometimes," she snapped angrily.

The madder she appeared to be, the more I laughed until she didn't have a choice but to laugh with me.

"Nancy, I seriously would like to spend some time getting to know you again. We could go to dinner or maybe go out for a drink or two."

Her eyes lost focus as she gazed into space and for a minute, I thought I had her, but when her eyes returned to my face, they were as cold as ice.

"I don't think so. The last time we were supposed to have dinner, your ass didn't show up." She started looking over my head, perhaps to the next person in the growing line of people who needed tickets to destinations unknown.

"I was young and simple then. Give a man a break, I've matured."

She seemed to be sizing me up. "I don't think so. You've fooled me before, I'll be damned if I'll allow you to do it to me again."

"Damn, girl, it's just dinner. What harm is there for two old friends to get together over dinner? I started to get an attitude. I didn't want to beg this bitch to do something I didn't want to do in the first place. With the way she was looking, she ought to have jumped at the opportunity to be seen with me. I tried to talk myself down from getting angry, but it wasn't working. Fuck it, I gave it my best shot.

"Fine, forget it. It was good seeing you anyway. Let me get a ticket to Baltimore on the next flight." I pulled my wallet out and dropped down my driver's license and credit card on the counter.

She started typing on her screen without meeting my eyes, which further pissed me off. Who the hell did she think she was anyway, *Beyonce*?

"Next flight is in three hours. Is that soon enough?" she asked before she swiped my card.

"That's cool."

"One-way or round trip?"

"One-way. Ain't nothing left for me in Atlanta. It's time I moved on."

"Were you being serious about dinner?" she asked with her arm raised in the air.

"Yeah, I was. But no worries. All things happen for a reason." I was sulking. I wasn't used to being turned down, and it didn't matter that I didn't really want to go out on a date with her. She continued the transaction without advising me of the cost.

"One drink, that's all." She handed me my ticket and clocked out.

"So what made you change your mind?" I asked once Nancy and I were seated in this bar called Ale Inn on concourse C of the Delta wing. I was truly curious about her abrupt change of heart because it wasn't like she owed me anything or had anything to gain by doing so. For a moment I thought she wasn't going to answer. Nancy and I had been inseparable at one point in time, but her attempts to rush me down the aisle, ruined our relationship.

"To be honest, I don't know. I thought I was going to hate your ass for the rest of my life."

"Damn, hate?" I wasn't expecting her to say that and I quickly took a sip of my drink just to have something to do with my mouth. I knew that I'd hurt her feelings, but never in a million years did I think my disappearing act would result in such a strong emotional response.

"Hey, don't forget, I was young too." She shrugged her shoulders and took a drink herself. She started rifling through her purse.

"True. So tell me what's going on with you? I don't see no ring on your finger. Are you married?"

She looked surprised by my question as her eyes shifted to my ring finger. "If I was married, I wouldn't be in this bar with you," she snapped back.

"What's wrong with having a drink with an old friend?"

"You are not my friend."

This was going to be a lot harder than I'd originally anticipated. While I didn't expect to walk back into her life and be greeted with open arms, I didn't expect this verbal sparring match. "Damn, Nancy. Even though things between us didn't work out the way you wanted them to, I've always considered you to be a friend." Part of me just wanted to throw some money down on the table and get the fuck out of there. I didn't need this bullshit.

"Whatever." She played around with the straw in her glass and kept looking at her watch like she had someplace else to be.

"Shit, you clocking your watch like I'm keeping you from something. Please don't let me hold you up any longer." I was done with begging a bitch. It wasn't like I was trying to get some pussy after all these years anyway. However, I said the wrong thing because I immediately sparked a fiery spark in her.

"You know what, fuck you, nigga!" She was stubbing out her smoke and trying to get up at the same time.

"Nancy, hold on. Why are you getting all upset? I was just trying to be respectful of your time. You didn't have to cuss at a brother." I was trying to hold back my laughter because her girth, coupled with her anger, may have contributed to her inability to get up out of the chair.

"No, *you* hold on. I didn't ask your sorry ass to have a drink with me. Did I? No, you asked me, and when shit ain't going the way you think it should, you want to do the same old shit you did back in the day—roll the fuck out." She was no longer trying to get up, but I could tell she was still mad as hell.

I looked around the restaurant to see if anyone was looking at us because sister girl was rather loud. "Why you got me on loud speaker? Take that shit down a notch before you get us thrown up out of here," I hissed at her. She had a right to be a little upset or even downright mad at me, but I was not about to allow her to show her ass on me in public.

278

"Because your ass threw me out like dirty dishwater once you were done with me." She was fumbling with her cigarette again, trying to get it re-lit, and I was glad we were in one of the few places in the airport that allowed people to smoke. Hell, she almost made me want to light up my damn self, but I'd kicked the habit years before.

"It wasn't like that and you know it. We just drifted apart," I said.

"You're a liar and the truth ain't in you." Any other time I would have gotten pissed by anyone calling me a liar, but she was so comical I couldn't stop myself from laughing.

"Oh, you think I'm a joke?" Once again, she tried to snub out her cigarette and get up at the same time in a confined space. She was butting people in the back of their heads with her big ol' ass, which only made me laugh harder.

I didn't stop laughing until I realized that she was actually going to leave me sitting there without answering any of my questions. "Nancy, wait. I wasn't laughing at you per se. I was laughing at the way you said it." I was sincere when I said it and I guess she must've heard it in my voice because she plopped back down in her chair. I signaled the waitress for another round.

"Just so you know, I don't take too kindly to being laughed at. By you or anybody else for that matter."

"I wasn't laughing at you. Never that. I thought about you often over the years."

"You didn't pick up the phone. Hell, my number ain't changed, just my disposition." Her one-liner comebacks were comical.

"I thought about calling, but I wasn't ready for you." Once again, I was being honest with her.

"You might have been worth something if you wasn't running up behind that other bitch who had your nose wide open." She was referring to Tilo, so I wasn't about to tell her that she was still in the picture. Tilo was running me even back in the day, much the same as I ran Nancy. But Tilo was like a drug to me and I just couldn't say no to her. She even had me asking Nancy for money and giving it to her. I should have had a problem with asking her, but I didn't, and that was one of the reasons we stopped kicking it. That and Tilo's threat to kick my ass to the curb if she even thought I was dishing out her dick to someone else. She didn't mind my getting money from Nancy, but she drew the line at sharing the dick.

"Like I said, I couldn't give you what you wanted." It made no sense to sit there and lie to her about my involvement with Tilo. She knew I loved her back then, and I assumed she wanted to know the deal now.

"I guess that shit didn't work out too well for you, did it?" She started laughing as if she'd said some kind of funny.

"Nah, it didn't work out." I wasn't really lying when I said it didn't work because, physically, Tilo wasn't around, we rarely saw each other, but she still resided in my heart.

"So what's in Baltimore?" She cocked her head to the side as if she genuinely wanted to know.

"I have family there, but actually I'm ready for a new beginning." We sat in silence for a few moments. I was trying to think of a way to bring the conversation around to the real reason I was sitting inside the airport with her in the first place.

"Humph, if I hadn't put in so many years at this airport, I'd leave too. I'm sick of Atlanta. I'm sick of the traffic, wages, and most of all, the men."

I knew better than to tackle the subject of men, especially since I knew that last part was directed at me. "You could transfer to another hub if you really wanted to leave."

"And get the shit end of the totem pole when it came to my schedule? Oh hell no, I don't think so. I'm gonna stick it out here until I can hang it up for good."

"I hear ya. I didn't think about what it would do to your seniority." I nodded my head in agreement. I admired the fact that she had a job she could retire from, and I was still flipping from spot to spot with very little stability to my income. That's another reason why I continued to fuck with Tilo. She was offering a means to get out of the rat race and live in the lifestyle I only dreamed about. Throw in some good pussy, it's a wrap. "Hey, did you know the dude who shot his ex-wife and her boyfriend?"

"Yeah, I knew him. It's messed up. They got shit all twisted around here." She finished her drink and looked at me expectantly.

I signaled the waitress. So much for the one-drink limit Nancy had imposed. I was grateful the liquor loosened her tongue and lightened her attitude with me. "What's his domestic battle have to do with you and your job? I don't get it."

"You know the drill, because of his clearance, everybody is on alert. See the media didn't tell the whole story. She filed for divorce and he wouldn't agree to it. So she turned things ugly on his job by telling the bosses that he was smuggling contraband through the airport. Now they're looking at all of us all crazy when we come through."

"Oh wow. That's fucked up. Is there any truth to her claims?"

"I'm not sure about that. I knew the guy, but I wasn't all up in his business." Her words were beginning to slur. I didn't know how much longer her spirit of cooperation would last.

"So I still don't understand why this presents complications for you unless you're doing a lot of traveling."

"Damn, nigga, do I have to spell it out for you?"

I wanted to choke the bitch and tell her yeah, but I just looked at her.

"Okay, it has nothing to do with travel. Seniority has its privileges, and one of those privileges is the ability to forego TSA screening. On a good day, screening can make the difference of being late for work, so it's definitely something I enjoy. Now this motherfucker done messed it up for all of us, and now we have to go through the line just like everybody else."

"That's fucked up. I can see why that would have you twisted."

"Yeah, like I said before, it's fucked up. Plus, his wife claimed he was smuggling drugs in and out of the country. The bitch gave names and we have to make sure we're not issuing tickets to folks on the list."

"That sucks because you don't even know if the bitch was telling the truth. How the hell did she know what the man was into?"

"Oh, I think she knew. All women aren't stupid. I don't know what all she said, but obviously there was enough truth to it to convince my boss to post the list. We're supposed to immediately alert security if the people named on the list even attempt to buy tickets. We have pictures posted at each terminal so they can't get past us. I was told if we messed up and issued a ticket to someone on the list, it was grounds for immediate termination and a possible criminal indictment."

"Shit, that's some bullshit right there. If someone calls security on me, I'm gonna turn this bitch out and sue the hell out of everybody in this motherfucker while I'm at it."

"Exactly. That's my point. The bitch must have been convincing."

"Shit, I'd love to see that list," I said, laughing.

"Ah, fuck that. I'm not gonna lose my job over no bullshit. Fuck that." She got up from the table like she'd finally put together why I was there in the first place.

I grew apprehensive because I did not want her showing her drunk ass now 'cause there was no telling what she would say now that she was fired up with a little booze.

"Fuck, I gotta go." She shook her head and backed away from the table as if she was suddenly afraid to turn her back on me.

I waited until she'd left the restaurant before I hightailed it out of the airport. I was pretty certain I wasn't on the list, but there was a good probability that Rome was. He was not going to like it either.

CHAPTER FORTY-EIGHT
ARIANA RAMSEY

I didn't start to feel apprehension until I rounded the corner to our house. Even though my mother-in-law didn't call me, I was still apprehensive about leaving my baby with her. As I put my key in the lock, I paused to see if I heard the telltale signs of screams to gauge how their visit was going. I was greeted with blessed silence.

"Hey, you okay?" I asked my mother-in-law, who was nodding out on the sofa. I smiled when I noticed the baby monitor on the end table closest to her.

She sat up as I approached. "You back already? I was just taking a catnap."

"Where is Mr. Ramsey?"

"Child, he's stretched out across the bed. He said the house was too quiet and he couldn't keep his eyes open."

"Quiet? Then I guess everything went well?"

"Shoot yeah. My baby got up, drank his bottle, played with us for a little while, and went right back to sleep. He was a perfect angel."

I breathed a sigh of relief as I settled on the sofa next to my mother-in-law. "Perfect. I was scared you were going to call me crying. I'm glad everything went okay."

"Honey, please, I have a way with men. Didn't my son tell you that?" She laughed and I could not help but to join in. Mrs. Ramsey was such a jovial woman, it was hard not to smile just being around her. "How's your dad?"

"He's doing fine. As long as he doesn't develop an infection, he should be coming home sometime next week."

"That's good, that's good. I know how worried you must be."

She didn't know the half of it. It was times like this that I missed my mother the most. She was my sounding board for a lot of things, and I missed having her around to talk to when I was confused and needed some guidance. I felt like I could talk to Mrs. Ramsey in the same manner, but I was hesitant to say a lot of things in front of her because a lot of my confusion surrounded her son. I didn't want her to think that I didn't love him or was unhappy in any specific way.

She said, "What's the matter, child? You look like you're carrying the weight of the world around on your shoulders."

I looked at her in surprise because she almost read my mind. Most days it was exactly the way I felt. "Huh? Oh, I'm fine. Just a little tired is all," I replied.

"Why don't you go upstairs and take yourself a nap. I'm here and I'll look after the baby while you get some rest."

"I'm not sleepy. You ever feel like it's too much effort to even comb your hair? I'm that kind of tired. I don't want to do anything."

"Honey, I feel like that every day, but you've just got to go on and press on through it. I think you and Moses need to spend some quality time together without the baby. Maybe a weekend getaway would be a good idea."

"Ah, man, I like the sound of that. I don't think I'd know how to act if I were to go someplace with my husband and not have to worry about feeding or changing the baby. Wow, that would be something else."

"Why don't you plan a little trip then? We can watch the baby for you while you and Moses go somewhere."

"I wish! Do you know that I've never been on a vacation in my entire life? I wouldn't know what to do with myself nor would I know where to go. Besides, Moses is so busy—"

"Nonsense. If there is one thing that child of mine knows how to do it is let go and have fun. He's been all over the world, so I'm sure he could plan a little trip for you two. It could be like a honeymoon for you, and it'll do a world of good for your marriage."

My head sprung up at the mention of our marriage. Was my mother-in-law trying to tell me something? Since Moses and I didn't have the typical courtship, I was unsure of how much of our relationship Moses revealed to his parents. I didn't know if she knew that I was married before or if she knew we were having an affair before my husband's death. I began to feel nervous and uncomfortable. "I think I might take you up on that nap idea. It's not often that I can go to sleep in the middle of the day." I stood up to leave, but Mrs. Ramsey pulled me back down next to her.

"Gabriela, what's wrong? At times you seem so distant. I don't want you to feel like I'm prying, I just want to help."

Ever since Moses told his family about us, Mrs. Ramsey was a regular visitor. She said it was one of the benefits of retirement and I truly appreciated her for offering love and support to me, but we barely knew each other. I was afraid that once she found out the sordid details of my marriage, she might not love me anymore, and I didn't think my heart could stand it. I wasn't as strong as I used to be.

"Mrs. Ramsey, there are a lot of things you don't know." I pulled away again.

"What did I tell you about calling me Mrs. Ramsey?" she warned.

"Sorry, old habit. But things are complicated right now. Maybe when things get a little better around here, I'll take you up on your offer."

"That's the problem with you young people today. You always assume there will be time to do the things you put off doing today. Life is not promised to you, so there is no better time than the present time. I've learned that over the years."

I wanted so much to open up to her, but my head just would not follow my heart. There was too much at risk. I stood up, ready to end our conversation.

"Honey, my son does not keep secrets from me. He tells me everything."

I was astonished by her admission, but still leery. I didn't believe Moses told her everything. "I'm sure he does. You two have such a wonderful relationship. I wish I were closer with my mother."

"Yes, he told me about your marriage and your affair. He even told me that he once wasn't sure that my grandchild was his." She chuckled, and it relieved some of the pressure I was feeling about being alone with her and confessing some of my sins.

"Wow, I wasn't sure you knew, and I didn't want to bring it up if he hadn't."

"Heck, he even told me he'd planned to kill you." She started laughing, but I guess she could tell by the look on my face that she'd gone too far.

"Wait, what? He tried to kill me?" I didn't know if this was some sort of ethnic colloquium that sounded like an insult but was actually a compliment.

"Oh shit."

I didn't know Mrs. Ramsey well, but I did know enough to know she rarely cussed. "I don't understand. Is that some kind of a joke because if it is, it isn't funny." I was ready to kick her and her husband out of my house. I didn't care who she was, she had to go.

"Damn, my husband said my mouth was going to be the death of me, and that I wasn't capable of holding water. I'm so sorry, sweetheart. I should have let you take a nap and kept my big mouth shut."

"What are you talking about? Why would Moses want to kill me? And more importantly, why did you find it funny?" Given all that I had been through over the last few months, she had to know anything related to killing me wouldn't be funny. I already had serious trust issues, this was only making it worse. I might not take my frustration out on his parents, but Moses would not get off so lightly. I was going to call that motherfucker and tell him exactly what I thought. Me and my baby would be gone by the time he got home from work.

"Hold on, before you run off half-cocked, let me explain. When Moses first told me what he'd planned, I was as outraged as you are. However, he wasn't thinking clearly. Tilo had messed up his mind, and that is the main reason he is so intent on finding her. She had him thinking that you played him."

"Here we fucking go again. What the fuck does Tilo have to do with this? You know what's wrong with me? I'm so frigging tired of hearing that woman's name every single day! To hear y'all tell it, she is the devil herself. Well, I don't think so."

"I don't know Tilo from a can of paint, but she is responsible for putting the idea of killing you in Moses' head. She had him believing that you played him and suckered him into a relationship. She told him the baby wasn't his and that you were lying the entire time."

"She did what? She didn't even know me!" I didn't know who I was madder at, Moses or Tilo.

"I know it sounds crazy, but she convinced him to shoot something into your IV at the hospital, and he honestly thought he'd killed you. He regretted it right away. But once he did it, he couldn't take it back. But Tilo tricked him, she didn't give him a drug to kill you, it may have been water in the syringe for all he knows. She did plant enough doubt and hatred in his heart to make him want to do you harm. He told me that when he found out you were alive, it was the happiest day of his life, but he was so scared he'd lose you if he ever told you the truth."

I sat back down. This was a lot to dump on a person at one time, and I felt like my head was about to bust. How could I ever trust my husband again, especially if he allowed a total stranger to convince him to commit murder? Shit, what was he going to do if I did something else to piss him off? Would he kill me in my sleep? And how could any of them rest at night knowing he was capable of murder? This whole family was nuts and I wanted to get as far away from them as I could. It was perfectly clear to me that I didn't even know my husband at all.

"I can't deal with this. Moses was right. I can't live looking over my shoulder and not knowing if and when it's going to be my last day on earth."

"Child, none of us know if this is our last day on earth. That was what I was trying to say to you earlier. God doesn't promise us anything when it comes to that. When He's ready to call us home, He'll call. The love Moses has for you prevailed, so please don't do anything foolish now."

"Foolish, are you kidding me? You just told me that the man I'm committed to tried to kill me! That's not like saying I got a booger hanging out of my nose. He wanted me dead, and I have a problem with that." Tears practically blinded me. As I struggled to leave the room, Mrs. Ramsey grabbed me.

"Stop, Gabriela, I thought for sure that Moses would have told you by now. That boy picked a fine time to listen to me. I normally don't like secrets in a marriage, but this was an exception to the rule. He really didn't want to kill you. Believe me. It's not in his nature, but he was so upset when he thought LM wasn't his. I told him that if he really loved you, he was going to have to accept your son as part of the package. But when I saw the pictures of LM, I encouraged him to get a DNA test because he looked just like Moses when he was born."

I felt like I'd just been punched in the stomach and busted in the head at the same time. Moses had my son tested without my knowledge or permission? How dare he? Who the fuck did this motherfucker think he was? I broke free of Mrs. Ramsey's arms and raced to the door. It was high time I had a conversation with my soon-to-be ex-husband, and it would be best not to have this conversation in front of his parents.

"Gabriela, where are you going? Oh God, you didn't know about that either? Me and my big mouth. Honey, I am so sorry. Seems like I'm doing more harm than good." Mrs. Ramsey was also crying. She knew she said more than she should have. Whatever the case, it had nothing to do with me.

"I need to have a conversation with your son. In fact, I think it's long overdue."

"You shouldn't be out there driving when you're this emotional. Why don't you wait until you've had a chance to calm down?"

"No, I need to go now. It won't take me long to say what I have to say." I slammed the door behind me as I fished around in my purse for my keys. At a time when things were finally falling into place for us, I learned this. This explained the changes I'd noticed in Moses' behavior. I reached in my purse for my cell phone to call my sister. I was hoping that she would be my voice of reason, especially since she was the most cynical person I knew. She would give me her honest opinion whether I asked for it or not, but she didn't answer her phone. It went straight to voice mail. I tried to sit still for a minute so she wouldn't be able to tell I'd been crying from the sound of my voice.

A little voice in the back of my mind urged me to go back in the house. If Moses had felt strongly enough to want to kill me, what would his mother do to my son, who was incapable of defending himself? I gave her a smoldering look when I walked back through the door. "Are you going to be okay with my son, or should I take him with me?"

"Gabriela, you are blowing this out of proportion. Moses loves you very much and wouldn't do anything to jeopardize what you have together."

"I wasn't speaking of Moses, I was speaking of you. You saw fit to keep this horrid secret, so now I have to question your motives as well." A look that could only be described as indignation crossed her face, but if anyone should have been indignant, it should've been me.

Her mouth fell open and snapped shut again. She repeated this several times before she was able to get the words out she wanted to say. "I know you're upset and that's completely understandable, but this also sounds much worse than it is. He really does love you; and, yeah, he had a fucked-up way of showing it because he wasn't thinking straight. None of you were."

She made a valid point, and if I allowed myself to sit back and think about it, I'd probably even agree with her, but right now I was filled with a blinding rage. I remembered all of the sleepless nights I suffered through trying to figure out why Moses was so distant toward me. It tore my heart out every time he walked past our son and never picked him up or offered to play with him. The whole time I thought it was me, and it pissed me off to learn that he was the one with the problem.

So many emotions were flowing through me. I was confused as to what I was supposed to be doing. How could I ever forgive and forget his plan to kill me?

"Honey, shut the door. I really botched this whole thing. I can see it in your eyes. You are looking at me like I'm the enemy. If you give us all a chance, you will see for yourself how much we love you."

I wanted to trust her. I needed to trust her because if I didn't then it would have meant everything was a lie and I refused to believe it, but something in the back of my head was warning me to tread lightly. I searched Mrs. Ramsey's face and I saw her sincerity. She may have been guilty of withholding the truth from me, but I honestly believed she did it out of love. I was no longer afraid to leave my child in her care. I could feel her pain and the love she had for me and my son. "I'm fine, but I would still like to go to my husband's office to speak with him. I cannot allow something this big to go unaddressed. Please do not call him and let him know I'm coming. Will you please do that for me?" If she failed this little test, I would know not to trust any of them again.

"He will be fine. Go handle your business, but try to remember what I said, he does love you." I wasn't sure who she was trying to convince, but I held on to the small hope, it was me.

CHAPTER FORTY-NINE
TILO ADAMS

I woke from another crazy-ass dream—soaked with sweat—but this time it wasn't Ariana standing over me with a gun pointed at my head, it was Moses. His face was fiery, his eyes sharp as laser beams aimed at my heart. When I woke from the dream, I was shaking so badly, I wasn't even able to make it to the bathroom. I peed right in the bed and sank back onto the soiled sheets, too tired to get out of my own piss.

"This shit is getting old." My voice was hoarse. It felt like I'd been screaming for a very long time. Almost like when you go to a sporting event and your favorite team was winning. My body was beaten down and broken. I hadn't had a full night's sleep since the murders, and I wasn't eating. Every time I forced myself to eat something, I threw it up in a matter of hours.

"I can't keep doing this to myself. I've got to find a way to deal with this shit and keep it moving, or I might as well roll over on my damn self."

I'd been having this same conversation with myself for months, but nothing was changing. I thought things would get better for me once I left Atlanta behind, but that wasn't working. I was also beginning to believe no amount of money was worth this shit. *I'd much rather be broke and happy than wealthy and miserable any day.*

"Get over it, bitch. It ain't like you could give the shit back and things would magically go back to the way they were." More and more I found myself talking aloud to myself, and sadly I was answering. The fact that I changed the face of an entire family, and the inability to talk to anyone about it, was slowly driving me insane.

"Fuck you. Why didn't you think about this shit before you pulled the fucking trigger? There were other ways to handle it."

"How? How the fuck do you steal money out of someone's hand and get the fuck away? Oh, did I forget to mention, they knew who the fuck you were?"

"Uh, we could have—"

"Bitch, please, you can't even get the thought out of your mouth. That's how stupid you sound right now. You and I both know that shit wouldn't work. We had to shut the door on the investigation because the bureau wasn't going to claim involvement. Killing them closed the investigation and you know it. There was no other way, trust and believe that."

I leaned forward and placed my head in my hands, trying to calm the beating drum inside my head. Fragments of conversations would flicker in and out like tiny light bulbs in my head. I needed for the voices and the visions to stop. I knew that what I was feeling wasn't right, but I didn't know what to do about it.

"So what do you want to do about it? Go to some shrink and confess all of our sins? They'll lock our ass up in a New York minute." I started laughing. The irony of the statement was that I was in New York, and this was one city where it was okay to walk around talking to yourself because nobody cared. From what I'd seen on television, the people were so busy getting from place to place, they didn't take time to see one another. This realization fueled me into getting up.

"I can be anyone I want to be in New York. Shit, I'm going fucking shopping." I rose from the wet bed, my panties clinging to me like a second layer of skin. As I walked past the mirror, I avoided eye contact. Despite my new look, I didn't enjoy looking at myself, not anymore. I turned on the shower, tossing my wet clothing in the trash. I had soiled so many clothes, shopping was not a want, it was a necessity because I was down to my last few pairs of panties. I turned on the water as hot as I could stand it and entered the shower, but no matter how hard I scrubbed, I could not undo my past.

I left the shower feeling rejuvenated and eager to cast aside my demons once and for all. My biggest threat was Moses. Although I didn't think he would come for me, I had to be certain.

"Rome, can you talk?" I was using another disposable phone, which I planned to throw away once I received confirmation.

"Yeah, what's up?" His voice was low, as if he was trying to keep our conversation on the down low.

I immediately got suspicious and paranoid. It was becoming increasingly difficult to determine which emotion reigned supreme in my head. "Motherfucker, are you tryin' to play me?" I demanded.

"Hold up, what the hell are you talking about? I ain't got time for no bullshit." Rome snapped back with a fire I'd never heard in his voice when he spoke to me.

This little bitch didn't know who he was fucking with, and if he didn't recognize it, I had no problem with writing another chapter to his life—the ending. "Bullshit? I think you'd better check yourself, motherfucker. I'm not the one. Why the fuck were you whispering?" Infused with anger, I hated the fact that cities separated us instead of miles. I would have handled his ass.

"Because I was in a motherfucking elevator and I didn't want everybody listening to my fucking conversation."

Damn, instead of me checking him, he checked me. I struggled for something to say after he reminded me that he wasn't sitting on his ass waiting for me to call. "What's the deal with the package you were handling?" I decided not to mention Moses to him. He had reason to suspect my judgment now, and I didn't want to put the nail in my own coffin.

"Uh—"

"What the fuck does that mean? Either you did or you didn't. It's a simple motherfucking question." I was heated again.

"Look, shit is kind of crazy around here. The narcs and Feds are everywhere, so I don't really have an answer for you."

"And, what are you telling me?" I tried hard to keep the rage I felt racing through my blood out of my voice.

"I got the stuff, but I'm trying to figure out how to deliver it," he said with a laugh that could only be described as nervous.

"Pussy, take the shit yourself. I'm trying to get ghost and I need my money." I was angry, but since I still needed his help, I was trying to play nice. But when he delivered my goods, I was gonna make sure he never rose his voice at any other motherfucker in life.

"Tilo, I—"

"Bitch, didn't I tell you not to call me that anymore? Fuck, you trying to mess my shit up?" I was enraged and ready to do damage. I flung a vase from the table at the paneled mirror and glass rang out through the air. Tiny shards of glass and ceramic pieces from the vase stuck in my exposed arms. I dropped the phone, covering my face.

"What the fuck is going on?"

Rome had to be shouting because I could make out his voice clearly, even though the phone was still on the floor. Obviously, flinging the vase wasn't the smartest move I'd made all day. Not only was I going to have to spend the next hour or so picking glass and shit from my body, I would have to pay for the horrible mess I'd made of my hotel room. I picked up the phone with hands that wouldn't stop shaking. I felt like a junkie needing a fix, but I didn't know what I should be taking.

"It's nothing," I lied into the phone.

"Nothing, it sounded like the motherfucking cops were kicking in your damn door."

"Why you got to throw salt on my plate, wishing the cops on me and shit?"

"Ain't nobody wishing shit. I'm just telling you how the shit sounded to me." He was huffing and puffing like he was big shit, which only fueled my irritation with him.

"Rome, if you want to get anywhere close to my Colombia connection, you'd better get me my money by the end of the week. I could probably find ten people who would like to make this connect if I wanted to, but I decided to offer it to you first. But it comes with a big price tag and time is of the essence. If you don't sell the shit then you lose big time, because my ass is about to be dead for real and I'm taking my connect with me."

"I'm gonna get the fucking money. Why you got to keep on threatening me and shit? I said I got you."

In my mind, I could see his face. There was nothing like a grown-ass man pouting like a ten-year-old child. It was fucking sickening, but there wasn't anything I could do about it. "It wasn't a threat..." I left the rest of the sentence unsaid. He knew.

"All right then," he said as he hung up.

For a second or two I stared at the phone, unable to believe he had hung up on me. It was ballsy on his part because he never knew where I would be coming from. I could've been around the corner from him and he'd never know it.

Shopping normally made me feel good, and shopping with money in my pocket should have fed my soul. However, the voices in my head continued to fuck with me and I wasn't able to determine which voices were real. I stopped at my favorite store to shop for some underwear. I liked Macy's selection much better than the highly advertised Victoria's Secret. To me the silk felt richer, and I enjoyed wearing underwear that caressed my skin. I held up a panty set and rubbed the crotch over my lips. As I rubbed the pink panties over my mouth, I thought of Ariana. My mouth watered as I sniffed the panties.

"You smell so good, baby," I muttered as I continued to sniff them, lost in a pussy-laden fantasy. Good pussy was like a large lobster soaked in butter. After you cracked the shell and pulled out the meat, your tongue was in for a treat. I sniffed again and sighed.

"You know what I want, I'm gonna suck on your fat clit until I get it." I was enjoying my personal vision so much I forgot I was in full view of everyone in the crowded store. I could smell her fresh scent and it was driving me nuts. I rubbed the panties over my chest, causing my nipples to peak against my blue tank top.

"Damn, baby, why you want to tease me? Stop playing." I urgently needed release. I felt like I'd been holding my nut in for years instead of a few months.

"Oh, you want me to take you home? Is that what you want? Ariana, why didn't you tell me?" I rushed to the doors of the store with one thought on my mind, busting a humongous nut. It had started to rain as I got outside, but I didn't care. I was on a mission.

"Excuse me, Miss?" I felt a slight tug on my arm.

"What the fuck?" I snatched my arm back and dusted it off. The pink panties were still entwined in my other hand, practically dripping with spit and perspiration.

"I'm going to need for you to return to the store," the buff security guard said.

My trance was broken. I looked around and I didn't recognize any of my surroundings. "Huh?" I had obviously walked out of a different door than the one I came in because I had no clue where I was.

"I need you to return to the store," the guard repeated and grabbed my arm again.

I misunderstood his intentions. "I'm lost, could you help me find my way back to the New Yorker Hotel?" I was in the beginning of a panic attack, and I needed to get back to my room so I could get myself together.

The guard was leading me deeper into the store; it felt like everyone was watching me.

"Hey, what is going on? I thought you were going to give me directions." I couldn't hear Ariana anymore, and I wanted to get back to that happy place where she was whispering in my ear. I needed to find that place.

"… shoplifting. Are you going to add resisting arrest, too?"

Hold the fuck up. This beefy motherfucker finally has my attention. Does he even know who he is fucking with? Hell, I could pay his salary. I don't need to shoplift. "What did you just say?" I had no idea what this man was talking about, but if he touched me again, he was going to be really sorry.

"I need to see your receipt for your purchase today."

I pulled back, suddenly conscious of where I was and what was going on. "What purchase?" I couldn't remember buying anything, but if he needed a receipt, surely I had one in my purse.

"If you grant me permission to check your purse, we can typically handle this without calling the police."

Police? He had my full attention now. The last thing I needed was having the police all up in my shit. Even though my identification was legit, there were some gaps in my life that I wasn't prepared to account for. I handed over my purse for inspection. After a few seconds the guard passed it back to me.

"What is going on? Is this the way the store handles its shoppers?" I was about to get Black on his ass; especially since he had searched my purse and didn't find anything stolen.

"No, it's not, but we also don't expect our customers to steal." He was looking down on me, and it was getting on my fucking nerves.

"I don't need to steal shit. I didn't see anything in this bitch that I wanted." I got up, ready to leave, but he stood blocking the door.

"Did you pay for that?"

Once again, I had no idea what he was talking about, but I followed his line of vision to my hand that was still clutching the pink panties.

"Motherfucker." The panties. I'd forgotten all about the talking panties.

"Excuse me? Are you all right?" He put the bass in his voice, but I also detected a little compassion.

I had to climb out of this shit in a hurry. "I am so sorry. I never intended to walk out of the store. I mean, who goes to the store and steals fucking panties, especially if they have a purse full of money. I didn't even realize I still had them." I tried to hand him the panties, but he refused to take them. When I looked, I understood why. The panties were damp and hanging limply from my fingers. They were no longer pretty. They felt soiled.

"Uh-huh. What's your name?"

Why the fuck did he need my name? I started to hyperventilate. I could not go to jail for stealing a fucking pair of twenty dollar panties. "Sir, I am so sorry. Could we please work this out? I have money." I pulled out a hundred dollar bill and gave it to the guard.

He just looked at me like I'd lost my damn mind.

"What? You don't want my money? My money ain't good enough for you?" I was starting to get mad, and it didn't make things any better because he just continued to stare at me. I threw him another hundred. "See, money ain't the issue. I'll take the panties, ring it up, and you can keep the change." I closed my purse and considered the matter closed. I would sit right there for him to bring me my receipt.

"You sucked the hell out those panties." His voice was low, but I heard him clearly and understood what needed to happen before I was allowed to leave.

"Shit, you act like I tried to steal a flat-screen television."

He shrugged his shoulders, but otherwise didn't say anything. His eyes said it all.

"Hell, I don't know your dick. How do I know if it's even clean?" I cried.

"Bitch, please. How do I know your mouth is clean?" Obviously he didn't like what I'd said, but, hell, this was 2014, and there was some dangerous shit floating around. This guy wasn't bad looking so he didn't really have to twist my arm to give him a tweet.

"If I suck your dick, will I be allowed to leave?" I didn't mind sucking his dick. Hell, I might even ride it, if it looked right, but I didn't want any bullshit when it was time to go.

"Yeah, we'll be straight." He unzipped his pants with confidence. He knew it was going to happen even though I was still considering my options.

To my knowledge, the door wasn't locked so I could technically make a run for it, but I would have to come out of the heels I was wearing to have any chance of getting away. However, I decided to take the easy way out and suck his dick, but I would not swallow.

"I'm not getting down on my knees."

"You don't have to. I just want you to wet my monkey like you wet those panties."

My pussy twitched when he pulled his dick out of his pants. It was lovely and I couldn't wait to taste it. He walked toward me, his dick jutting out at me like a wand.

"Don't try no funny shit," he warned. He didn't have to worry. His dick looked like a chocolate pipe and I loved chocolate. I licked it as I would a Fudgesicle, but my mind was not on his dick. In my head, I was making love to someone else. He, this unnamed guard, got the benefit of my love and he didn't even know it.

CHAPTER FIFTY
ARIANA MENDOZA

"I'm not feeling this, Moses. It's too easy. Why would the gate agent even know which hotel Tilo chose to stay at?" We were sitting in the lobby of the New Yorker Hotel hoping that the information given to us by the gate agent at the airport was correct.

"I know, it has been easy, but your girl is losing her damn mind and creating a scene everywhere she goes. The agent said he put her in a cab and told the driver where to take her. So we'll see if she's still here."

I was nervous about seeing Tilo again. "So what is the plan if we see her?"

"Tonight we watch. I spoke to one of the bellhops and he said she left a few hours ago and hasn't returned."

"How does he know she hasn't checked out?" I wanted to get up and walk around. All this waiting was only adding to my anxiety.

"Would you relax, Ariana? Didn't you know detective work is a whole lot of hurry up and wait?"

"I guess that's why I'm no detective."

"Well, you are tonight, so sit back and act like we're comfortable. We don't want to be like your friend and draw any attention to ourselves." Moses was laid back in his chair with the newspaper like he was in his living room at home.

I sat back and tried to mimic his calm persona. "Are you going to confront her?" I was thinking about best-case scenarios and it wasn't looking good. We didn't have any weapons, so if things turned ugly, it would be like target practice for Tilo on our asses.

"Ariana, if we find her, I have to report it. I can't go with my first instinct and shoot her. I wouldn't be able to live with myself. Plus, I don't want to go to jail for the rest of my life."

"Humph, life behind bars wouldn't bother me a bit," I replied.

"Yes, it would. You're allowing your emotions to govern your good sense. We need proof that she's alive so the FBI can handle it. They have to know how much of a threat she is to your family and quite possibly to their organization."

Moses was disappointing me with his talks of reason. Where was the man who vowed to get Tilo and claimed finding her was personal? I wanted to give Tilo a dose of the same medicine she had given me. Letting the bitch get away with killing my brother and shooting me wasn't going to fly.

"What makes you think the FBI will listen to you now? They haven't been listening to you up until now. What then?" I was frustrating myself thinking of all the what-ifs. And, through it all, the only thought that kept coming back to me was killing Tilo. The rest of the bullshit was irrelevant.

"I'll make them believe. I just have to get the evidence that she exists," Moses proclaimed. His confidence irritated me.

"Have you ever asked yourself why the FBI didn't search for her? They see some blood in her car and boom, she's considered dead. Now they want us to believe this headless body is hers. They just are making up shit like she didn't exist." If my words disturbed him, I couldn't tell.

"Truth be told, I don't think they wanted to find her. If my theory is correct, they needed her to go away. It was that or own up to their involvement."

"Whatever. The cat's out of the bag and they still haven't done anything about it," I insisted.

"We don't know what the hell they are doing. For all I know, they might be doing an investigation, but I was told that they believed Tilo was an innocent victim."

"That's another thing, why haven't they been around questioning me to find out what really went down?" I never thought about it before, but it seemed logical to me that someone would have come around just to make sure all the loose ends were tied up.

"Damn, my bad. I still have some connections with the bureau so I stopped that from happening because Gabriela said you didn't need anyone reminding you what happened."

"Shit, your wife needs to stop babying me. I'm a grown-ass woman and the last time I checked, my mother was dead." My voice rose louder, and for a moment, I completely forgot why we were sitting in the hotel lobby.

Moses reached over and shook my arm. "Ariana, get a grip. You're going to mess up everything."

My mind was racing as it became abundantly clear to me that Moses was going to pose a problem for me. I needed to get rid of him and I knew just how to do it. "What are you going to tell your wife?"

"I, uh…"

Moses was in my way. He wanted to hand Tilo over to the very people who facilitated her escape. Fuck that, I needed justice for me and my brother.

My heart practically stopped when I saw Tilo come through the door. Even though she'd changed her outward appearance, I knew it was her. "There she is." I gasped. I felt my heart pounding loudly in my ears. My quarrel with Moses was temporarily forgotten. In less than a minute, I went from not wanting Moses around to being grateful he was with me.

"Where?" Moses asked. His face was rigid with emotions I could identify with.

"Over by the elevator with that man." Seeing her with someone else inflamed me. It took everything in me not to rush toward her and strangle her until she was limp in my arms. She appeared to be enjoying herself and this made me mad. I couldn't remember a single day of joy since she shot me, but this bitch had clearly gone on with her life.

Moses said, "Damn, if I didn't see it with my own eyes, I wouldn't believe it. She's fierce."

I tore my eyes away from Tilo to examine Moses. Lust was written all over his face and once again, I was questioning his relationship with her. Did something sexual happen between them? Is that why he was here, because she jilted him too? "So, are you

309

gonna just sit there and gape?" I asked angrily. "She could get in the elevator at any moment and we wouldn't be any closer to bringing her to justice."

"Right." Moses moved in closer to Tilo and snapped a few pictures. She was in her own little world and didn't notice either of us as she openly groped the man she was with. Jealousy surged through my veins because it was clear she had forgotten about me, while I was stuck in this warped time capsule she left me with. Unable to move forward and in constant confusion of our past.

"Ms. Adams," the lady at the front desk called out. She was looking right at Tilo but she didn't respond. "Hello, April Adams." She snapped her fingers and shook her head while coming from behind the desk. Several people were still waiting for assistance and seemed to resent having to wait while the lady sought to get Tilo's attention.

"What the hell is that about?" Moses asked.

"Who is April?" I wasn't paying attention. I was still checking out Tilo. The elevator came and went several times but neither of them bothered to get on it. They were so busy fondling each other, I doubted if they even realized what was going on around them.

The clerk stopped in front of Tilo, tapping her on the shoulder. "Ms. Adams, the manager would like to speak with you a moment before you go to your room."

"Excuse me?"

If looks could kill, the lady would have withered and died on the spot.

"I'm sorry, I was calling you and you didn't answer," the lady defended herself.

"And that gives you the right to put your hands on me?"

The man who was with Tilo attempted to pull her back, but she pushed him off.

"What kind of place is this? Let me speak to the manager." She swayed on her feet, confirming my suspicions about her being drunk. Once again, the man with her attempted to grab her arm. She wasn't having it. She snatched it away from him with an evil snarl on her face.

"If he expects to get some tonight, he'd be wise to stay out of whatever is going on," Moses whispered.

I wanted to get closer so I could hear better, but I was afraid Tilo would see me. The woman appeared to use her two-way radio to call the manager.

"The manager is coming. I'm sorry if I've upset you, Ms. Adams," she apologized and walked away. She appeared to be upset as she went back behind the desk.

Moses walked over to the sofa and sat with his back facing Tilo. I didn't realize what he was doing until he placed his phone over his shoulder. He was not only taking pictures of Tilo, he was recording the entire encounter.

"Ms. Adams, can I speak with you alone?" the manager asked.

"Alone, for what? Don't you see I'm busy?" She was loud and belligerent.

I'd seen this side of her before, and it normally happened when she was drunk.

"Ms. Adams, it is very important." The manager acted like he needed to borrow someone else's balls because Tilo had him ready to shit in his pants.

"This"—Tilo grabbed the man's dick in a serious grip and continued her statement—"is very important."

I wanted to laugh. The manager turned so red he was almost purple.

"I see. Uh, there is a matter with your room that I need to discuss," the manager said.

This obviously got her attention because she released her firm grip on dude's dick. He visibly relaxed and started stepping back toward the doors.

"She won't be riding that dick tonight," I said, laughing.

"What did I miss?" Moses asked.

"Her man just slunk his happy ass out the damn door."

I wanted to leap up and rub it in her face but I couldn't. Moses and I shared a smile. I assumed he didn't want her getting the dick either. I filed that bit of information away for later.

"Ms. Adams, there was considerable damage done in your room, and the neighbors are complaining of noise coming from your room."

"What fucking neighbors? I'm in the presidential suite, and the only person on my floor is at the other end of the hall. Shit, if they could hear me inside my apartment, you have a bigger problem than a little bit of damage."

"I have an itemized bill that must be paid before you can go back to your room. And since you are paying in cash, we will require an additional deposit if you decide to continue to stay with us."

I waited for the explosion, but surprisingly, it didn't come. Tilo stood there staring at him as if she was weighing her options. A few minutes passed before she held out her hand for the bill. I was so glad they didn't take this conversation out of our earshot because this was better than a movie with the popcorn.

Tilo pulled out her wallet and counted out several thousand dollars and gave it to the manager. "This should handle it."

"I'll be right back with your receipt."

"Have someone bring it to my room. I've got some unfinished business to handle." She looked around and I had to duck to keep her from spotting me. She must have been looking for her man, but he was long gone. Shrugging her shoulders, she impatiently pressed the button for the elevator and finally disappeared from sight.

"Wow, that bitch is crazy," I said.

"Damn. That was off the chain, and I've got it all on tape. Plus, we learned which room she is staying in and her alias."

"Great, now what?" I was getting annoyed. I wanted to go catch the next elevator up and snatch the life out of the bitch.

"We take the information back and persuade the FBI to arrest her. With your testimony, she will be put away for life."

"Fuck all that, Moses. You don't understand what she did to me and my family. If I let her leave this hotel, it will be like saying I don't give a fuck, and trust me, I give a fuck."

"I'm not saying to let her go free, Ariana. I just think we need to go through the proper channels.

I've got a wife and kid and I'm not trying to lose them behind Tilo's stank ass." Moses' voice turned hard. For the first time I heard the love he had for his family.

"So what happens if we leave and she checks out? We might not be so lucky in finding her again."

"One of us has to stay here and watch her. You wouldn't have to sit outside her room or anything like that. I could place a bug in her room to alert you of her movements," Moses said.

"How did you go from one of us to me? How you gonna volunteer me like that, especially since you know how badly I want to kill her?"

"Ariana, you can't kill her. You just can't. Your sister would kill me if she even thought I would get you involved like that. Promise me you won't do anything that will get you in trouble."

"Wait, what's going on here? Why do I get the feeling that you're setting me up or something?" The itty-bitty committee in my head was working overtime.

"Huh? No, that's not it at all. I need to go back and I think someone needs to stay here in case Tilo decides to run."

"I got all that, but why all of a sudden do you need to go back? That's what I don't get."

"I told you I was going to go get help."

I could tell he was getting agitated but I didn't care. "Why can't you just pick up the phone and call someone? This is the day of technology so anything you can say in person you can pretty much say and do over the net."

A myriad of expressions crossed his face until he finally settled on one that resembled defeat.

"Gabriela sent me a text that said if I didn't get my Black ass home, the next time I saw her or my son, it would be in court."

I could tell he was worried and I tried really hard not to laugh, but I knew my sister and she wasn't playing.

"Fine, I'll do it. What do I do if she runs?"

"Promise me you won't kill her. Just follow her and I'll be back as soon as I can."

I crossed my legs. "I promise," I said sweetly, but keeping that promise was the last thing on my mind!

CHAPTER FIFTY-ONE
ROME WATSON

"Fuck." That bitch was getting on my last nerve. Getting involved with that crazy heifer was the dumbest thing I'd ever done. I stomped around my apartment thinking of what to do next. Greg wasn't answering his fucking phone, either, so I had no choice but to deliver the money to the airport myself. I sent him an urgent text and told him to meet me at the airport.

"Damn, I wish that fucker would phone in to let me know whether or not the coast is clear. Shit!" I wasn't worried about getting bagged at the airport because I didn't go there enough to arouse suspicion, but I disliked making the drops myself because there was always a chance something could go wrong. My problem was I didn't know who else was involved in the shakeup with airport security. But my time had run out. The longer I waited, the more likely it was that I'd get caught. I needed to get paid so I could replace the drugs I'd removed from the evidence room.

"Fuck." I grabbed the duffel bag from under the bed and drove to the airport, unsure if Greg would actually meet me there. My head was pounding. I desperately wanted to stop for a drink, but I fought off the urges. Besides, I needed to have my mind right. I was supposed to meet my connect at ten o'clock and I didn't want to be late. I only had to check the bag and the connect would tag it and make sure it got through security and on to its final destination. When the package was delivered, I would receive a wire letting me know where to collect my money.

I was sweating profusely as I parked the car. This was my first drop and I didn't like it one bit.

"I ain't doing this shit no more. Lord, if you get me out of this mess, I promise I ain't never gonna fuck around again."

It wasn't really a prayer, but it was the closest I'd been to speaking to my Highest Power in years. Funny, I would remember Him now after all the shit I'd done, but it was what it was. This was another thing I would work on once my shit was clear. I parked the car in the short-term lot and carried the bag with me. It seemed heavier to me for some reason. I wiped the sweat off my forehead and tried to mix in with the other travelers. I dialed Greg again to see if he would finally answer his phone. I was going to have to do the deed myself.

"Fucking answering machine. I hate them." I tried to mask my frustration as I stood in line to check my bags. My connect was working the counter and it made me feel a little better, but it wasn't over so I kept my guard up. I was ready to bail at the first sign of trouble.

"Sir, we've opened up another line to serve you better."

"Huh?" I said.

"Another service representative can take you in this other line." The man from the airlines was pointing to another line next to my girl.

"No, I'm good. Thanks." I prayed that he would go away, but he stood looking at me for another few seconds before he moved on to bug someone else. Sweat trickled down my balls and I resisted the urge to scratch. I pulled out my phone and sent a text to Greg. After this, I was done with that motherfucker.

Finally, it was my turn. I pulled out the passport I was using for identification and placed my bags on the scale. My girl processed my ticket and took my bags. Relief flooded through my body as she handed me my boarding pass. I scratched my balls, and I didn't care who was watching. As I was turning around to leave, I was grabbed from behind and forced to the ground. My hands were cuffed and I was placed under arrest.

"Rome Watson, you are under arrest for interstate trafficking of drugs and currency."

"Fuck." When I looked over my shoulder, my girl winked at me as she handed my bag to the officer next to her. I'd been fucked, double-dutch style.

CHAPTER FIFTY-TWO
GREG CARTER

"It's a good fucking day." I was grinning my ass off as Rome was being led away from the airport in handcuffs. I should have felt badly, but I didn't. If he hadn't sent me all those fucked-up text messages, I might not have told Nancy to bag his sneaky ass when he got to the airport. Actually, he did it to himself really, I just helped. It would be a cold day in hell before Rome ever saw the light of day as a free man. His ass was going down. I was tying up my loose ends in Atlanta and Rome was my biggest threat.

"Adios, Rome."

He turned when he heard my voice and the look on his face could've been used to promote a movie called *Oh shit, I've been fucked,* 'cause ol' boy was definitely out-dicked by me.

Rome yelled, "You fucking bastard. What did you do?" He was pulling away from the officers, trying to get at me.

"Chill, bro," I said, laughing. It did my heart good to see Rome in handcuffs. It was about time he saw the business end of a jail cell.

"I'm gonna fuck you up when I get my hands on you." He continued to buck as he was led away through the security doors.

"Detective Carter, thanks for your cooperation," another officer said as he handed me the duffle bag they took from Rome.

"Did you get his cell phone? I'll need to book it into evidence as well."

"Yeah, sure, we'll get it."

I waited for the officer to return with Rome's phone. I had a hunch I would find everything else I needed to know from it.

"Thanks again," the officer said as he handed me the phone.

"All in a day's work, my man. All in a day's work," I replied. I felt so good, my dick got hard. I'd been taking shit from Rome for a minute, but, tonight, I shoved it straight up his ass. After giving Nancy $5,000 for her help, me and the duffle bag boarded the plane for New York. It was time I paid another bitch a visit. I was tired of being fucked doggie style with no Vaseline. Rome, just like Tilo, thought they were going to come up on the sweat off my back, but I was about to turn the tables on her too.

Things worked out much better than I'd planned. I'd been searching for a way to get Rome out of the picture, but I never could catch him with his pants down. When he sent me the text saying he was at the airport, I damn near nutted in my pants. I had the bitch where I wanted him. From there it wasn't hard to set up a sting with a bunch of greedy motherfuckers wanting to get their hands greasy. With Rome's arrest, I was able to even the score.

The drugs from the evidence room would be returned, but the cash, I would be keeping that and I was cleared of any involvement.

Rome fucked himself when he told me to go to the airport and speak to Nancy. If he hadn't, I wouldn't have known about the sting operation that Tilo had orchestrated. My only problem was, I didn't know who the trap was intended for, me or Rome, so I didn't have much of a choice than to take them both down. Tonight taught me a valuable lesson— "never trust a big butt and a smile." Tilo was my poison; however, she'd grossly underestimated me if she thought I would go away so easily.

Rome made his first mistake when he let me know the drugs seized in the cartel raid weren't destroyed. The FBI dictated the disposition of drug seizures, but when I looked in the logs, the disposal date had been altered. The Atlanta Police Department did not have authority to hold the drugs for any reason unless under the directive of the FBI. This directive was duly noted in the computer and logged in the binders used by the evidence room for tracking. Tilo's badge number was used to remove the drugs from the records room and Rome was the issuing officer. The only way Rome would know her number was if she'd given it to him. Putting together the rest of the puzzle wasn't hard from there. Tilo must have been fucking both of us and playing me to the left. Common sense told me to cut my losses and run, but my ego wasn't hearing that shit. I was going to fuck Tilo up and keep it moving.

♠ ♠ ♠

"April, where you at, Ma? Holla at your boy. You're scaring me, boo, get back with me." I was gritting my teeth by the time I ended the plea on Tilo's answering machine. It wasn't the first message I'd left her since I arrived in New York, but I'd hoped it would be my last because I didn't know how many more nice calls I had in me. I was not in the best of moods as I checked into my hotel for the evening. It wasn't how I wanted to spend my first night in New York, but I wasn't surprised.

Tilo never operated on my timetable and over the years, I'd come to expect this type of behavior from her, but it didn't mean I liked it. I would have rather spent my time between her thighs instead of beating my meat in a ridiculously overpriced hotel room. Since there wasn't anything I could do about it, so it didn't make much sense getting myself all worked up about it. After I settled into my room, I decided to go downstairs to the bar to have a drink.

My flight from Atlanta was delayed for two hours, and we had to sit on the tarmac the entire time. That was the kind of shit that pissed me off about flying. Airlines had no problem at all leaving your ass if you weren't on the plane fifteen minutes before departure, but would park your ass on the corner lot for hours and offer little by way of an apology. I could understand weather-related delays and mechanical issues, but it blew me away when the delay was due to congestion over LaGuardia. What the fuck did that mean? I thought scheduling landings were a part of the duties of an air traffic controller, but obviously not when it comes to New York. I just didn't get the hype of New York. The streets were overcrowded with traffic, and now they were telling us the air was littered with planes, too. I couldn't wait to finish my business with Tilo and get the fuck out of New York.

CHAPTER FIFTY-THREE
ARIANA MENDOZA

I approached the front desk. I was relatively sure that Tilo was drunk and more than likely passed out in her room. Tilo could not handle her liquor and was probably loudly snoring as I spoke. "I would like to get a room please."

"I'll be happy to assist you. How many nights would you like to stay with us?" The smile on the receptionist's face was so different from the grimace it held when she was dealing with my nemesis, Tilo.

"A week, maybe two. I've never been to New York before and I heard there is so much to do. I want to make sure I have enough time to do it all," I said with fake enthusiasm.

"I heard that. I have a room with a king-sized bed on the tenth floor, or would you prefer to be up higher?"

"Actually, I'd rather have a suite if you have one."

"Certainly, let me check on availability." The fever in the lobby had calmed down and I was ready to get a room and relax. I hadn't realized how tired I was until I started thinking about a hot bath. I'd never spent the night in a hotel, and I was going to take advantage of the opportunity being in New York afforded me.

"You're in luck, we have one available. Will you require assistance with your luggage?" As she looked around me, the smile disappeared from her face.

"Not at the moment. The airport has misplaced my bags, but I hope to have them soon. I'm really missing my toothbrush right about now," I said in a joking manner, but she had to know if it was really true, the last thing I would be doing was joking about it.

"Okay, I will need your credit card and identification please. And just so you know, we have a wonderful gift shop that is open for any incidentals you may need. And of course, we do have some courtesy items in your suite."

She handed me the key and my information after I signed the receipt.

"Thanks." I exhaled a deep breath as I walked to the elevator. I was relieved to have someplace other than the lobby to hang out.

"Enjoy your stay."

I waved my hand, acknowledging her wishes. As I exited the elevator, I bumped into the same bellman I saw assisting Tilo earlier in the lobby.

"I'm sorry, Miss. Are you okay?" the bellman asked as I read his name tag.

"No problem. I wasn't paying attention."

He kept on moving, but I couldn't get him off my mind as I entered my room. He was definitely sexy, but something about his eyes bothered me and I couldn't put my finger on it.

I checked out the bathroom to see what toiletry items I needed and wrote a list using the pen and pad from the desk. Knowing Tilo, I was feeling pretty confident that she was in for the evening, but I didn't want to take a chance on losing her. I was going to need assistance. With Moses being out of pocket, I wasn't sure how I was going to get it. I was about to order from room service when I got a call from Moses.

"You must have been reading my mind," I said.

"Oh yeah, how so?"

"I was trying to figure out my next move, and I started thinking about you, that's all."

Moses was still an enigma to me. I wanted to believe that he was on the up and up, but my trust level with people in general had been shattered, so I was still leery.

"What's Tilo up to?"

"She's probably sleeping it off in her room."

"What do you mean probably?"

I didn't like his tone of voice. "Hell, I can't see through walls, shit. So I can only assume she is asleep."

"Ariana, chill. I didn't understand what you meant."

I was tired and hungry and didn't feel like any shit from him, or anyone else for that matter.

"Yeah, all right. I got myself a room and I'm going to eat something before I go back downstairs, but I seriously doubt she's going anywhere else today."

"Good, I'm glad you're getting some rest. I managed to get on the last flight out. I've been on the phone since I left you and I'm still trying to get someone to listen to me. I will be back as soon as I can."

I didn't like what he was saying and wondered just how long he expected me to maintain this vigil. If I knew how to get into her hotel room, I was ready to end it tonight, but first I needed a weapon. "Moses, room service is at the door. Let me know when you're headed back this way." I lied to get off the phone before he could say anything else that might piss me off. Part of me realized I was being irrational, but the other part of me didn't give a fuck. Patience was never one of my strong suits, and mine had been stretched past its tolerance level.

As I waited for my sandwich to be delivered from room service, I made up my mind to end this shit one way or the other tomorrow. I finally understood why Gabriela wanted to let this go, because it was tearing me up inside. I was thumbing through the yellow pages when someone knocked on the door. It scared me until I realized it was probably room service with my food.

"Coming," I shouted as I went to get my wallet for a tip. As I opened the door, I realized it was the same bellman who I'd bumped into earlier. "Can you put it in the sitting room?" I asked as I allowed the door to close.

"Sure."

I followed him as he unloaded my food from his small cart to the table. "Hey, I remember you. Are you the only one working here?" I said jokingly.

He chuckled. "Sometimes it feels that way, but, trust me, there's a boatload of us. Oh snap, I remember you too. Weren't you with that dude who was asking all those questions?" He tipped his head from side to side. He caught me off guard because I thought we'd done a good job at being less than visible.

"Yeah, that was my brother-in-law," I was embarrassed about being busted.

"You should tell that dude he needs to step up his tip game, especially if he wants some information on our guest. He could have me losing my job over a lousy ten dollars."

"I hope you won't hold it against him, he wasn't trying to insult you." I didn't know what else to say to him, but I did get more money out of my wallet to make up for Moses' shortcomings. He was staring at me as I went through my wallet and it was starting to make me feel uncomfortable.

"No offense taken. I was just letting you know, just in case you needed something else," he said. He looked out the window, as if he didn't see the elephant that he allowed into the room.

I held out a hundred dollar bill for him to take. But he shook his head no.

"Sorry, lady, I can't break that bill for you."

I wasn't offering him the money expecting change, I was baiting him with a promise of more.
"Oh, I wasn't asking for change. I was trying to make up for my brother-in-law's mistake." I smiled to let him know, I knew what time it was and I was fine with it.

"Cool, appreciate it." He reached forward and took the money from me. "So, what did she do?" he asked after the money disappeared into his pocket.

He was one step ahead of me because I wasn't sure how to answer his question. My gut told me that I could tell him the truth, but my gut had also lied to me before, so I was hesitant to listen to it now. I continued to stare at him for a few more seconds before I answered him. "See that right there?" I pointed to my head so he could see the trace markings of the bullet that grazed my head.

He jumped back in surprise. "Ah, damn! She did that shit? I thought you were going to tell me she screwed your man. I'm sorry, shorty. That's messed up." He pulled the money back out of his pocket and tried to give it back to me.

"It's okay, keep it, because I really do need your help."

He lowered his arm, but didn't immediately put the money back in his pocket. "I feel for you, boo, but I ain't into none of that gangster shit. I knew that chick wasn't right the moment I laid eyes on her, and that's the only reason why I'm talking to you now." He was clearly nervous and I understood his fear. If I hadn't been so mad at Tilo, I might have been afraid too.

"Do I look gangster to you? That woman killed my brother and shot me and left me for dead. The only thing I want to do is keep an eye on her until my brother-in-law returns with the police to put her ass behind bars where she belongs."

"So what do you want me to do? I believe you and I want to help, but I can't afford to lose this job. I'm paying my way through college, and this job gives me spending money. Plus, I can sneak away and study when I need to."

I couldn't get mad at him for trying to do something with his life. After all, he was no different than I was before Tilo came into my life. "If you help me keep an eye on Tilo until help comes, I could contribute twenty thousand dollars to your college fund." I was scared. I didn't really know this guy from a can of paint, and for all I knew, he could bash me over the head and no one would be the wiser.

"Yeah, right. I may have been born at night, but it wasn't last night," he said, laughing. He turned around to leave, taking away the only hope that I had at the moment.

"I'm dead serious." I really needed his help but I wasn't going to beg.

He said, "She has a gun."

I shouldn't have been surprised, but I was. Where the hell did she get a gun? I sat down to think. I didn't know anything about guns or how to go about getting one.

"Figures, but I'm not trying to kill her. I just need to make sure she doesn't disappear again. She faked her death, and we're trying to prove that she's still alive so she can stand trial for the murder of my brother." Waiting for him to respond one way or the other seemed like an eternity.

"You're still going to need a gun. That lady is crazy. I could see about getting you one, but it's going to cost a little more."

For some reason I trusted him. Maybe it was because I didn't have much of a choice, but regardless of the reason, I did. "Fine, I'll have the money tomorrow."

Instead of leaving, he took a seat and got comfortable. "I just hope this mess ain't gonna come back and bite me in the ass, because I really can't afford the trouble, you know what I mean?"

"I feel you, but if I let her get away with what she did to my family, she's going to keep on destroying lives and I can't live with that."

"She's been here about a week and doesn't go out much, but when she does, it's always a big production. I think she's having a nervous breakdown because she's always talking to herself. Housekeeping hates her. She's creeping us all out, so I hope your brother-in-law gets back soon."

"You and me both." I wanted to say more, but it wasn't necessary. I could tell he knew where I was coming from just from the look in his eyes.

Craig wrote his number on a piece of paper and handed it to me. "Call me if you need me and I'll let you know if she moves."

"Thanks, Craig. You won't be sorry for helping me."

"I hope not."

CHAPTER FIFTY-FOUR
TILO ADAMS

I knew I was teetering on the edge of insanity and little things would send me into tantrums. I remembered going shopping a few nights before, but I couldn't find any of the items I bought. I scoured the entire suite and couldn't find a single bag from the store. All of my underwear were soiled, and I didn't have anything else to wear. I walked out of the bathroom wearing a towel after a brief shower. I lost track of the days and had no idea how long it had been since I ate anything. The only thing I was doing consistently was drinking until I passed out.

I needed to allow housekeeping into my room today because it had started to stink. "What the fuck am I going to put on?" I still had some clothes that I hadn't worn, but the thought of my southern lips kissing the inseam of my jeans wasn't something I wanted to do. I poured my first drink of the day as I contemplated what to do. I damn near dropped my glass on the floor when the door opened.

I panicked. "Greg, what are you doing here?"

He put down the bags he was carrying and looked at me real strange. "Are you fucking kidding?" He was staring at me like I was crazy or something.

"What?" I snapped. I had so many questions to ask, but I was afraid of his answers. I obviously had invited him to come because there was no other logical reason for him to be here. This only made me question what else I'd done that I didn't remember.

"For real, Tilo, I think you need to lay off the booze. I've never seen you act like this before, and you're starting to freak me out." He walked over to the bed and handed me the bags he had brought in. He dumped the underwear on the bed and walked over to the bar and fixed himself a drink.

I stared at the underclothes, afraid to touch them. Evidently, I had a few gaps in my memory, but I didn't know how to get them back without admitting my confusion to him. I continued sipping from my glass as if nothing abnormal was happening to me. I was going to follow his lead until I could remember what the fuck we were supposed to be doing.

"Are you going to get dressed?" he demanded. He had a stank attitude and it was starting to piss me off.

"Look, you can check your attitude at the door. I'm not your child."

"I can't fucking tell," he mumbled.

I tried to ignore his comment because I was still trying to understand why he was in New York. Things were so tense in the room, I could feel it like a current. I didn't know whether I should consider Greg to be friend or foe.

"I'm sorry. I'm not myself, but I'm going to get my shit together." I wasn't used to playing this contrite apologetic role, especially with him. I had always been the dominant one in the relationship and overnight it appeared as if this had changed.

Greg's face softened. He put down his glass and came over to me. Pulling me to my feet, he wrapped his arms around me. I felt so comfortable and secure, I started crying.

"Stop crying, baby. I'm here now and I'll make sure nothing else happens to you."

Happen to me? What was he talking about? My mind was spinning and it wasn't from the booze. I forced myself to remember as he stroked my back. I remembered coming back from the store. The people from the hotel were upset because I'd trashed my room. I lifted my head from Greg's shoulder and surveyed the room, but nothing appeared to be out of place except for some suitcases near the door. At the risk of sounding like a complete nut, I inquired about the bags.

"Whose bags are those?"

Greg turned his head and followed my gaze. If he thought I was cuckoo for Cocoa Puffs, it wasn't etched on his face.

"Ours. We can't show up for a cruise without any luggage. What will people think?" He started laughing.

"Yeah, that would draw some curiosity." I chuckled nervously. I didn't remember telling Greg about going on a cruise. "I got to go to the bathroom."

He dropped his arms to his side and I slowly backed away from him. I grabbed some underwear off the bed and my clothes. I stumbled to the toilet and kicked the door shut.

"What the fuck is going on?"

CHAPTER FIFTY-FIVE
GREG CARTER

"Fuck," I whispered. I didn't expect to see Tilo on her feet. Before I left, I managed to slip two roofies into her glass, which should have knocked her out for the rest of the night. I picked up her glass and realized why it didn't last. Tilo didn't finish drinking the cocktail I had prepared for her when I showed up at her door unannounced. She was so drunk, she thought she'd invited me and I played along. I'd just about given up on finding her until I went through Rome's phone. When I saw that she'd been texting Rome, I almost lost it. I couldn't believe she would tell him where she was staying and not me, but it also confirmed my suspicions that she was fucking him too. It was the push that I had been looking for.

Part of me wanted to grab the suitcases and run, but the other part of me knew I had to get rid of Tilo once and for all. Using the little time I had left, I wiped clean all the surfaces I remembered touching. Not that it mattered, because my plan was to leave the country as soon as I'd disposed of Tilo's body. I refreshed our drinks. Since Tilo had made a name for herself with the hotel staff, I didn't want to kill her in the same hotel. I would find somewhere to ditch her after we checked out. For now, I needed her compliance. I opened the door and rolled in the baggage cart I'd hijacked from the hotel lobby and loaded the luggage onto it. She came out of the bathroom as I stowed the last piece.

"We going somewhere?" She looked frightened. If she weren't such a bitch, I might have felt sorry for her, but I didn't. I walked toward her and handed her the drink. "Didn't you tell me you were ready to leave this dump?" I said, laughing. I was winging it and hoped she wouldn't put up a fuss.

"I did?" She drank from her glass, which lowered my anxiety level by a few degrees.

"Uh, yeah. After the way they treated you downstairs, you said you didn't want to spend another dime of your money in this—to use your words—bitch of a dump." She drained her glass and sat back on the bed.

"Yeah, I remember that." She nodded her head, but her eyes still held remnants of doubt.

"I got us a room over in Times Square. We can leave for the boat in a few days."

She started to lie back down on the bed, but I couldn't allow that to happen. I put her shoes on. As I pulled her to her feet, I handed her purse to her. She looked at it for a few seconds as if she didn't recognize it, but she finally took it. The drug was working faster than I anticipated, but that was probably because she hadn't been eating. She didn't complain as I led her out of the room and into the elevator. When the elevator opened, she had this goofy grin on her face, but she followed me like she knew where she was going.

As we approached the desk, Tilo started for it and I started to panic. "Honey, where are you going?" She was going to mess everything up, and I couldn't afford to let that happen.

"I got to check out." She was rocking on her feet and slurring her words.

My heart was beating double time and I was starting to sweat. "No, you don't. We paid in cash, remember?" I coaxed. I didn't know if she paid in cash or not, I just needed to get her away from the front desk. When I turned back, Tilo was pointing a gun at my head. Instinctively, I reached for mine too. "What the hell are you doing?" I yelled as I tried to think of a plausible reason for her pulling a gun on me.

Her eyes were wide and wild, and I was beginning to believe she was on to me.

"It can't be," she murmured as she swung her head from side to side. Spit flew from the corners of her mouth. It appeared as if she was waging some sort of internal battle.

"Tilo," I hissed. I needed to diffuse this situation or I was going to have to cap the bitch in the lobby and make a run for it before anyone called the police. "Shit," I yelled as the sound of multiple gunshots filled the air. My arm felt like it was on fire. I looked down in disbelief because Tilo's gun wasn't the first one to go off. My finger tightened on the trigger as I was pushed to the floor by some dude. I swung my head around to see what was going on as Tilo's bullet caught me in the chest.

Pandemonium had broken loose in the lobby. People were scurrying like roaches when the lights are turned on. This woman, who looked vaguely familiar, kicked the gun from my hand and it slid across the shiny floor. I wanted to go after it, but the pain in my chest wouldn't allow me to.

Tilo was shaking like a leaf and screaming obscenities. Her head was still whipping back and forth like she was trying to escape from an awful dream. "No, why won't you leave me alone?" she shouted. And just as suddenly as the screams started, they stopped. She raised her arm and pointed the gun to her head and pulled the trigger. Her lifeless body dropped to the floor.

CHAPTER FIFTY-SIX
ARIANA MENDOZA

I waited a full ten count after the shooting stopped before I rose from my position off the floor. It all happened so fast, I couldn't tell where it started. My eyes were focused on Tilo so I didn't see who fired the first shot. When I heard it, instinct took over, and I dropped to the floor with my finger curled around the trigger of the gun Craig had given me. I rolled under the sofa and prayed that my shelter was sufficient.

As much as I wanted to believe I could actually fire the gun, when the opportunity presented itself, I choked. Now that it was quiet, my bravado returned. I knew from the many movies I had seen, that there was a chance Tilo had dodged the volley of bullets just like I did. I clutched the gun to my chest as I cautiously peeked over the sofa. If Tilo managed to survive the bullets, I would finish the bitch off myself. For a brief moment, I kind of wished she did. Looking her in the face while putting a bullet through her skull would've been a perfect way to end this mess.

I stood up and was completely blindsided by my sister. She rushed me and threw her arms around my neck. She said, "If I wasn't so happy to see that you are okay, I would shake the hell out of you." Moses stood next to his wife with a sheepish grin on his face. He didn't have to say a word. I already knew what happened when he got back to the house. Gabby climbed in his ass and he folded like a deck of cards.

I felt confused and betrayed by Moses. He was supposed to be on my side, and now I was questioning my decision to trust him. I pushed Gabriella away. She was the last person I wanted to see, especially since I had a gun. She was lucky I didn't shoot her when she rushed me. I tucked it in the waistband of my jeans before she could see it. Without giving her a chance to say anything else, I turned on Moses. "How the hell did you get back here so fast? And why did you have to bring her with you?" I was so mad I could have punched him.

Gabriella pushed Moses aside and got all up in my face. "Hold on a damn minute. I don't need him to bring me anywhere! I was already on my way without him."

"Oh, please, give me a break. You didn't even know where we were, unless he snuck off and sent you a text or something."

Moses held up his hands trying to shush me. "Trust me, I didn't tell her anything." He tried to push us toward the elevator, but I wasn't going anywhere until I saw Tilo's body twitching on the floor!

"Don't be pushing me. Unlike you, I need to make sure this is finished."

"I'm not trying to push you. Look around, this ain't the best place to be having this conversation." People were milling around looking dazed.

He had a good point, but I still wasn't ready to concede it. Besides, I was still mad at him for snitching. I saw other people trying to get into the lobby, but the hotel staff blocked the doors. This was a crime scene now and we wouldn't be able to leave even if we wanted to. I tried to see over the people standing around, but my view was obstructed.

"Well, we sure as hell can't leave now, the police are here. Did you see the shooters? Could you see if they got Tilo?" I demanded.

Moses nodded. "Yes, she's dead. I saw her go down."

I was satisfied, but I still wanted to verify it. "Good, but I'm still mad at you. Did y'all bring the baby too?" I asked sarcastically.

Gabriella huffed loudly. "The baby is home with daddy. You got your nerve being mad. If anyone should be upset, it should be me. I asked you both to let this go and y'all ignored me. When he didn't come home or answer my calls, I knew something was up. Obviously, you both forgot, I used to work for him, so I know how to find somebody, if I need to. When he stepped off the plane, I was waiting for him."

I opened my mouth to say something, but shut it. It made no sense to argue about it now. "So, if you're mad about it, why did you come?"

"Because you were here. When I found out Moses left you here alone, I could have killed him. I might not agree with what you two were up to, but you're my family and family sticks together. Tilo didn't just hurt you, she hurt me too! I tried to shoot the bitch myself, but her friend got in the damn way."

"You did?" My heart swelled with pride as my sister nodded her head yes. I felt vindicated in some way. My sister's hurt was different from my own. We both lost a brother, but I also lost my lover at the same time. I couldn't explain this to her in a million years, nor did I want to. What was the point? I was going to let this deception die. It was finally over and the only thing left to do was move on. I turned to Moses. "Any ideas as to how we're going to get out of here now that the circus has arrived?" Once again, my sister spoke up.

"I got this. Chill."

CHAPTER FIFTY-SEVEN
GABRIELA RAMSEY

"What else do you want from me?"

"Mrs. Ramsey, I know you're tired, but we need to get your story on record. Can you just repeat for us, what you told the officers on the scene?" the officer asked.

I turned to my lawyer, Mr. Lewis, for his advice. I was ready to go home and be with my family. He gave his approval with the nod of his head. I could see my husband, Moses, and Ariana outside in the waiting area, and I was eager to join them so we could leave this hotbed of activity behind us.

"I drove to New York to surprise my sister. She'd been having a rough time and we were going to spend some quality time together. However, when I got to the hotel, I saw that woman who killed herself pointing a gun at my sister. I fired a shot to scare the woman, but the man she was with got in the way. Now, can I go?" I was scared about lying to the police, but they were going to have to catch me in the lie before I'd admit to them that I came to New York to kill Tilo.

"Do you have a license to carry a weapon?" the officer asked.

"Yes, I do," I answered confidently. I had my license and the gun belonged to Moses, so I had every right to have it.

"Then we have no further questions at this time. You're free to go."

Relieved, I walked out of the interrogation room a liberated woman. Greg Carter died of his injuries, but the shot from my gun wasn't the one that killed him. The bullet from my gun got his arm. Tilo's gun fired the fatal shot. As we left the police station, I felt vindicated. I did what I needed to do to protect my family, and now we were going to go about the business of living.

"Okay, y'all, I'm done with all that drama," I said as I got into the passenger seat. I have some rest I need to catch up on.

"I'll second that," Ariana said as she closed her door.

Moses laughed as he got behind the wheel. "Remind me not to fuck up with either of you ladies. Y'all don't play," he said, laughing.

"Believe that," I said, closing my eyes to the deceptions of the past. Tomorrow would be the beginning, and I was looking forward to it.

"Well, I want to know when the hell did you get to New York? Last I heard, you didn't want to have anything to do with chasing Tilo," Ariana said.

"I didn't, but since you two kept running around after her ass, I had to put an end to it somehow. I just want everything back to normal."

"I guess you're right, Sis, and thanks for having my back. She could have shot me."

I smiled. "Not on my watch."

Moses said, "Thanks to Ariana, we got the bonds back. The bellhop rolled their luggage out of the way when the bullets got to flying. The cops never saw them."

I could tell he didn't know what to think about this family that he married into, but given time, I was sure he was going to find out. We still had some issues we needed to work out, but thankfully, we had time to do it.

ABOUT THE AUTHOR

Tina Brooks McKinney began her writing career as a dare. As an avid reader, writing was the next step for her. Armed with a very active imagination and a story to tell, Tina penned her first novel All That Drama. Readers fell in love with Tina's no-nonsense characters and her comedic style of weaving a story. Since then, Tina has written eight novels and two novellas. Her titles include, All That Drama, Lawd, Mo' Drama, Fool, Stop Trippin', Dubious, Deep Deception, Snapped, Got Me Twisted, Deep Deception 2, Snapped 2: The Redemption, Betta Not Tell and Catch Fire.

Catch Fire 2 is anticipated for a December release.

A wife and mother of two, Tina uses real life situations to entertain and inspire her readers. You can find out more information about her by visiting her website, www.tinamckinney.com or drop her an email at tybrooks2@yahoo.com. She would love to hear from you.

www.ingramcontent.com/pod-product-compliance
Lightning Source LLC
Chambersburg PA
CBHW031430240626
47154CB00001B/275